Princess ON THE RUN

The Royals & Rebels Series
BOOK 2

BY
MEREDITH BOND

Princess on the Run by Meredith Bond

Published by WOLF Publishing UG

Text by Meredith Bond
Edited by Chris Hall
Cover Art by Victoria Cooper
Paperback ISBN: 978-3-98536-128-1
Hard Cover ISBN: 978-3-98536-129-8
Ebook ISBN: 978-3-98536-127-4

WOLF Publishing - This is us:

Two sisters, two personalities.. But only one big love!

Diving into a world of dreams..

...Romance, heartfelt emotions, lovable and witty characters, some humor, and some mystery! Because we want it all! Historical Romance at its best!

Visit our website to learn all about us, our authors and books!

Sign up to our mailing list to receive first hand information on new releases, freebies and promotions as well as exclusive giveaways and sneak-peeks!

WWW.WOLF-PUBLISHING.COM

Also by Meredith Bond

The Royals & Rebels Series

This new, exciting, and sweet Royals & Rebels series tells the stories of Prince Nikolaus, his sister Princess Louisa, and their accidental ally Lucinda North as they each discover romance, adventure—and clues as to who wants the prince and princess dead.

#1 In Lieu of a Princess

#2 Princess on the Run

#3 A Prince Among Spies

Prequel: Christmas Intrigue

Princess ON THE RUN

Chapter One

-Day 8: Isa Tries To Make Friends-

Princess Louisa of Aachen-Düren sat down at a table in the dining room of the Abingdon School for Girls. She smiled at the other girls already sitting at the table. She knew most of their names as they were in many classes together, but despite the fact that she'd been at the school for nearly three months, she'd never actually spoken with any of them beyond the most superficial pleasantries.

A week ago when Isa had dinner with her brother, he'd scolded her for not making more of an effort to make friends. Now, knowing she only had four days before she would have to tell her brother exactly how that was going, she decided she might as well make an effort.

With a sigh, she pasted a smile on her face and sat. "Good evening," she said to the four girls.

"Good evening," Miss Leventham said before looking over to Lady Elizabeth Smyth, daughter of the Duke of Pentreth. At the frown from the young lady, Miss Leventham's gaze dropped to her hands neatly tucked in her lap.

Isa sighed. It seemed as if she would need to befriend Lady Elizabeth before she could even hope to become friends with any of the others. She was slowly, with the help of her companion Frau Schmitz, beginning to understand how these things worked. Never in her life had she had to actually work to make friends. Well, she'd only ever had the daughters of the courtiers in her father's court to be friends with, and they hadn't had any choice but to be nice to her. This was a very, very different situation.

These girls not only didn't have to be friends with Isa, they clearly didn't even feel the need to be nice and were barely polite.

"Did you enjoy the assignment in our watercolor class today?" Isa asked, trying again.

The four girls were silent, so Isa continued, "I found it to be quite challenging. I can somehow never get my colors mixed just right." She turned to the leader of the group. "Lady Elizabeth, I noticed your colors were quite beautiful. Do you think you could give me some hints—"

"It takes practice," the girl snapped.

"It's true," Miss Leventham agreed. "Lady Elizabeth, indeed, all of us have been working at it for years. You've only—" She stopped speaking abruptly at Lady Elizabeth's frown.

Their dinners were placed in front of them. There was no serving one's self, no taking as much of whatever one wanted here. Full plates already made up were simply placed in front of each young lady. They were expected to finish it all, but even if they did, there were no second helpings. Isa was still getting used to this. She found the food here to be bland and tasteless. Very little of what she'd eaten did she actually like, but she was trying her best if only to keep from being sent back home.

Miss Leventham looked relieved to have something else to do besides try to be polite. The other two girls hadn't even made an attempt. Isa supposed they were experienced enough—or completely cowed by Lady Elizabeth—to know not to do so.

After they'd eaten in silence for a few minutes, Lady Elizabeth looked up at Isa with an unpleasant smile on her face. "Do you read the newspaper, Princess Louisa?"

"Please, call me Isa," Isa told her. "And, er, no, I generally don't. Why? Was there something of interest recently?"

Lady Elizabeth widened her eyes in mock surprise. Miss Leventham winced. She knew what was coming. Isa tried to brace herself. "Oh! Well then, perhaps I shouldn't... but, of course, I'm sure you already know."

"Know what?" Isa asked.

"About your brother?" Lady Elizabeth tried her hardest to hide her smile and adopt an expression of worry or concern.

Isa stopped breathing for a moment. "What about my brother?"

"Let me see if I have a copy..." She reached down into her bookbag at her feet. They weren't supposed to bring their books with them to meals, but no one was ever reprimanded for doing so. Lady Elizabeth pulled out a copy of a newspaper, carefully folding it to the second page and then in half so it was easier to hand over to Isa. "First column, about halfway down," she instructed.

Isa let her eyes skim down the first column of print and then saw it.

In an unfortunate accident, amid rough waters, the ship carrying the Prince Heinrich Nikolaus Alexander Guelf, heir to the throne of Aachen-Düren, sank yesterday as it was crossing the English Channel while taking the young prince home. There were no known survivors. The prince leaves behind his only sister, Princess Louisa Catherine Anneliese, and his father, Prince Heinrich Norbert Albrecht of Aachen-Düren. We extend our condolences to His Majesty, Prince Heinrich.

Isa suddenly found herself on her feet. "No! It's a lie! Is this some trick of yours? You are a cruel girl, Elizabeth, but even this, this is, is beyond... beyond..." she shouted.

"Princess, what is the matter? Lady Elizabeth?" the headmistress, Mrs. Clark, asked as she rushed over.

"Nothing, Mrs. Clark, I just—" Elizabeth began.

"She made this up. She lies!" Isa screamed, shaking the newspaper at the headmistress.

The woman took the newspaper and looked to see what Isa was referring to. She glanced at it but clearly had seen it before since she didn't even bother reading it. "I'm afraid..."

"NO!" Isa snatched the newspaper back and ran from the room. It wasn't true. It wasn't true. It couldn't be true. She stopped to look at the paper and read the all too brief article again.

No. She'd know. She'd feel it if Nik was... It was wrong. She'd *know*.

She calmed herself. Of course she would know.

Isa couldn't sleep that night. She kept pulling out the newspaper and looking at it. Reading it and re-reading it. She would know. She was absolutely certain she would know if Nik was dead.

She lay back down, but her eyes were wide open, and she didn't think she would be able to close them any time soon. She could hear Herr Mueller, her bodyguard, snoring in his cot in her sitting room. Frau Schmitz was in her own bedroom next to Isa's.

There was only one thing to do, and Isa knew it. The only way she would be able to rest would be if she went to see her brother for herself. But she couldn't go tonight. If she weren't in class in the morning, that horrid Lady Elizabeth would know she'd won. No, Isa thought, she would bide her time, and when no one expected it, in a day or two, she would go and find Nik. He was probably in his room in Oxford, studying away and completely oblivious to the fact that he'd been declared dead.

-Day 13: Isa Goes in Search of Nik-

Isa waited a full five days before deciding it was time. No one would suspect she would disappear now. She'd stayed quiet on the topic of the article and had just gone about her days as normal. It hadn't been easy. She'd been even more antsy than ever, and it had taken all her self-control not to simply jump on her horse and ride off. But the last thing she wanted was to alert anyone as to her intentions. She would simply slip away in the middle of the night, go and see Nik, and be back, most likely, by morning.

She packed a change of clothes just in case. Moving about silently in her room, she bundled a dress and the appropriate underthings into her saddle bag, along with her journal and a pencil. For tonight, the ease of riding was paramount, so she donned her breeches and riding coat and carried her boots in her hand. Neither her father nor her brother minded her unconventional riding clothes; they understood it was easier and safer if she were properly attired. How anyone could gallop or take fences comfortably in a skirt, Isa just didn't know.

Just before she left her room, she thought she should, perhaps, leave a note for Frau Schmitz, just in case. She quickly scribbled something and left it on her dressing table. She would probably be back before they even awoke, but just in case...

As she snuck past Herr Mueller, she saw he had emptied his pockets and left the contents on the table by his cot. There was a watch, a few scraps of paper, but most interestingly, a little leather pouch in which she knew he kept his money. Well technically, she suspected it was her money because, whenever she wanted to purchase anything, he would pay for it from this pouch. She grabbed it on her way out the door.

Isa was proud of herself for making as little sound as possible. She hadn't even woken the stable boy when she'd walked Lilli out into the yard. She saddled the horse quickly and efficiently and was on her way galloping toward Oxford and Nik. Merely an hour later, Isa made her way through the quiet streets of Oxford. At three in the morning, there were only a few people about—mainly students returning home from an evening out. She just hoped her brother didn't kill her for waking him at this ungodly hour.

As she attempted to ride past the guard house on her way to her brother's rooms, a man came out and stopped her. "Ho there! Just where do you think you're goin', me lad?"

"I am Princess Louisa of Aachen-Düren, here to see my brother," she informed the man from atop her horse, pulling off her cap so he could see her better.

"Oh! I beg yer pardon, Yer Highness, I didn't recognize ye," the man said, doffing his own cap. "But, uh, ye do know that yer brother..."

"What? Where is he?" she asked. He wasn't going to tell her he believed that falsehood in the newspaper, now was he?

"Er, ye didn't see..." he hesitated awkwardly.

"The article in the newspaper? I did and I don't believe a word of it," she informed the man.

"I'm awfully sorry, Yer Highness, but I ain't seen him since a week ago when he took off in a tearing hurry."

"In a hurry? Where was he going, did he say? How was he traveling?"

"Didn't say, I'm sure. And he was in a coach, his traveling coach, so I suspected he was going far—to the coast."

Isa controlled her horse as the animal tried to step forward, perhaps feeling Isa's own tension. "But..."

"I'm awfully, awfully sorry..."

"No! I don't believe it. I don't believe he's... he's dead. He's not," she informed the man. "And I will prove it."

She turned her horse around and headed back south. She had to find Nik. Why had he left in a hurry? Why in his traveling coach? Where had he gone? The newspaper had said he was on his way home, but why? He'd had no plans to return to Aachen-Düren—not unless he'd received some news that made it imperative he return immediately. But if that were the case, he would have informed her.

No. She didn't believe for a moment that he'd actually been on that ship—if one had sailed at all. She supposed she had no choice in the matter now but to go after him.

She knew their ship was docked in Margate—the ship they had used to come to the horrid country nearly three months ago in the most stomach-churning crossing of the English Channel. Crossing the channel in January had been awful, and Isa had no desire to go through that again, but if she had to do so to find Nik, she would. The only thing was... he had their ship, presumably.

Either that or it was sitting at the bottom of the English Channel with his lifeless body, a small voice whispered inside of her. "No!" she shouted to no one. And thankfully, there was no one to hear. He was not dead. She would go to Margate. He was probably there, or some place nearby hiding out, or-or taking a holiday, or-or she didn't know what. She didn't know why he might have left Oxford.

If anything had happened to their father, Nik would surely have come to get her on his way south. That couldn't be it. There had to be another reason—a good reason—why Nik had left in a hurry, and she would find out why.

She was too tired. She couldn't think just now.

Isa walked her horse to a tiny little posting house she'd passed a number of times. No one would know her there, and no one would ask. A boy was standing outside and came up to hold her horse's head as she dismounted.

"Can I take yer 'orse for ya, miss?" he asked.

"Yes." She fished a small silver coin from Herr Mueller's purse and gave it to the boy. He smiled and doffed his cap and walked her horse off in the direction of the stable as she went inside.

A man was sitting behind the counter in a chair, snoring away.

"Excuse me, I need a room for the night," she said loudly.

The man jumped. "Eh? What?"

"I need a room for the night," she repeated.

The man smiled down at her while rubbing his extended belly. "Oh, do ya, now?"

She didn't like the way he was looking at her. She took a step back.

"Here now, miss, we don't cater to the likes o' you," a woman said from behind her, making Isa swing around.

"I beg your pardon?" Isa said, affronted. The likes of her? What did that mean? She'd thought her English was pretty good, but she didn't understand the implications of such a statement.

"Oy, you a noble?" the woman asked.

Isa didn't want her true identity known, so she just nodded.

"Where's yer maid, then?" the woman asked. "An' why are ye dressed like a boy?"

"Looks like a runaway to me," the man said. "Wantin' a little fun, eh, girl?"

"No, ye don't," the woman growled. "Come along, then, I'll take ye to a room, and ye'll lock the door," she said pointedly while looking at the innkeeper.

Isa followed the woman up the stairs to a room that, if one were kind, one might say was small. In fact, it was little more than a filthy closet, but it had a bed in it, and that was all Isa cared about at that moment.

"This will do," Isa told the woman.

She just huffed and walked away. Isa followed her advice and locked the door behind her. In the morning, she would head south and find Nik.

Chapter Two

-Day 13: In Which We Meet Our Hero Making a Bet-

"It can't be done, and she's driving me mad repeatedly asking me to even try," Viscount Wythe told his friends before emptying his glass of the excellent rum that could only be had at Powell's Club for Gentlemen.

"I don't know why you think it can't. I could drive to Shropshire and back in four days," Sam, the Marquess of Ranleigh said, leaning forward and refilling Wythe's glass before doing the same to his own.

"Oh, come now, what is it? Nearly two hundred miles?" said the Earl of Devereaux, or Dev to his friends.

"About that," Sam said, sitting back again.

"A bit less. Somewhere between one-fifty and two hundred, depending on how you go," Wythe admitted.

"And you can't do that in two days? And you want to be considered for the Four in Hand Club? Really, Wythe, I'm ashamed." Sam chuckled and shook his head. He could see Wythe grind his teeth.

"And all for what? A bleeding necklace to wear to a ball!" the man said through his clenched jaw.

"Not just any ball, the first ball of the Season. Of course, your mother wants to look her best," Dev pointed out.

"She just wants to flaunt her wealth into the face of Lady Wraxely —not that she has any beyond what that necklace is worth," Wythe added under his breath.

"It's all about show, isn't it?" Sam said with a shake of his head.

"Do you really think you could drive there and back in four days?" Dev asked, giving Sam a side-look.

"*Puff*! Of course I can. Easy."

"I'll bet you a monkey you can't," Dev said, his skeptical look turning into a grin.

Sam opened his mouth to accept the bet, then remembered he'd decided to turn over a new leaf this Season. He was going to be responsible. He was going to actually look for a wife and settle down. No more silly bets. No more late-night drinking and gambling with his friends. No more... fun.

His father's death the year before had made him realize he was wasting his life away. Not only that, but since the demise of the marquess, Sam had learned his father had done an excellent job at depleting the family coffers and nothing to keep them flush. In other words, he'd gambled away the family's wealth and let his estate rot. Sam was determined not to follow in his father's footsteps, no matter what anyone said.

All his life, he'd been compared to his father. Just because he looked like him didn't mean he had to behave like him. Of course, it had taken Sam twenty-seven years and his father's death to come to this realization, but at least, he had done so.

And now here he was faced with this dilemma. Did he take this one last bet or tell his friends of his decision? The responsible thing would be to tell his friends and turn down the bet.

"I can't believe Ranleigh's actually thinking about it," Wythe said with a burst of laughter. "It can't be done!" His words were a challenge. Sam knew it. Wythe was doing it deliberately, and he knew that, too.

"It's not that it can't..." Sam started.

"Well, then?" Dev asked.

"It's that I had decided to turn responsible, you know," Sam hedged.

"Responsible? Why, in heaven's name, would you want to do that?" Wythe scoffed.

"Is it because of your father?" Dev asked, getting it immediately. Sam wasn't surprised. Dev was clever that way. They understood each other. Always had.

"Oh, come on!" Wythe said, still not getting it. "Lord Ranleigh's dead. You're the marquess now, yes, but that doesn't mean you can't still have fun. I mean, I'm sorry for your loss and all that, but really."

Sam ran a hand down his face, rubbing at the stubble beginning to roughen his cheeks. "It's time I started behaving responsibly. I've got an estate now, tenants and all that. I need to marry and—"

"Don't even say it, man!" Wythe nearly shouted, making some heads turn their way in the relative quiet of the reading room. He quieted down immediately, giving an apologetic nod to those who'd turned to look. He leaned forward and said with his voice low, "You can't, Ranleigh. You cannot turn on us that way."

"I wouldn't be turning on you, first of all," Sam said, lowering his voice as well. "But we've all got to do it some time, and now is the best time for me."

"Is it your mother? Is she putting pressure on you?" Dev asked.

"No." Sam gave a sad little laugh and shook his head. "She doesn't even think I'm capable of acting responsibly. Thinks I'm just like my father."

"But you are! And what a great life he led," Wythe said, admiration tinging his words.

Sam just sighed. "The man died trying to swim the Thames for a bet—in February."

"Can't believe he even got into that disgusting water," Dev said, shaking his head.

"True enough. We still don't know if it was exhaustion, the cold, or something in the water itself that actually killed him, but he's dead, nonetheless." Sam drained his glass. "And I don't want to follow in his footsteps."

"All right, but one bet, Ranleigh. One last bet," Wythe teased.

"Before you go off and get leg shackled to some shrew who will put you back on leading strings."

Sam just frowned at him.

"Yes, Ranleigh, one last bet. One last hurrah," Dev said, adding his weight to the argument. "To Shropshire and back in four days. You return with Lady Wythe's necklace and collect... we don't even have to make it a monkey. It could be a century instead. Would that make you feel better about it?"

"It's not the money," Sam started.

"It's that he can't do it," Wythe said, sitting back with a smirk on his face.

"You know I can."

"Prove it."

Sam's two friends looked at him in expectation. He sighed. "All right. One last bet. I will go and fetch your mother's necklace and be back in time for her to wear it to the ball."

His friends broke into cheers, calling for another bottle of rum.

Chapter Three

-Day 14: Pleading for the Mail Coach-

The room Isa woke up in was even more disgusting than she'd thought. The dark had hidden a good deal of the dust and grime. The pillow on which her head had lain was gray with dirt. She tried to repress a shiver of revulsion. She supposed she would be lucky if she didn't walk away with ticks in her hair. Just for good measure, she gave her head a good strong brushing, grateful she'd thought to bring her hairbrush.

There was no water to bathe with and no bell to pull to request some. After braiding her hair in a simple plait, she dressed in her gown, carefully packing her riding clothes into her saddle bag. She supposed she had better get used to this if she was going to travel south to Margate to find Nik. Never in her life had she done so much for herself.

Being a princess meant you never had to brush your own hair or pack your own bag. Thank goodness her governess had taught her to braid when she'd learned stitching and knitting. She'd hated every moment of those lessons and had escaped from them the very second she could, but now she was grateful she'd learned something useful.

Down in the common room, now filled with men and a few women, Isa ordered breakfast and then sat down as far from the window as she could get. She wondered, as she ate, if Herr Mueller was already out looking for her. If so, he would most certainly be passing by this inn. She could only hope he did just that—pass by and not stop. She hurried her meal.

The lady who'd assisted her the night before was no where to be found, so Isa approached the innkeeper. "What do I owe you for the night?"

He looked up from the ale he was pouring out and looked her up and down with approval. "Look more like a toff this mornin' than ye did last night," he commented.

Isa just frowned at him. "How much do I owe?" she asked again, pulling out the pouch of money she'd taken from Herr Mueller. She had no idea how much things cost and wasn't at all certain she understood the currency in this strange country. She poured the contents out into her hand. There weren't very many coins there, but there were two large gold ones and a few of the smaller silver ones like she'd given to the stable boy the night before.

The man plucked a gold one from her hand. "That's fer the room," he said. "And that's fer breakfast." He took the second.

Isa grabbed the coin back from between his fingers. "My breakfast does not cost as much as the room."

He snatched it back. "Consider it an added fee fer comin' in so late an' causin' trouble."

"But that's not fair! I caused no—" Isa started.

"Whoever told ye life was fair? Have a good journey," the man said, interrupting her. He turned away rudely, a sly smile lifting one corner of his mouth.

"I am not done!" Isa said, stomping her foot for emphasis. "How dare you be so—"

"Well, I am done. Now, I suggest you get goin' before I charge ye more for disturbin' the peace," he said, not even turning back around to address her.

Isa just stood there, unsure of what to say or do. Was there anything she *could* do? The man was very large, and Herr Mueller wasn't here to defend her. He would have known how much to pay the man, but she had no idea how these things worked. She was a princess; she wasn't supposed to deal with such common interactions.

Fine. She would allow the man to get away with this injustice. She lifted her chin. "Send someone to fetch my horse from the stable," she commanded in a tone that would brook no arguments.

The man turned back. "What stable? I don't have stable."

Isa's stomach clenched. "What do you mean you do not have a stable? A boy took my horse last night and headed off toward some stable with her."

"What? Next door? Those ain't mine. I don't have a stable, I tell ye."

"Then who was that—" She stopped as the man shrugged and went back to pouring out ale for customers. Well, she would find out herself. Her horse had to be somewhere.

She picked up her saddle bag and went out to the stable next door. There was a young man there brushing down a horse, which looked as if it should have been put out to pasture years ago. "Where is my horse?" she asked as she walked past him to look into the stalls.

"I beg yer pardon?" he asked, looking at her.

"My horse. A boy took it when I arrived at the inn last night and brought her here," Isa informed the man.

A smile twitched on and off his face. "Did he, now?" He shook his head. "That would be Tommy—known horse thief around here. And if he took yer horse, you can be sure it's long gone by now. Sold to the highest bidder and gone."

"What?" The word screeched from her mouth. "My horse? My beloved—"

"Look, miss, didn't no one ever tell ye not to just leave yer horse with anyone?"

Isa could only look at the man. Her heart pounded in her head, and she was having trouble breathing.

"Yeah, I know. Tommy pretends he's from this stable, but he ain't. I tell ye, he's got a good thing takin' horses from people who stop at the inn, but ye'll never catch 'im and ye'll never see yer horse again, of that ye can be sure." He shook his head sadly and then went back to brushing down the horse in front of him.

Isa resisted the urge to either fall to the floor in tears or jump up and down, screaming in fury. Neither one of them was going to move this man or bring her horse back. What could she do? What could— She fought back a sob. She'd loved her Lilli. The sweetest goer that never hesitated to take a fence. Isa put a hand to her mouth.

"Look, miss, I'm sorry, truly I am, but there ain't nothin' no one can do," the man said, clearly feeling something for her.

"Do you... do you have another horse? One I can buy or... or..."

He shook his head. "All I got is Betsy, here, and, well, she ain't mine to sell."

"No. She wouldn't do. I need to ride south to... to Dover." Isa said, quickly changing her destination so as to not tell this man where she was really going, just in case.

The fellow laughed. "No, she certainly wouldn't make it to Dover." He laughed again and then went back to his work.

"Is there nothing I can do?" Isa wasn't about to give up, not now.

"Well, there's the Angel on High Street. Ye'll be able to catch the mail to Dover from there."

"The mail?" Isa asked. She had never heard of this.

"The mail coach. It'll take ye to Dover. Don't know when it leaves, but there'll be somewhat there who knows."

Isa nodded. It looked like she was about to learn what this mail coach was and hope it left soon.

Luckily, it wasn't a very long walk back to High Street, and she'd seen the Angel before. It was the coffee house that constantly had coaches coming in and out. She now supposed some of those were mail coaches, whatever they were.

In fact, there was a large coach there just as she walked up. She found a large, burly man tying luggage to the back of the coach. "Is this the coach to Dover?" she asked him.

"Naw, it's goin' ta Brighton, miss."

"Do you know if there's a coach to Dover leaving soon?"

"Ask 'im," the man said, nodding toward a man standing off to the side, overseeing passengers and their belongings.

She strode over to the man. "I'm looking for the coach to Dover," she told him.

"Inside. See Mr. Bulby," he said shortly.

So, Isa went into the bustling inn. She hated being so open where anyone could see and recognize her, but she didn't think she had a choice, not if she wanted to find Nik, and that she wanted more than anything. For him, she would risk everything.

"Mr. Bulby?" she asked a man standing at a tall desk near the door.

"Yes? How may I help ye, miss?"

"I've been told I need to catch the mail to Dover?" It was all nonsense to Isa, but it seemed to make sense to this man.

"It comes in at 10:45 a.m., leaves at 11:00 precisely," he told her.

"Oh, excellent," she sighed with relief, then began to turn away to wait.

"That'll be a half-guinea, two bob, if ye please," he said, making her stop and turn back to him.

"I... beg your pardon?" she asked. Had he been speaking another language?

He repeated himself more slowly.

"I... I don't know what that means," she told him.

"Money. It costs money for a coach ticket, miss," he explained, as if she were an idiot.

"Oh!" Goodness, she was feeling particularly stupid today. It must have been from sleeping in that disgusting room the night before. "Of course." She pulled out the few coins she had left. "Is this enough?"

"Ye got two tanners there. A shilling," he explained. "The ticket to Dover costs twelve shillings, six-pence."

"Oh." She looked around. Where could she get more money? "I... er, if you send the bill to—"

"I ain't sending a bill nowhere. Ye either got the money or ye don't." He looked at her sternly. "And it looks as if ye don't. Sorry, miss."

"But... but... I need to get to Dover. Well, actually Margate, but Dover—" Tears were pricking at her eyes. She tried to blink them away, but they were being very stubborn.

"I'm sorry, miss, there's nothin' I can do—"

"But you don't understand. Someone stole my horse," she cried. "And then the man who told me this said I could catch the mail from here. I need to find my brother."

The man just shook his head and pursed his lips.

"How can I get... surely, you can understand," she pleaded. Never in her life had Isa pleaded. Not with anyone, anywhere, ever.

He stood there and just stared at her.

"If you give me a ticket, I'll... I'll make sure you are paid. Double! You'll be paid double! If you just—"

"I'm sorry, miss. I don't send out bills. I don't want to be paid double. You either have the half-guinea, two bob or ye don't." The man was intractable!

A tear rolled down her cheek. "My brother is in Margate. I'm sure he'll pay as soon..."

"I say!" Another man's voice came from behind her. "Did you say you needed to get to Margate?"

She spun around to face a handsome man with brown, wavy hair, strong cheek bones and deep forest-green eyes. He was dressed to the height of fashion and had a small portmanteau in his hand. "Yes! Yes, I do. But I don't have enough..." She held out the two coins in her hand to show him.

"Er, yes, so I see."

"I had two gold coins this morning, but the innkeeper at the other inn took them. One for the room and one for breakfast. And then I found that a boy had stolen my horse!" She did her best to keep her tears in check, but they were escaping ever faster now.

The man's mouth dropped open. "A sovereign for a room and another for break—" He paused and shook his head. "Oh, my poor girl. You have been horribly swindled. And your horse was stolen as well?"

Isa pulled out her handkerchief and wiped at her cheeks as she nodded. "I... I just don't know what to do. I need to find my brother."

"In Margate?"

"Yes."

He smiled at her kindly and said, "Well, your luck has just changed. I happen to be heading there myself and would be happy to take you up in my phaeton."

Isa widened her eyes. "You would?"

"That is much too kind of you, my lord," the man behind the counter said with a sad shake of his head.

"Yes, well, how can I resist a damsel in distress?" the man said with a little laugh. "My vehicle is just being brought 'round." He walked to the open door and looked out.

Isa turned back to the man behind the counter. "Do you know that man?" she asked quietly.

"That is the Marquess of Ranleigh, miss. I've known him since he was a student here at Oxford."

"Oh!" For the first time in days, Isa's spirits lifted. A marquess. And he was heading to Margate! She ran out the door after the man.

Chapter Four

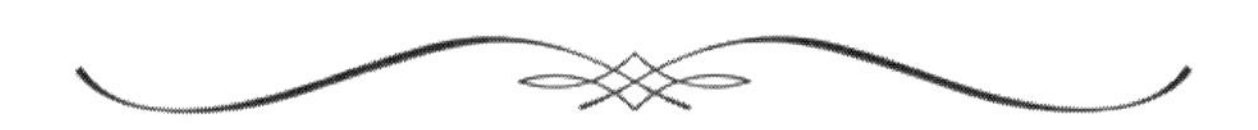

-Day 14: Getting on the Road in the Wrong Direction-

Sam didn't know what had come over him. He wasn't usually swayed by a pretty face and tears, and yet he found himself heading south to Margate rather than west to Shropshire. He was never going to make that bet now. He wondered if Dev would forgive him the hundred pounds since he was, after all, just doing this to help a lady in distress.

On the other hand, it was most certainly a much more responsible thing to do rather than driving all the way to Shropshire just for Lady Wythe's diamond necklace. The woman could live without her necklace. The young lady, however, seemed desperate to get to her brother. She was also, obviously, a total flat. A very pretty flat with her dark-blond hair, cute little turned-up nose, and delicate figure, but a flat, nonetheless.

Honestly, who didn't know money? Either she was an idiot or...

"I do beg your pardon, but I don't believe I even introduced myself to you," he told the girl as he directed his horse out of Oxford. "I'm the Marquess of Ranleigh."

"How do you do, my lord," she said, giving him a slight tilt of her head which he took for a bow.

She didn't introduce herself immediately, so he asked, "And your name?"

"Isa," she said quickly and then added, "Er, Isabelle, but I'm normally just called Isa."

He nodded. "Do you have a last name, Isa?"

"G—" She held the sound for a second and then said, "Günter. Isa Günter."

All right, so clearly that wasn't her actual name. He wasn't surprised, only she hadn't been prepared with a made-up name already on the tip of her tongue. He did think Isabelle was her first name, but she was keeping her surname to herself—probably because he would recognize it if she told him. She was clearly from the nobility, although...

"So, who is coming after you?" he asked in an offhanded way.

Her head swung toward him so fast he almost started laughing. "What makes you think anyone is coming after me?"

"Well, you're clearly a gently bred girl, which means you've probably run away from home," he told her.

"I... I, er, *am* gently bred, as you say, only I haven't run away. I am going to see my brother. I think I mentioned that."

"Hmm," was his noncommittal reply. There was something about the way she spoke. She clearly wasn't English, but where was she from? He couldn't quite place it. It was either German or Dutch, or... he didn't think it was Russian, not that he'd ever heard a Russian accent before. But it certainly wasn't French, Spanish, or Italian. Those were all languages he'd studied, and he knew what they sounded like. No, it was definitely Northern European. "And how long have you been in the country, Miss Günter?"

He heard a quick inhalation from her before her eyes dropped to her hands clasped in her lap. "I don't know what you are talking about. I told you. I'm just going to see my—"

"Brother in Margate, yes, I got that. But where are you from? You're not English."

"Why do you say that?"

He gave her a disbelieving look. "You are either a foreigner with a pretty good accent—I have to give you that—or a simpleton. You don't know the money. You got taken in by some unscrupulous innkeeper, who stole just about all you had, and gave your horse away to a lad on the street who happily absconded with it. And you tried to cry your way onto a mail coach. So, which is it? Are you a foreigner or an idiot?"

She stayed quiet, just pressing her lips into a flat line.

"I'd like to give you the benefit of the doubt and say you're a foreigner," he told her, thinking to himself that she was probably, in truth, both. "Well, wherever you're from, it's clear you're completely naïve. I mean, honestly, who allows themselves to get taken in so very thoroughly? Don't you know any better than to go to disreputable inns? Don't you know—"

"Well, obviously I did it on purpose because I love having my money stolen," she snapped. "And I didn't like that horse anyway, so I'm happy someone stole her. She was going lame in her foreleg, anyway." She turned toward him, anger flashing in her bright blue eyes. "What do you think, *my lord*?" The way she said "my lord" almost made it sound like a curse.

He adjusted himself on the bench. "All right, clearly you didn't know and were taken in, but honestly, if—"

"If you would just be quiet, I think this journey will be a great deal more pleasant," she said, cutting him off.

"Now, listen here, my girl," he started.

"I am *not* your girl, and I have no desire to listen to you berate me for my obvious stupidity. Now, do just drive and leave off talking."

Well, at least she admitted she'd been a flat.

-Day 14: An Apology and an Introduction-

Being in no great hurry, Sam stopped at midday to have a leisurely luncheon and change horses. At least that had been his intention. Miss Günter, or whatever her name was, refused to come inside the inn with him and claimed she wasn't hungry.

He couldn't very well enjoy something nice to eat with her sitting outside waiting for him. With a sigh and a longing look at the steak and kidney pie another customer was enjoying, he went back out as soon as a fresh horse was hitched up to his phaeton and was back on the road merely half an hour after they'd stopped.

They reached Reading in the afternoon, and Sam decided that was as far as he was going to go for the day.

"Why do we stop?" Miss Günter asked as they pulled into the Rose and Barrow.

"Because I'm tired and hungry. We'll spend the night here."

"Spend the night? I... I can't spend the night. I have no money, and it would be wrong—" she started.

"It's all right. I'll spot you. But before anything else, I need something to eat." Sam jumped down and was about to turn to help Miss Günter when she leapt down by herself and walked toward the inn. "Get my saddle bag," she commanded as she strode past him.

Sam's mouth dropped open. No one had ever commanded him to do anything—not since he was a boy, anyway. Damn it, he was a marquess and doing this girl a favor. A huge favor at no little expense to himself.

He growled quietly as he grabbed her saddle bag and his own portmanteau and followed in her wake.

He was shocked to find her speaking with a lady and gentleman who were sitting at a table not too far from the door. "... need of a ride south to Margate," he overheard her telling them.

What the hell did she think she was doing? He listened some more as the man and woman shook their heads sadly and said they were heading north. Miss Günter nodded and started toward another table where two gentlemen were sitting. Was she trying to find another ride? After all he'd done?

Sam clenched his jaw and strode over to her before she could say a word to them. "I beg your pardon," he said and grabbed her by the arm, dragging her away. "Just what the hell do you think you're doing?"

"Trying to find someone kinder to take me to Margate, what does it look like?" she asked, staring up at him, her eyes flashing.

"How dare you? I go out of my way to—"

"I do beg your pardon," a trim older woman with graying hair interrupted him. She turned to Miss Günter. "Is this man bothering you, my dear? Is everything all right?"

The girl gave the woman a grateful smile. "Actually…"

"Actually, my friend here was trying to solicit a ride from a stranger—a very dangerous thing to do," Sam interrupted whatever she was going to say.

The older woman looked distressed. "You weren't—?"

The girl had the grace to nod. "I was, but it isn't as if I know this gentleman either, and he's already offered to take me south."

"What?" the woman looked from Miss Günter to Sam and back again. "I think you had best tell me everything, perhaps over a calming cup of tea?"

"I don't know about tea, but I certainly need something to eat. I swear I am feeling lightheaded from lack of food," Sam said. "Ladies," he indicated an open table toward the back of the room. On their way there, he stopped a serving maid and ordered a full dinner for himself and Miss Günter. Perhaps with some food in her, she would begin thinking clearly.

As he sat down, he said, "Before she spills out her entire story to you, perhaps you might introduce yourself, ma'am?"

"Oh! Of course. I am Mrs. Margaret Brompton. I have been a lady's maid to the Countess of Teviot for the past thirty years. Sadly, my lady has gone on, and her son kindly suggested I retire. I'm on my way to Dover where my sister lives."

"Gone on?" Miss Günter asked, looking confused.

"Passed. Died," the older lady explained.

"Oh!" She nodded.

"I am sorry for your loss—of both your employer and your position, Mrs. Brompton," Sam said.

"Thank you. It was not unexpected," the lady said. She looked between Sam and Miss Günter. "And you?"

"I am the Marquess of Ranleigh," Sam told her. "And this is… well, she *says* her name is Isabelle Günter."

Miss Günter frowned at him. "My name is Isa. I was on my way to find my brother in Margate when I had nearly all my money and my horse stolen from me. I was trying to get onto the mail to Dover when Lord Ranleigh offered to take me there himself."

"Oh, how horrid you were robbed! You simply cannot trust people these days," Mrs. Brompton said with a sad shake of her head.

"No, apparently not. Lord Ranleigh has fully informed me of how much of a flat I was to allow myself to get taken in. I found him to be extremely rude and cruel. I want to find someone else to take me to my brother," Miss Günter told the woman succinctly.

Sam tried his best to keep from laughing at her choice of words but clearly didn't fully succeed. Miss Günter turned to him, her blue eyes flaring with anger. "What do you find so amusing here?"

"Where did you learn the term 'flat'?" he asked.

"From my brother." Her eyes widened, losing the anger as quickly as it had come. "Did I not use it right?"

"You did, but it's not something young ladies say," Mrs. Brompton told her. She paused as their meal was served. "But, my dear, this situation is not so simple. And clearly Lord Ranleigh is going to a great deal of trouble to take you up in his carriage," the woman added after the serving maid had left.

Sam immediately began eating and so was unable to comment on the woman's good sense.

"But he has insulted me," Miss Günter said, beginning to pick at her food.

"Perhaps, but you must admit he might have a point. I'm certain his criticism was said in kindness, so you might learn not to allow such a thing to happen again, isn't that right, my lord?" the older lady said, pouring herself some tea from the pot that had been put on the table in front of her.

"That is absolutely right," Sam said as soon as he had swallowed his mouthful. "I assure you, madam, I was not being rude."

"You see, my dear, it was not said maliciously. And truly, you would be hard pressed to find anyone willing to take you up as he has done. I would not throw that away lightly if I were you."

Miss Günter played with her food. "I suppose you are right."

"You see? You should count yourself very lucky to have found him. Why, I am here waiting for the mail coach, myself."

Chapter Five

Miss Günter looked up at that. "Are you taking the mail to Dover?"

"I am," the lady agreed.

Miss Günter looked to Sam, and he knew immediately what she was thinking. He had to agree; it was the perfect solution. "Mrs. Brompton, one thing has been bothering me ever since I offered Miss Günter a ride. It's the fact that she is a gently born girl without a chaperone," he started.

"Indeed, my lord, I was thinking the very same thing," the woman agreed.

"Might you be willing, in exchange for a ride to Dover, to take up that role for the duration of the journey?" he finished.

A smile spread across the older lady's face, crinkling it like a crumpled piece of paper that had been smoothed out again. "What a wonderful idea!"

"You would be willing to do this?" Miss Günter asked.

"I would be happy to do so," the older lady said.

"That is excellent," Miss Günter said. "I am not used to traveling without my companion. Sadly, I, er, was forced to leave her behind."

"Where did you leave her?" Sam asked, trying to get some information out of this girl. He had no idea who she was, where she came from, or what her story was. How did a gently bred girl end up in Oxford, searching for a ride south?

He knew the moment she stopped to think he wouldn't get a straight answer. "I left her at home," she said with an expression that clearly said she was pleased with herself.

"And where would that be, Miss Günter?" Mrs. Brompton asked sweetly.

"That is not your concern, nor that of Lord Ranleigh. I was not able to bring her, that is all," Miss Günter said with a lift of her chin.

Mrs. Brompton was clearly taken aback at first, but then her lips twitched, as if she were holding back a smile. "I see. Well, you shall tell us, perhaps, when we have got to know each other a little better."

"I cannot see that happening," the girl said with certainty.

Sam gave a sad shake of his head. What had he got himself into—traveling with this girl who behaved as if the world should obey her every command and not ask questions while doing so?

He sighed.

"It will be a tight squeeze. I only have my phaeton with me," Sam said apologetically. "But tomorrow we can correct the situation. My estate is not far. We can stop there, and I can get my traveling coach, and then we will go on in comfort."

"It sounds perfect," Mrs. Brompton said, all smiles. "And I thank you."

"It is acceptable," Miss Günter agreed. Not exactly the note of thanks Sam expected, but he supposed it was the best he could expect.

-JOURNAL ENTRY #1-

My dearest Nik,

I'm writing this letter in my journal because I don't know when I will have the opportunity to actually send it to you. If When I do, I promise you, I won't hesitate to cut out the page. The integrity of my book is nothing to me, especially when compared to sharing my adventures with you.

It's funny now that I think about it. I have shared my entire life with you. I have lived it with you, in your ever-present company. I value that now... now that you are missing. These things we just take for granted, my dearest brother! Things I just took for granted—like my older brother always being there.

Please excuse the drips on this page. I will try to blot them away as best I can.

Isa paused to wipe away the wetness on her cheeks and then blot her paper carefully. As she did so, she glanced over her words. It felt good... it felt comforting to write in her native German. It felt like it had been forever since she'd done so. She gathered together her thoughts and then continued:

So, let me begin by telling where and with whom I am! You would never believe this, but I am currently in Reading, traveling with the Marquess of Ranleigh and, as of today, an older lady to act as my chaperone, Mrs. Brompton. The marquess is insufferable, and I am grateful I will have the chaperone to deal with him, for I have no desire to do so any more than strictly necessary.

So, what puts me into such company, I hear you ask? I have left Herr Mueller and Frau Schmitz behind at school. I knew they would not approve of this journey, and to be honest, I thought I would find you at university and return soon enough. I don't know what they might be thinking of my disappearance, but it is of no concern to me, except the fact that they may be out searching for me. I will deal with that should it come to pass. I know they stay with me only because they are paid to, so I have no thoughts as to whether they are worried for me. I'm certain they are not.

I have never felt at ease with others like you, nor had your charm. Give me an animal and a quarter of an hour, and they will be devoted to me for life. Put a person in my midst and they will surely despise me within the first five minutes. I try... but... well, I can only hope Herr Mueller will take his time in sending out the search party. (Do you remember that fox I saved from the hounds? It upset the gamekeeper so!)

In any case, I am on my way south to meet you. Well... to find you, really. I fully believe you are in Margate or somewhere near there. Why? I don't know, but I have faith there is an excellent reason which you will share with me when we meet.

Did someone threaten you? Have you done so poorly in your classes that you were forced to leave school? (I hardly believe that one—you are cleverer than most people I know.) Have you got yourself into some other trouble with friends? (So far, to my mind, the most likely scenario.) Or perhaps you just wanted a break from your studies? But then, wouldn't you have informed me? I don't know. I would have thought so, but...

All I know is that you are missing, and the newspapers have announced your death–which I know absolutely for a fact to be false. So, there must be something...

I am determined to find out what it is and find you. I am coming my dear, sweet brother. I am coming!

-Day 15: Fathers-

"Are you looking forward to going home, my lord?" Isa asked after a couple of hours on the road.

She was bored beyond belief. She had listened to Lord Ranleigh and Mrs. Brompton chatter on for most of the journey, but they'd sat quietly for the past quarter of an hour. It had been so quiet she felt it incumbent upon her to continue the conversation.

Mrs. Brompton was sitting in between them on the bench of the phaeton, and it was rather a tight squeeze. But as they were now headed to Wendover and his lordship's estate, so he could get his traveling coach, Isa couldn't really complain. And it was better to have the older woman along. She fully acknowledged that.

It wasn't that Isa couldn't manage for herself, although buttoning her gown had been a little tricky. It was more that she was used to having someone take care of everything for her. All her life she'd had her own maid, not to mention housemaids, footmen, and a governess entirely devoted to see to her every need. There had been courtiers around every corner of her father's palace if she'd ever wanted anything the servants couldn't provide, including company.

"I suppose I am," Lord Ranleigh said, not sounding entirely convinced.

Isa gave a little laugh. "Why do I get the impression that you're not enthusiastic to be going home?"

He smiled. "Well, I have been spending a great deal more time there recently than I've been used to. My father died a little over a year ago," he said, as if that was an explanation.

"I'm sorry to hear that," she said, knowing it was the appropriate response. Then, she thought about it and added, "I would be horribly upset if I lost my father."

"Really? Are you very close?" he asked.

"Well, not *very* close, but..." In truth, she hadn't seen much of her father in recent years. He kept to himself more and more as he grew older—either that or he simply avoided her. Once she asked someone about it and had been told she was growing to look just like her mother. Isa had never known the princess since she'd died soon after Isa had been born, but she'd heard her parents had been very much in love.

And then there was the issue that, if her father died, Nik would become the ruler of the country. Isa didn't know if her brother was ready for such responsibility. He was preparing for it; indeed, he had probably been doing so for many years. But it would certainly be a dramatic change—not just for her but for the entirety of Aachen-Düren. She imagined her brother was going to be a very different sort of ruler than their father.

There was the small matter that, at the moment, Nik was missing. But she was certain she would find him soon enough.

Instead of finishing her sentence, she instead asked, "Were you close to your father, my lord?"

"No, I can't say that I was. He was a... a peculiar man, I suppose you could say. He was much more interested in his own pursuits than his family or his estate." She noticed he kept his eyes on the road as he said this, his expression bland. Or was he seeing off, to something in the past?

"Oh, well, I believe most men are like that," she said. "My father is usually too busy with his own work to spend much time with me or my brother. I just thought that's what fathers did."

"Not all. I've got one friend, Dev... Lord Devereaux. His father has always made time for him whenever he was down from school. Sometimes I would go to his home for school holidays, and we would always go fishing or hunting with his father."

"That sounds lovely," Mrs. Brompton commented with approval. "It's such a shame when gentlemen do not spend time with their children."

Isa was a little shocked the woman joined in their conversation. She wasn't used to servants talking, except when spoken to. On the other hand, she *was* sitting right in between them.

"And your mother?" Isa asked. "Is she still with you?"

"Oh yes, she will be at Ranleigh. She rarely leaves and has overseen the estate for the most part—my father had no interest. Of course, when I inherited it, she informed me I could very well take over."

"And have you?" Isa asked.

"Yes, although it did take me awhile to learn how. It's mostly what I've been doing for the past nine months since my father's death. It wouldn't have been right for me to be in Town, so I spent the time learning how to manage—agriculture, tenants, and such."

"Have you returned to Town since then?" At home, one was supposed to mourn a parent for a full year, but Isa didn't know what the customs were here in England.

"Yes, of course! Goodness, nine months was long enough!" he said with a laugh.

"Aren't you supposed to be in mourning for a year, my lord?" Mrs. Brompton asked with a slight frown.

"Oh, well, yes. I haven't been living it up in Town or anything. Been keeping it quiet, not attending parties and such," he said quickly. "Just going to my club. Meeting friends. That sort of thing."

"Your mother approved?" the woman asked.

"Nearly threw me out!" he said with a laugh. "She wasn't used to having anyone home with her. Oh, she wanted me to manage the estate, but she wanted me to do so from a distance."

Isa laughed. "It sounds like it was best for both of you that you returned to Town."

"Absolutely!" He paused, then added, "I love my mother and all that, but well, we haven't actually shared a home since I was a boy, and certainly not for as long as nine months."

"So, I assume you'll be happy to just stop in quickly to get your coach and be on your way," Isa commented.

"Oh yes. No worries. We'll be on our way soon enough. I, er, do think it would be better for you both to stay in Wendover, however. A little too much explaining, otherwise. You won't mind, will you? I'll take care of the charges, of course."

"That is very good of you, my lord," Mrs. Brompton said with a nod.

"I don't mind," Isa added. And she was happy to avoid having to share her lies with anyone else.

Chapter Six

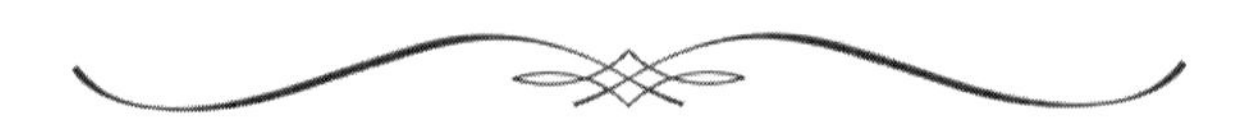

-Day 15: Mother!-

They stopped to change horses and refresh themselves midway through the day.

"Poor Mrs. Brompton," Sam commented after assisting the lady down from the phaeton and watching her slowly and stiffly make her way into the inn.

"Oh, it's all right, my lord," the lady said gamely. "I'm just not used to sitting for so very long. I'm sure it would have been just as bad, if not worse, in the mail coach. The way they pack them so full of people it's just awful."

"Why do they do this if it is so uncomfortable?" Miss Günter asked.

"So they earn more money, I suppose," the lady said before excusing herself to see to her personal needs.

"We'll be much more comfortable once I get my traveling carriage," Sam commented as he and Miss Günter sat at a table.

"Good. Your phaeton is definitely not made for three people," she stated.

He frowned at her. "No, no it's not. Nor for such long journeys."

He left the women at the Hare and Hound in Wendover and then headed home, not without a little trepidation tingling under his skin. When he faced his mother later that day, he was very happy he did so without Miss Günter by his side.

"Why, Ranleigh, what a pleasant surprise," his mother said after he walked into the drawing room.

"Good afternoon, Mother." He bent over and gave her a peck on her cheek.

"To what do I owe this pleasure? You aren't in trouble, I hope?" she asked, looking up at him with a hesitant smile.

"No, no trouble at all. I just stopped by to collect the traveling coach," he told her, settling on the tapestry-covered sofa across from her. It perfectly matched the hanging just behind it, making the piece of furniture almost difficult to discern in the busyness of the design.

His mother tilted her head in curiosity. "Are you going some place?"

"Just to Margate," he said. "I'm, er, escorting a young lady to meet her brother—properly chaperoned, of course," he added for good measure.

The edges of his mother's mouth turned up into a little smile of disbelief. "I see. And where is this young lady and her chaperone?"

"Oh, I left them at the Hare and Hound. I thought it would be easier for you if I didn't suddenly bring in unexpected guests."

"How very thoughtful," she said, fully skeptical now.

"I'd hoped you would think so," he agreed.

"So, who is this supposed girl? Anyone I know?"

Sam frowned at his mother. "No. No one you know. She says her name is Isabelle Günter, but I think that's a sham. She may be running away from somewhere, or possibly running to someone. She claims she is not, merely going to meet her brother. She hadn't much more than a tuppence in her pocket, however, when I met her trying to wheedle her way onto the mail in Oxford."

Now it was his mother's turn to frown. "Is this some sort of joke, Samuel? What ridiculous story are you spouting?" She quickly lost her frown and began to laugh. "It's a lark, isn't it? Something you and your friends are up to?"

Sam sat up. "No! I am telling you the truth."

"Hmm-hmm," she said, clearly not believing a word.

"Mother, I am behaving responsibly. I am assisting a young lady who was in distress. Ducked out of a bet with Dev and Wythe to do so, I might add."

"Yes, dear," she said, looking back down at the embroidery in her lap and picking it up again.

"You don't believe me!" he snapped.

She looked up at him, opened her mouth, and then closed it again, clearly considering her words. "My darling, you are just like your father. I didn't believe half the falderal he told me, either. But it doesn't mean I love you any less."

As if that made up for thinking him a liar, Sam thought to himself as he stood. Maybe he *should* have brought Miss Günter and Mrs. Brompton here and let his mother cope with having guests suddenly thrust on her.

"I shall be off first thing in the morning," he told her on his way out the door.

"Don't forget, I keep country hours. Dinner will be at six," she called after him.

-Day 16: Another on the Journey-

"My lord! My lord," a man's voice called. Sam was heading to the stable the following morning to speak with the head groom about getting the traveling coach ready. He turned and found Mr. Wainsbridge, his estate manager, jogging up. "I wonder if I might have a word, sir," the man asked slightly out of breath. He really could stand to lose a pound or two.

Sam sighed, then realized it wasn't polite, and turned his lips up into a smile. "Of course, Wainsbridge, what is it?"

"Er, it's one of the tenants, my lord, and, er, the livestock. There are a few issues with which I need your assistance, actually."

"I'm sorry, can't it wait? I've got people—"

"I do beg your pardon, my lord. I've written, but perhaps if you've been out of London, you haven't seen it. It's really quite urgent," the man insisted.

"Very well. Just give me a minute to send a note to the village." He turned and went back into the house.

The few issues ended up taking most of the day just as he feared. It was nearly dinner by the time the man let him go. The very moment he was allowed to go free, however, he immediately headed to stable. This time nothing was going to stop—

"My lord! If I might have a word," another voice called from behind him. Sam dropped his head for a moment before turning around. At least it wasn't Wainsbridge. Strangely enough, it was Thomas Davies, one of the footmen. He was an older man, which was odd for a footman. As Sam's mother managed the household staff, and Sam was almost never here, he supposed she could hire whoever she wanted. He waited for the man to catch up to him.

"My lord, Lady Ranleigh mentioned you were off on an escapade. I was wondering if you might need a man along with, just for a helping hand, er, with anything?"

Sam frowned at him. "I am not going on an..." He sighed. "I am escorting a young lady and her chaperone to Margate, that is all."

"Oh. Well, do you need assistance with that?" the man asked.

"Can you drive the traveling coach?"

A grin spread across Davies' face. "Of course I can, my lord. I worked for many years in the stable."

"Oh, that's right, you did. And then you were moved into the house, is that right?"

"Yes, my lord. I was looking for a way to advance—knew I'd never make it to head groom with Smith in there. He's a good man and not likely to leave his position anytime soon." Davies said, still smiling brightly.

"Huh! Yes, of course. Makes perfect sense. Well then, yes, if my mother doesn't mind, I *could* use you. I don't know how long we'll be gone..."

"Quite all right, my lord. For however long it takes. I can drive the coach during the day, assist you in the morning and evening should you need, er, assistance—shaving and the like?"

"I shave myself, thank you, but very well. I'll check with my mother, and if she has no objections, we'll leave first thing in the morning."

"Very good, sir. I'll go and tell Smith to have the coach ready." He tugged at his forelock since he wasn't wearing a hat and walked off.

"Is he escaping from a woman or just, as he says, trying to advance? Knowing Davies, it's most probably a woman," Sam said to himself with a laugh as he headed back inside.

-Day 16: Shopping for Clothes-

The morning after Lord Ranleigh left them, Isa came down to the common room to partake of a little breakfast. She found Mrs. Brompton already there sipping a cup of tea. The lady looked her over critically.

"I do beg your pardon, Miss Günter, but have you any other gowns with you?" the lady asked delicately.

"Only my riding outfit, I'm afraid," Isa admitted. "I hadn't planned on such a long journey when I set out."

The lady looked at her curiously. "But certainly, you knew it would take a few days for you to reach Margate, did you not?"

"When I left, I thought I'd find my brother in his rooms at Oxford, actually. I expected to be... home within a day," Isa explained carefully, not giving away where her home was.

"Oh, I see! Well, I have received a note from Lord Ranleigh, and he sends his regrets. He has estate business to take care of this morning and asks us to await him. I'm thinking we might take advantage of this time and see if we can't find you another gown." She smiled kindly at Isa.

"An excellent idea!" Isa said with some enthusiasm. Shopping wasn't her favorite activity, but if her only other choice was to sit here and wait for Lord Ranleigh, she would take it.

They set out to explore Wendover after Isa had eaten and quickly found a dressmaker. Mrs. Brompton took charge, which Isa was more than happy to allow her to do. She was the expert here. Isa, herself, didn't care much what she wore so long as it was comfortable.

After greeting the shopkeeper, Mrs. Brompton smiled at her and asked, "Do you happen to have any half made-up gowns. We're just passing through and find ourselves in an awkward situation."

"Of course, ma'am." The woman pulled out six gowns of varying sizes, which only needed a bit of fitting.

Mrs. Brompton turned to Isa. "Is there one you prefer, Miss Günter?"

Isa shrugged. They were all pretty much the same in her eyes. There were two blue, one pink sprigged muslin, two white, and one yellow. "I'm told I look good in blue. It matches my eyes," she said.

"The paler blue, then," Mrs. Brompton directed the woman.

Isa submitted to being pinned and pricked while the dress was fitted to her.

"Very good, ma'am," the shopkeeper told Mrs. Brompton after Isa had been helped back into her own gown. "If you could come back this evening, I'll have this ready for you. Will you be paying now or then?"

The chaperone looked to Isa who looked back at her.

"Miss Günter?" Mrs. Brompton prompted.

Isa suddenly realized that the woman thought she had money. "I have a shilling, but that's all. The innkeeper in Oxford took all my money," she said.

Mrs. Brompton's mouth dropped open a touch. She snapped it closed again and then turned to the woman. "I'll pay for it now." She pulled a purse out of her reticule, and Isa had the strangest sinking feeling in the pit of her stomach. Never in her life had she had to think about money, and now within the space of only a few days, she'd found the need for it again and again. She had no idea how Herr Mueller or Frau Schmitz, her companion, managed.

As they walked back to the inn, Isa said, "I shall repay you when I find my brother."

"Do not consider it now, miss."

Isa wished she had the words to thank her for her kindness, but she was torn between embarrassment and the knowledge that the woman would be well compensated once Nik was found—she would be sure of it. So, she stayed quiet.

As she was thinking about this, Mrs. Brompton took her arm and hurried her across the street just in front of a cart that nearly hit them.

Chapter Seven

"Mrs. Brompton, what are you doing?" Isa cried, jumping out of the street and pulling the older woman with her.

"There were two men," the woman whispered furiously. She continued walking quickly toward the inn, every once in a while glancing back behind them. "I think they are gone."

"Two men? I don't understand," Isa said, keeping up with the woman.

"I noticed two men looking in the shop window while you were getting fitted for your dress. They were still there when we left the shop just now, and they began to follow us."

Isa widened her eyes and began to walk even faster. Mrs. Brompton could hardly keep up. She began breathing heavily. Isa slowed down again to allow the woman to breathe. They entered the inn and went straight up to Isa's room.

The lady dropped onto Isa's bed, her hand to her rapidly rising and falling chest. "Who do you think they were?" she asked.

"I have no idea." But Isa had a very good idea who they were—men hired by Herr Mueller to find her! That was the only thing that made sense. She'd been gone for nearly four days; surely, her bodyguard had men out searching for her.

"We should send a note up to Lord Ranleigh," Mrs. Brompton started.

"What? No! No, I'm certain they will be gone soon enough. Maybe they saw you take out your purse and wanted to steal it," Isa suggested. The last thing she wanted was Lord Ranleigh to become more suspicious. Mrs. Brompton was probably too innocent to think it could be anything more, but his lordship seemed to be the savvy sort. He would immediately think something dubious was going on, and sadly, he would be correct.

"Yes. Yes, I'm sure you're right," the lady said, now calming down. She gave Isa a little smile. "Well, why don't you rest until his lordship —" She was interrupted by a knock on the door.

Isa stood back and looked to Mrs. Brompton to answer it. She took a moment and then got herself to her feet and opened the door. It seemed to be one of the serving girls from downstairs.

"This came from 'is lordship while you was out," the girl said.

"Oh, thank you." Mrs. Brompton took the note and closed the door. Isa was about to hold her hand out for it when the woman had the tenacity to open it and read it herself.

"Is it addressed to you?" Isa asked, surprised.

The woman looked up with widened eyes. Surely, she knew she had just committed a faux pas. She just looked at Isa and then back down to the note. "I do beg your pardon, miss. It is addressed to both of us, actually. Lord Ranleigh says he won't be able to get away in time for us to make any headway today and suggests we leave first thing tomorrow morning."

"But does he not know I am anxious to get to Margate? Why is he wasting my time?" Isa snapped.

She wasn't sure she liked the temerity of these people. Lord Ranleigh addressing a note to both her and her servant? And then the servant in question reading the note herself first? Never in her life had she been treated—Isa stopped herself. No one knew she was a princess. No one knew she should be treated with deference. They just thought she was some common girl trying to reach her brother.

Mrs. Brompton just stood there, looking at her with mild disapproval on her lips. "Miss Günter, the gentleman is doing us a favor in taking us to Margate. We will go at his convenience."

Isa sighed in disgust. She didn't like not leaving when *she* wanted to go. How she hated being common! How did others deal with this? No wonder Lady Elizabeth from school was always in such a foul mood. Isa probably would be too if she had to be ordinary all the time.

"Why don't you rest for a while?" Mrs. Brompton suggested gently. "I'll meet you downstairs for dinner at six."

Isa didn't know what she would do until then, but she supposed she didn't have much of a choice. She couldn't go out for a walk—those men of Herr Mueller's were out there looking for her. She didn't have a horse to ride, or she would have been gone on her own in a heartbeat. She could do nothing but sit here and wait.

She ended up pulling out her journal and continuing her letter to Nik. A little before six, Mrs. Brompton knocked at her door, carrying a tray.

"I'm sorry, Miss Günter, but I thought it might be better for us to take our dinner here, just to be safe."

Isa stood and allowed the woman to place the tray on the table where she'd been writing. "Have you seen those men again?" she asked.

"They're in the common room. I saw them when I went out to collect your dress. Oh, let me fetch that for you. It's in my room. I think you'll be pleased. The woman was kind enough to add a touch more lace around the neckline, and I think it looks very pretty." She bustled off, returning a moment later with the dress. Isa allowed her to chatter away about dresses while they ate—together. Isa reconciled herself to this by remembering that Frau Schmitz had done the same on their journey from Aachen-Düren. Of course, Frau Schmitz was the younger sister of a markgraf, but perhaps Mrs. Brompton was of noble birth as well. Isa had never asked her.

-Day 17: Commotion and an Escape-

The following morning, Mrs. Brompton helped Isa dress in her new gown. "Oh, it looks lovely, Miss Günter," the older woman gushed.

Isa just smiled at her. It didn't look too bad, she had to admit to herself. And she did feel better about having more than just one dress to wear. Sadly, she didn't think it would be appropriate to wear her breeches—she'd probably give the old woman an apoplexy, she thought with an inward laugh.

"I do hope those men are gone," Mrs. Brompton said as they made their way down with their luggage.

They paused at the entrance to the common room and, not seeing them there, sat at a table near the window, so they would be able to see Lord Ranleigh when he drove up. They shared a pot of tea and some toast, and Isa had just seen the approach of a large traveling coach when Mrs. Brompton gasped.

She looked over toward the door. The two men from the day before were standing in the hall by the entrance.

"You go out and wait for his lordship," Mrs. Brompton whispered.

"That may be him," Isa said, nodding toward the coach now pulling up to the front of the inn.

"Good. You go on ahead, and I'll follow," the older woman said.

"But—" Isa started to protest.

"You go on, now." Mrs. Brompton stood and smoothed down the front of her dress.

The two men were talking to the innkeeper and had their backs to the door to the common room when Isa slipped out. She went quickly to the front door of the inn.

"There she is!" she heard one of them say.

There was a loud *oof,* and then she heard Mrs. Brompton screech. "How dare you! He touched me! He touched me!"

She turned to help the woman, but Mrs. Brompton seemed to have things well in hand.

Her companion slapped one of the men across the face and grabbed hold of the arm of the other before he had a chance to go after Isa. "You! You disgusting creature! You have some nerve touching a woman like that!" Mrs. Brompton yelled. The innkeeper, the barkeep, and a maid all immediately surrounded the woman and the two men. Isa escaped.

Lord Ranleigh had just stepped down from the coach when Isa ran out of the building and jumped straight into the coach. "Come, my lord, quickly."

"But where is Mrs.—" he started.

"She's coming. Get in!" Isa told him shortly. And indeed, a moment later, Mrs. Brompton came hurrying out. She climbed into the coach and knocked on the roof to signal the driver to start.

"I do beg your pardon, my lord. I'm certain you want to get going as quickly as possible? Of course you do! After losing a whole day on our journey, we definitely want to get a move on," the woman said as the coach rambled away from the inn.

"Is everything all right, Mrs. Brompton?" Lord Ranleigh asked.

The lady's hat was askew, and her face was flushed. "What? Oh yes, yes, of course, my lord."

"Yes?" Isa asked, giving her a meaningful look.

"Indeed, my dear. My lord—" Mrs. Brompton started to turn toward Lord Ranleigh, who was still looking at her a little strangely.

Isa put her hand on the woman's arm to stop her. When Mrs. Brompton turned back at her, Isa gave a little shake of her head before turning a smile onto the man.

"Yes, Mrs. Brompton?" he asked, waiting for her to finish.

"Er, did you notice Miss Günter's new gown? We purchased it yesterday," Mrs. Brompton said, clearly thinking fast.

"Oh, er, no. She ran past me so quickly I didn't have a chance to notice," he said, turning to Isa and looking at her dress. She was wearing her old pelisse over it, but she held up the skirt for him to admire.

"Actually, Mrs. Brompton purchased it for me, but I shall repay her as soon as we meet my brother," Isa admitted.

Lord Ranleigh turned toward the older lady. "That was very kind of you, ma'am."

"Oh no, it is nothing. And she had only the one dress." The woman fanned her hand in front of her face. "Can't let such a lovely young girl live in one dress for a week, or however long it will take us to reach Dover."

"Truly, too kind," he reiterated.

Chapter Eight

~Day 17: In Which our Hero Realizes that the Heroine is a Nice Person~

Sam couldn't figure out what was wrong with Miss Günter and Mrs. Brompton when they stopped for lunch that afternoon. They both seemed to be inordinately jumpy and hurried. It was only when they were back in the coach and on their way once again that either one of them relaxed.

Mrs. Brompton relaxed so thoroughly she actually fell asleep. As soon as Miss Günter realized this, she switched seats so she was next to Sam. After she did so, he noticed how nice she smelled. Surely the inn at Wendover hadn't provided her with rose-scented soap. Yet as she settled in next to him, he was overcome with a delicate floral smell that strongly reminded him of his mother's rose garden at the height of summer.

"So, my lord, did you enjoy your all-too-brief visit home?" she asked, showing how very straight her teeth were and how pretty her smile.

He couldn't help but return her smile and wish his teeth were as perfect. His weren't bad, certainly not as awful as some he'd seen, but not as perfect as hers. He pushed the odd thought from his mind and turned his thoughts back to his visit home. "I can't say that I exactly enjoyed it, Miss Günter," he told her in as quiet a voice as she had used so as to not wake Mrs. Brompton.

"Oh?" she cocked her head ever so slightly.

"Well, when I told my mother why I wanted the coach, sadly, she didn't believe me. She thought I was embarking on some lark. I tried to tell her about you and Mrs. Brompton, but she just laughed and brushed me off," he admitted, not quite certain why he was being so open and honest with her when she had been anything but with him. He supposed it just wasn't in his nature to skirt the truth. He hadn't done so when she'd asked about his family situation before they'd arrived at Wendover, and he wasn't going to now.

She frowned at him. "I am so sorry. Is this normal for her to not believe you when you tell her something?"

He sighed. "Not precisely. Well, I mean, I usually don't tell her everything I get up to, so she doesn't usually have a chance to believe me or not."

"Ah, I see. You do not want to risk her disapproval should you want to engage in some activity she might not deem entirely appropriate," she said with an understanding nod.

He looked at her curiously. "Yes! That's precisely right. How... I can't imagine you have ever been in the same situation."

She gave a little laugh. "Well, unfortunately I never had an opportunity. My father always—but always—knew exactly what my brother and I were doing."

Sam chuckled. "Had his spies, did he? Your maid or governess, I suppose?"

She nodded. "Among others."

"Well, I suppose in that way, I am lucky. I have had the freedom to do as I liked, and if I ever did anything of which I was certain she wouldn't approve, then yes, I simply wouldn't tell her." He frowned thinking about it. "But she always seemed to know anyway, or at least hinted that she did so."

Miss Günter laughed quietly. "Parents always know."

"Well, my father knew because he was up to even more outrageous things than I was."

She turned toward him in surprise. "You mentioned before that he was very involved in his own occupations."

"Yes, well, those occupations, as you so gently put it, usually entailed gambling and drinking. He was the sort to bet on anything and would do anything for a wager. He once rode a horse backward through the park at the height of the promenade." Sam shook his head, remembering his mother's horrified expression when she'd caught sight of him. Sam was there and had seen the entire thing. Lady Ranleigh had been driving her phaeton with Lady Blakemore and had been so embarrassed, she immediately turned her carriage around and headed back in the other direction. It had caused quite a disturbance, almost more so than his father. Now that he thought about it, it was about that time that his mother had retired to their estate and rarely returned to Town.

"Goodness!"

"Yes, so... well, you can imagine that when I tell my mother I am helping a young lady out of a difficult situation, she might not believe me."

"She *expects* you to behave as your father did?"

"Yes, that is precisely what she expects of me."

"Oh, I am sorry."

He gave a little shrug. "The world certainly didn't lose anything when my father died, I'm afraid."

She looked at him in silence for a moment and then asked, "When you die, would you like people to believe the world has lost something? Would you like to make your mark on the world—in a positive way?"

Sam was startled at the depth of her question. His comment about his father was just an expression to his mind, but she'd taken him literally and turned the tables. He thought about it. "Yes," he said slowly. "I have not yet taken my seat in Parliament—only inherited the title a little over a year ago—but I would like to do so. I would like to do something good for this world, and I would like to be thought of well." He sat digesting his own words. He added, "It's why I am determined to become responsible."

She gave him a little smile. "Have you not been responsible up until now?"

He chuckled. "No. I was told at a young age that I was exactly like my father—I look just like him. I've always done my best to live up—or, I suppose, down—to their expectations."

"So, you have wagered and drank and behaved..."

"Badly," he said, summing it up in a word.

"But you will do so no longer?"

"No. I have decided to turn over a new leaf as they say. I want to do something good, something constructive. I want to help those I can and take up my responsibilities."

She nodded in an approving manner.

"It was the other thing that kept me so long at Wendover. My estate manager needed my attention on some issues dealing with the home farm. I thought it would just take an hour or so, but it ended up occupying me most of the day, I'm afraid. I am sorry for the delay."

"It is all right. I do have to admit to being anxious to get to Margate. I am rather concerned—" She stopped speaking abruptly and then shook her head. She gave an embarrassed little smile. "Well hopefully, we will be able to get there without too much further delay." She paused and then said again more softly, "Hopefully."

Sam frowned. There was definitely a great deal she wasn't telling him. "Why would we not?" he asked.

She widened her eyes and placed a polite smile on her lips. "No reason. No reason at all."

"I don't suppose you would care to share your concerns with me?" he asked gently.

She blinked rapidly a few times but shook her head. "I wish I could, but... I do not think it would be a good idea."

"I wish you would be more honest with me. I am going to a great deal of trouble and expense to see you to Margate."

"I know. And I promise you will be compensated—"

"I don't want compensation. I want honesty."

She bit her lower lip and fluttered her eyelashes again, as if she were blinking back tears. "I... I cannot," she said with a little shake of her head.

"What is it? Are you running away from someone, from something?"

"No! No, at least, I do not think so. No, I just need to get to my brother. That is all. I fear... well, no matter. We shall be there soon enough, yes?"

"I certainly hope so." There was so much more to this girl. He didn't know how he knew, but he was certain of it. She had a great number of secrets she was keeping from him, and he didn't like it. Oddly enough, it only made him want to help her even more. He felt a strong surge of protectiveness for her. She was running either away from something or to something—he didn't know which—all he knew was she needed help and he wanted to be the one to provide it.

-Day 17: Meeting Davies-

Isa, as always, was the first out of the coach the moment they arrived at the inn where they'd be staying the night.

"If you'll just wait a minute longer, miss, I'll put down the step for you," the coachman said with a twinkle in his eye. He was a very handsome, if older, man with broad shoulders and thick dark hair with silver shot through it.

"That's all right. I have to admit I am not used to being couped up in a coach for so long. I am anxious to get out and stretch my legs," she told him.

"I understand. Well, you're welcome to join me on the box anytime you like, just to get a different view or some fresh air."

That was a thought! Isa had never considered riding on the front bench with the coachman before. She nodded. "I will think about that."

The man bowed and said, "Davies, miss. My name is Davies." He turned to Mrs. Brompton who had descended from the coach. She took up her position a step behind Isa and gave her a smile.

"How do you do, Mr. Davies," the older woman said. "I am Mrs. Brompton, Miss Günter's chaperone for the journey."

"A young thing like you? Why, I would have thought you would be needing a chaperone of your own!" he said.

The woman smiled but said, "Oh-ho, a charmer, are you?"

The man tried to look innocent, widening his eyes. "Me? Oh, I don't know, I suppose some ladies have thought me charming in my day."

Mrs. Brompton gave a little giggle and then ushered Isa into the inn where Lord Ranleigh was already making arrangements for their stay.

Isa glanced at her chaperone and was shocked to see the woman had turned quite pink. Was she attracted to the coachman? Isa suppressed a laugh as she followed Mrs. Brompton up the stairs to their room for the night.

Chapter Nine

-Day 17: Some Truths Are Revealed-

"What? I beg your pardon, my lord, I missed what you said," Mrs. Brompton said, her eyes snapping back to Sam. They were wide and looked apprehensive.

He smiled at her reassuringly. "I said, I hope this journey isn't taking too much of a toll on you."

"Oh!" She gave a little flustered laugh. "No, no, not at all. Certainly, nothing compared to what the mail would have been like."

"What is it then, Mrs. Brompton? What has you so distracted and, if I may, disturbed?" They were waiting for Miss Günter to join them for supper. Sam hoped she would take another few minutes so he would have the chance to speak to the woman confidentially.

"Disturbed? Me?"

He just looked at her, waiting for the truth. He had reluctantly accepted that Miss Günter was keeping secrets from him, but he wasn't going to give the same grace to Mrs. Brompton who, so far, had been completely open and honest with him.

She sighed a little dramatically and then seemed to recall herself.

Her eyes shifted over to her left. "Do you see those two men sitting at that table close to the wall?" she asked quietly.

Sam allowed his eyes to shift in that direction without moving his entire head. "Yes."

"We saw them at Wendover. They were following us. First, when we were on our way back from the dressmaker, and then again later that evening, they were in the common room of the inn. They were there again this morning when Miss Günter came down for breakfast. You might have noticed I was a little, er, befuddled when I left the inn?"

He nodded. "But surely, they were also just visitors to Wendover staying at the same inn. It's not uncommon—"

"When Miss Günter walked past them on her way out to the coach this morning, I heard one of them say 'There she is!'," she told him. "I had to use my wits to ensure they couldn't follow immediately after us. Sadly, they seem to have managed to do so, anyway."

Sam frowned and allowed his eyes to look over at the men as inconspicuously as possible. "Who do you think they are?"

"All I know is that they're looking for Miss Günter. She was trying to make out they weren't after her, but I could see the fear in her eyes both yesterday and this morning."

Sam nodded. "If you'll excuse me for just a moment, Mrs. Brompton, I'll see if I can secure a private dining room for our use." He got up and went over to the innkeeper. Luckily, there happened to be one on the premises, and it was unoccupied.

He motioned for Mrs. Brompton to join him. Before she entered the room, however, she stopped. "I'll just go up and fetch Miss Günter, so she knows where we are and doesn't go into the common room." At Sam's nod, she went up the stairs.

He, in the meantime, ordered a bottle of wine. He figured they could all do with a glass.

When the two women came down again, he said, "So, Miss Günter, did Mrs. Brompton tell you why I have had to go to the extra expense of hiring a private room?"

The girl's eyes became worried. She nodded.

"Then, would you care to explain why there are two men looking for you?"

She lowered herself to a chair and clasped her hands in her lap. Finally, he would get a straight answer. It was about time!

"No, my lord. I have no idea why those men are looking for me if it is, indeed, me who they are looking for. I have certainly never seen them before in my life," she said, looking him straight in the eye.

Sam jumped to his feet, his patience at an end. "Surely, you don't expect me to believe such nonsense?"

The girl, too, stood, all pretense of submission gone from her demeanor. She lifted her chin to stare him down. "I do not care what you believe. I tell you all I know. I do not know who those men are or who they are after. *Gute Nacht*." With that, she spun around on her heel and left the room.

Sam couldn't believe it. "That girl has some nerve!" he exclaimed.

"Oh, my lord, do, please, be patient with her. Clearly, she is terrified. And in all likelihood, feeling all the worse for having put you to such trouble and expense already. Pointing out to her that you are going even further probably just made her feel worse," Mrs. Brompton said, trying to calm him.

"You would think she would manage to be polite about it. Apologize? Tell us the truth?" He sighed in disgust and grabbed the bottle of wine and a glass. "I do beg your pardon, but I think I, too, will retire for the night. Please feel free to order dinner for yourself."

He went up to his room and was surprised to find Davies there, laying out his shaving kit.

"Oh, my lord, I didn't expect you up so soon."

"I didn't expect to be so, but it seems Miss Günter is being followed," Sam ground out. He put the bottle on a side table and filled his glass.

"Being followed? I don't understand." Davies stopped what he was doing.

"There were apparently some men following her at Wendover, and Mrs. Brompton has seen them here as well. I just can't believe that girl! I should have known she'd be trouble. No one can be that pretty, on her own, and not be trouble." He drank down the contents of his glass. "If only she were honest with me. If she would tell me anything, anything of what was going on I would probably be able to do something."

"What could you do, my lord?"

"Well, I could confront those men, for one," he said. He actually hadn't thought through what he could do, truth be told. "I can only suppose her father sent them to find her," he admitted.

"Sounds very likely, in which case you would have a decision to make—do you turn her over to them and allow them to escort her home, or do you aid her in escaping from them? I suppose it's a question of whether you believe she ran away for a good reason or... or not."

"Well, if she would bloody well tell me—" he exploded. He calmed himself immediately. It wasn't Davies' fault this girl had not spoken an honest word to him since they'd met. "I do beg your pardon, Davies. I'm extremely frustrated at this whole situation."

"Naturally, my lord. No offense taken at all."

Sam sipped at his second glass of wine. "The question is, as you say, whether she escaped her home for good reason. There is, of course, no way to know. If I ask her, I can be pretty certain whatever she tells me *won't* be the truth, or she'll somehow skirt around the question and not give me an answer at all." He took another drink.

"You do know where she is going, though?" Davies asked.

"To Margate. Presumably to meet her brother." He paused and then added, "I actually believe that one. She seems very insistent on that."

"Well then, it could be possible she isn't running away from her family, but *to* family—perhaps from a difficult situation," Davies suggested.

"Yes." He thought about it a bit more. "Yes, that is possible."

"In which case, it would be better to help her and not turn her over to these men. And really, who sends men after a girl?"

Sam looked up. "Someone who is unlikely to have her best interests at heart. Otherwise, they would have come after her themselves. You're right! No father would hire men to chase after his daughter."

Davies nodded. "It sounds to me like you're doing the right thing, my lord, in helping this girl get to her brother."

"Yes!" Sam stood, refilling his glass again. "Yes, I think I am. All right, then, we leave at first light."

"Very good, my lord. I will have the coach ready. May I assist you in preparing for bed before I go check on the horses and inform the stable?"

"Yes. And on your way out, stop by the kitchen and tell them to have a basket with some cold meats and cheese for us to take along. We won't have time to eat here."

"Very good, my lord."

-LETTER TO NIK CONTINUED-

That man is completely insufferable! If I didn't have to maintain this pretense as an ordinary girl, I would love to give him a piece of my mind. How dare he accuse me of not telling him the truth!

Oh, very well, I am not doing so, but I cannot!

If he knew who I truly was, he would turn me over in a heartbeat to those men following us. Goodness, Herr Mueller has probably set a hefty reward for my return. It would certainly explain the men's persistence.

But I can't let them take me back. I can't! Not now! I am determined to find you, my dearest Nik. Absolutely determined. I don't care what expense that man goes to. I don't care who follows us. I will find you!

Oh, drat! I need my handkerchief and, as always, it is no where at hand.

Isa took a deep breath and tried to calm herself.

Mrs. Brompton, the chaperone who is now accompanying me, is an extraordinarily kind woman. I am ever so grateful she has joined us. I am certain I don't know what I would do without her. Do you know she purchased a dress for me with her own money, so that I would not have to either wear the same gown day after day or my riding clothes? (Truly, I would not want to shock her by wearing my breeches, which is all I have with me.) It was an act I am not likely to forget—ever. Oh, I'm certain she will be reimbursed, but the money is not the issue. It is her kindness, her generosity. She is clearly not a woman of means. She has been a lady's maid for thirty years. And yet, she did not hesitate to open her purse for me. I wonder if she is a relation of some lesser noble. She certainly behaves as if she is.

On the other hand, even those who I know to be of noble birth have never acted with such generosity. Never have I experienced anyone like her. We have only ever known people who have wanted something from us, be it wealth or prestige. At this moment, in this guise, I have neither, and still, she stands by me and assists me in every way possible. I am truly in awe of such selflessness. I'm not even certain I ever knew it existed.

I do pray you have known such people, my dearest Nik. Indeed, that you are experiencing this even now... wherever you are... whoever you are with. I hope you are safe and happy and know in your heart that I am with you in spirit as I will soon be in body.

-Day 18: Making a Run for It-

Isa was woken early the following morning. So early in fact, she'd thought it still night. The sun hadn't even risen when there was a knocking on her door.

Mrs. Brompton, who was sleeping on a small mattress at the foot of Isa's bed, got up to see who it might be.

Isa could only hear the low tones of a man's whisper before the door closed again. Mrs. Brompton then lit a candle from the embers of the fire before turning toward the bed.

"What was that, Mrs. Brompton?" Isa asked.

"It was Lord Ranleigh, miss. He wants us to leave now before those men have a chance to follow us again. Come, let me help you get dressed."

Isa got up and dressed as quietly as possible. They then tiptoed down the stairs and found his lordship standing just outside the door, waiting for his coach to be brought around. If the coachman, Mr. Davies, thought it odd they were slipping out so early in the morning, he didn't say a word.

Chapter Ten

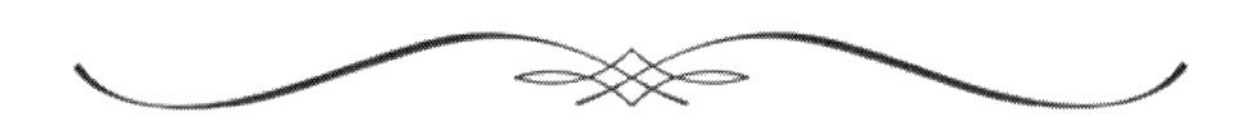

-Day 18: A Side Trip to a Tree-

Isa fell back asleep soon after they were back on the road. There didn't seem to be any reason not to, so she snuggled down in one corner, using her saddlebag as a pillow. When she woke a few hours later, she found herself curled up on the seat with her feet up, and Mrs. Brompton sitting across from her, next to Lord Ranleigh. The two of them were reading, making Isa jealous that they both had something to do on this tiresome journey.

"Oh, good. We'll be arriving soon," his lordship said, looking up from his book. He slipped a piece of paper into the pages to keep his place.

"Arriving? Not at Margate already?" Isa asked, looking out the window. It all looked the same—just rows and rows of crops or endless stretches of meadow. The English countryside could not be said to have been interesting. Pretty, she supposed, but definitely not interesting.

Lord Ranleigh gave a little laugh. "No! Not Margate. We won't arrive there for a few days. No, I thought we'd stop at Runnymede. I arranged for some food to be packed for us last night. We can stop and see Ankerwyke Yew if you like. Have a bit of a picnic there."

Confusion must have been writ all over Isa's face because he smiled and explained. "Ankerwyke Yew is where the Magna Carta was signed."

"Oh. Why would we want to stop there?" Isa asked. She had a vague recollection of being taught something about the Magna Carta, but truthfully, she couldn't remember what it was. Clearly, she supposed, it was something important in Britain.

"It's very impressive. I've seen it once before. My lady went once with her children to see the spot," Mrs. Brompton said.

"I am afraid I don't understand the importance of it—or even what it is," Isa admitted.

They both smiled at her. "You'll see when we get there," Lord Ranleigh said.

When they did arrive, Isa could see why Mrs. Brompton was impressed. The Ankerwyke Yew was the largest tree Isa had ever seen in her life. It was probably two and a half meters across.

"They say it's thousands of years old. Can you imagine what this tree must have seen?" Lord Ranleigh asked, looking up into its branches.

"Nothing, actually. Trees do not have eyes," Isa pointed out.

She received a frown for that comment.

"Perhaps, then, what it may have witnessed," Mrs. Brompton suggested. "We don't know they aren't aware of their surroundings. They are living beings."

Isa just shrugged.

"It's a very old tree," Lord Ranleigh stated.

"And you are not worried about the men who were looking for me?" Isa had to ask.

"No, I think we gave them the slip. And if we didn't, they're certainly not going to expect us to stop here. In fact, the more I think about it, the more convinced I am that taking our time would be the best plan." He sat down at the foot of the tree and began to dig into the picnic basket provided by the inn.

"What do you mean?" Isa asked, settling herself across from him.

She wished she were wearing her breeches. It would have been so much more comfortable for sitting on the grass.

"Well, they surely know we're heading for the coast. Probably figure we'll want to get there as quickly as possible." He opened up a cloth filled with bread and then another with a chunk of cheese. He began cutting off slices for each of them as Mrs. Brompton settled herself with a slight *oof*.

"Either that or they will assume we are heading to London. Do you not think?" Isa suggested.

He nodded and looked impressed for a moment. "They could, although we're not headed in quite the right direction for that. Would have taken a different road were we going to London."

"Oh, so you think they are expecting us to head to Dover."

"Yes. Do you think you might want to share with us any thoughts you have on who these men are, and what they might want with you?"

"This is lovely cheese," Isa said around a mouthful.

"Right. As straight forward and honest as always, Miss Günter," he said, frowning at her.

Isa kept her attention on her food, but she could feel his stare.

"Very well. Do you think that, whoever these men are or whoever sent them after you, knows where you are headed?" he tried.

"No. They would not." She could tell him that much.

"Do they know where your brother is? Is it still your brother who you are going to see?"

"Most definitely. And I doubt very much they know where he is. They might know he is at a port but not which one," she said, helping herself to another piece of cheese.

"All right, then. We'll give them a bit of a red herring and start off in the direction of Portsmouth tomorrow before coming back toward Margate."

"A herring?" Isa asked, wondering what a fish had to do with this.

"A red herring," Lord Ranleigh said with a laugh. "It's used as a lure. We'll make them think we're going in one direction when really we're headed in another."

"Oh! How clever!" Isa was impressed—and very grateful this man was on her side—he was devious!

He basked for a moment in her compliment and then continued, "Yes, and we'll continue to take it slow because they'll also believe that we'd want to reach our destination as quickly as possible."

"I do!" Isa agreed immediately.

"Right, which is precisely why we won't." He turned toward Mrs. Brompton. "You're not in any great tearing hurry are you, Mrs. Brompton?"

"Me? No. I've got all the time in the world. I'm heading to my retirement. Why would I want to rush to get there?" she asked with a little chuckle. "I may drop my sister a note and tell her I won't be arriving as soon as expected, however, just so she doesn't worry. I'll tell her I'm making a bit of a holiday of the journey."

"Excellent idea! And precisely what we should do. We are heading in the direction of an area of extraordinary beauty, you know. I see no reason why we should rush through it," he said happily.

"You do not have anywhere you need to be?" Isa asked.

He gave a little shrug. "There's nothing I need to do that can't wait a week or so."

"A week or so!" Isa nearly screeched. "You surely do not anticipate taking that long!"

"Oh, I plan on it, Miss Günter. I plan on it."

-Day 18: Getting to Know Davies Better-

Isa followed Mrs. Brompton down for dinner that evening and was surprised to find Lord Ranleigh sitting with the coachman! What was *he* doing at their table? It was already odd that Mrs. Brompton ate with them, but Isa figured it was necessary since she was supposed to be chaperoning her. But the coachman? At least he wasn't wearing his livery.

"Oh, good evening, Mr. Davies," Mrs. Brompton said with a smile. "What a lovely surprise this is."

"I hope you don't mind. I invited him to join us. I thought those men searching for you might overlook the four of us sitting together.

And it doesn't hurt to have another set of eyes keeping watch for them," Lord Ranleigh said, helping Isa take her seat.

Isa's own bodyguard never actually sat with her and Frau Schmitz, her companion, but always at a table nearby. But she supposed Lord Ranleigh was right, and the men wouldn't look twice at the four of them together. They were looking for one woman, possibly traveling alone. Being in a group was definitely safer.

She decided the wisest thing would be to stay quiet. Perhaps it is an English tradition to eat with the servants, or maybe it was simply the extraordinary circumstances of traveling that made it acceptable. This was altogether the oddest situation. Isa didn't know whether it was her or whether rules were, in fact, being shoved aside.

"Miss Günter, you are quiet this evening. Do you have an objection to Mr. Davies joining us?" his lordship asked, taking the seat across from her.

"Oh, no, I, er, I am sure you are doing whatever is correct," she answered quickly. "I have to admit I was friendly with my groom at home. It is the same sort of thing, is it not?"

"Yes, I suppose it is," Lord Ranleigh acknowledged.

Isa turned to the man with a smile. "Have you been a coachman for very long, Mr. Davies?"

"Actually, miss, I've been a footman for her ladyship for the past few years. I was in the stable before that. But I'm hoping to move up the ranks. Wouldn't mind being a valet, actually," the man answered her.

"Well, you're getting some practice with that on this journey, so that's a good thing," Lord Ranleigh commented. "But won't the maids at Ranleigh miss you while you're gone? Or was that the point?" He gave the man a pointed look.

"What? I don't know what you're talking about, my lord," Mr. Davies said, clearly trying his hardest to look innocent.

Mrs. Brompton just gave a little snort of a laugh. "Oh, he's *that* type, is he?"

"What type?" the man protested as Isa asked the same question silently in her own mind.

Just then the serving maid came up to their table with a mug of ale for Mr. Davies and a bottle of wine for the rest of them to share. As she placed the mug down in front of the coachman, however, Isa noticed she deliberately bent over him so low that she brushed her chest against the top of his shoulder and turned her face toward his. Had she whispered something to him as she passed his ear? Isa couldn't tell, but she understood enough to know this was inappropriate behavior.

Mr. Davies' cheeks turned bright red, but the maid just gave a little giggle before sauntering away with a swing in her hips.

The coachman cleared his throat uncomfortably. "Sorry, she and I were, er, talking earlier."

"And expect to, er, talk some more later?" Mrs. Brompton asked with a lift of her eyebrows.

He pursed his lips, clearly trying not to smile. "Might."

"And that is most likely the reason why you requested to come along on this journey," Lord Ranleigh summarized.

Mr. Davies gave an embarrassed little laugh. "Not my fault women find me attractive, my lord. Honestly, I don't do anything, they're just drawn to me."

Mrs. Brompton gave another snort of laughter.

"Well, you are very handsome," Isa said, understanding that women might be attracted to him.

"Thank you, Miss Günter," the man said, nodding to her and then giving Mrs. Brompton a smile as if to say, "No need to laugh at me!"

"Are you kind as well?" Isa asked.

"Am I kind?" he repeated, not understanding her meaning.

"Do you do little things for ladies, er, women? Do you behave gentlemanly toward them?"

Lord Ranleigh cocked his head and looked at her curiously.

"Women like that sort of thing," she told him in answer to his unasked question.

"Oh, of course," he said quickly.

"Have you ever courted anyone, my lord?" Isa asked with a laugh.

Chapter Eleven

"Er, no. I've called on a few young ladies and danced with a fair number as well, but I've never actually courted anyone," he admitted.

"Well if you ever do, do not forget to buy them flowers and do small kindnesses for them. Girls like that," Isa told him.

"I can't agree more, Miss Günter. Some gentlemen go for those grand gestures—emerald necklaces and the such, but it is absolutely the little things that really turn a girl's head," Mrs. Brompton agreed.

"Have you ever been courted, Miss Günter?" Lord Ranleigh asked, turning the tables on her.

"No, but I have certainly thought about it. I had one, er, friend mention that it was the small kindnesses that made her fall in love with the man she married. I thought it made perfect sense." That the friend was not actually a friend but a courtier didn't make a difference. Nor did the fact that she hadn't actually been talking to Isa when she'd said this, but to another lady of the court, and Isa had merely been in the room and overheard their conversation.

"Hmm, thank you, I will have to keep that in mind," Lord Ranleigh said, before digging into the food that had just been placed in front of him.

"Sounds like good advice to me too," Mr. Davies agreed.

"Oh, Mr. Davies, I don't think you need any help making women fall in love with you," Mrs. Brompton said with a laugh before beginning to eat her meal as well.

-JOURNAL #3-

Nik, I think I'm going to go mad! Lord Ranleigh wants to take a week or more to reach you! He thinks it will keep the men chasing after me off our scent. I pray he is right. Tomorrow, we're going to head toward Portsmouth for a good part of the day before returning to our eastward journey.

Herr Mueller's men caught sight of me. While I managed to fob off Lord Ranleigh from questioning me too closely as to who they were, it's taking some doing to get them off our tail—hence, our extremely slow progress to Margate. I do so very much hope Ranleigh is right, and this will confuse the men so much they begin seeking me elsewhere.

I have to say I thought it clever of Herr Mueller's men to find me so quickly. I hadn't anticipated that. I suppose he knew where you might be, and this was the most reasonable route there. I can only hope we confuse them so much they don't actually find me. The last thing I want is to be dragged back to school before we've met again.

I wish so very much I knew where you were! I could send you this letter so you would not worry for me. On the other hand, you probably believe me to be at school and so would have no worries, anyway. No, I suppose the only one doing the worrying right now is me.

In any case, I truly do feel I am in good hands. Now that I am getting to know Lord Ranleigh, he really is not as bad as I originally thought. He, at least, is trying to make something of himself and do so through his own strength and effort, striding forward on his own feet—unlike a good number of the courtiers we have known our whole lives, who have merely attempted to hang on to our coattails and hoped we would take them with us wherever we went.

In any case, while I am frustrated at our slow progress, at least I am safe. I pray you are as well.

-Day 19: A Romantic Breakfast and Some Truth-

Sam found Miss Günter at breakfast the following morning and joined her. After giving his order to the serving maid, he noticed she was looking around the room in a rather nervous manner.

"How did you sleep?" he asked, thinking that perhaps she was just tired.

"Very well," she answered, turning her gaze back to him. "And you?"

"Like the dead," he said with a smile. "I always sleep well no matter where I am."

"How very lucky you are," she commented. Her eyes began to wander the room again.

It almost looked as if she were looking for someone—but, of course! He didn't know why he hadn't realized it immediately. "I do believe we lost them after we left Hayes. I think that side trip to Ankerwyke Yew put them off our trail."

Her eyes snapped back to him. "I cannot imagine—"

"Miss Günter, do not take me for a fool. You were looking about the room. Clearly, you were searching for those men," he said, taking a sip of the coffee that had just been placed in front of him.

She gave him a tight smile. "That is not what I was going to say. I was going to say that I cannot imagine we have lost them for long. At least, well, I hope we have, but I am not counting on it. It is rather disconcerting knowing you are being followed." She toyed with the eggs on her plate.

Sam frowned and felt bad for having snipped at her. "I'm sure that it is. And you truly have no idea who they might be or why they want to find you?"

She shook her head, but then said, "I have an idea, but as you have probably surmised, I do not want to be found and returned to where I came from."

"Was it not your home?" He thought that maybe if he asked smaller questions, he might learn more.

"No. I was... I was at school if you must know."

Ah-ha! "And you didn't like it there?"

"Well, no, but that is not the point. I learned… I heard something happened to my brother. He was at university in Oxford, which is why you found me there. I was looking for him."

"And you think he went to Margate… why? To go back to wherever your home is on the Continent?"

She nodded.

"So that's what your hurry is. You think he's boarding a ship, and you're afraid you'll miss him." So many things were becoming clearer!

"No, actually, I think he is trying to make it look as if he *has* boarded a ship, but I do not think he will. Our father would not be pleased if he returned."

"So, you believe him to be staying in Margate."

"I do not know!" She looked like she was ready to burst into tears.

Sam reached out and placed his hand on top of hers. "Please, Isabelle, do not worry. I will get you to Margate, and we'll find him. It may take a little longer the way we're going, but if you're right, and he's waiting there for… for whatever reason, he'll still be there by the time we arrive."

"I hope you are right," she whispered. She turned her hand over, so she could intertwine her fingers with his.

A warmth spread through him as she sought comfort from him. An act so simple as holding hands did something to him… something he'd never experienced before. It wasn't just the heat of lust—although there was a touch of that, too. No, it was the warmth of a connection. It was a tugging at his heart. It was the drive to protect this sweet, innocent young woman.

The serving maid came over and placed a plate filled with food in front of him. Reluctantly, they released hands.

For some reason, their conversation at dinner the night before came back to his mind. Miss Günter had said it was the little things, the small touches and courtesies that really touched a girl's heart. Just now, Sam wanted nothing more than to touch Miss Günter's heart. To make her feel safe and comforted.

An idea came to him as he ate his food and stared at her half-eaten breakfast of eggs and ham. He lifted a hand and called the serving maid to them. "Do you have any pastries ready in preparation for the day?" he asked.

The girl blinked at him and nodded. "I believe Mrs. Murphy has just pulled a few cakes and a tray of biscuits out of the oven."

"Good. Please bring a piece of cake and a few biscuits over for my companion."

The girl nodded and went off to do as he'd asked.

He gave Miss Günter a smile. She was looking at him curiously.

"I noticed you like sweets," he admitted. "Perhaps a piece of cake would be welcome?"

Her beautiful lips spread into a smile. "Yes, it-it would. That was very thoughtful of you."

He nodded and went back to his own breakfast. "Good. I like seeing you smile."

-Day 19: Boredom Sets In-

Isa heaved out a sigh. They had rushed to leave in the morning, and Lord Ranleigh had loudly proclaimed to the entire common room—in the guise of speaking to her—that they were heading to Portsmouth and would hopefully reach there before too many days had passed.

Trap set, they did, in fact, head in a southwesterly direction, as if they truly were heading to Portsmouth. Isa braced herself for more such rude behavior from his lordship at the next inn, just to secure the red sardine or whatever it was he had called it, that would hopefully send Herr Mueller's men off in the wrong direction while they swung around and headed east to Margate.

But even then, after sitting in a coach for so many days in a row, Isa was bored and antsy. She wished with all her might her horse had not been stolen, and she could ride. On the other hand, then Herr Mueller's men would certainly have caught up to her, and she would have had no recourse against them. At least with Lord Ranleigh and Mrs. Brompton, she had allies to keep her safe and hidden.

"Mrs. Brompton, tell me a story," she told the woman sitting across from her happily reading her own book.

"A story?" the woman asked, looking up.

"Yes. I am bored," Isa said.

"Why are you so rude?" Lord Ranleigh asked, nosing into their conversation.

Isa turned toward him. "I am not rude."

"Yes, you are. You never say 'please' and never say 'thank you.' You don't ask people to do things, you command them. You're an exceedingly rude young woman," he informed her. He gave a little laugh as Isa just sat there with her mouth hanging open.

"How dare you?" she finally managed to gasp out.

"Oh, it's all right, Lord Ranleigh. I'm used to such—"

"No! You should not be. You should not have to put up with it. You're an independent woman now. You are no longer in service."

The woman just chuckled. "I have always been in service. Probably will always behave as such as well."

"Well, you shouldn't. You need not. You are the one doing Miss Günter a favor and has she ever said thank you?"

"Well..." the woman started.

"For any of the innumerable things you do for her every single day, not to mention you even went so far as to purchase a gown for her? A gown!"

"She will be repaid!" Isa exclaimed.

"I don't need—" Mrs. Brompton started.

"Well, I should very well hope so. She should be well compensated not only for the gown but for her time and patience as well," he informed Isa.

"No, really, it's—" Mrs. Brompton tried again.

"Well, she is getting a free journey to Dover. She said she would be happy to help us in exchange for that," Isa pointed out, ignoring the old woman.

"Yes, and who is paying for that? For our journey south? Me! So, it is to me she is beholden to for that, but it is you who she is waiting upon," he insisted.

Isa frowned at him. "Do you wish for her to assist you in dressing and undressing?"

"Oh now, really, miss!" Mrs. Brompton protested.

"No. I am not in need of assistance. I'm saying you could be a little kinder to the woman, especially since she is helping you out of the goodness of her heart."

"But I—" Mrs. Brompton started.

"And how do you know I do not thank her every night? How do you know what I say to her as we are climbing into bed?" Isa challenged him.

He kept his mouth shut at that.

"Right. So why do you—"

"If you ever say a kind word to her, then I apologize for my assumption. But I have never heard you say as much, and you certainly don't ever show any gratitude to anyone who gives you anything or waits upon you in any other way," he said, interrupting her. "No, it's simply *commands* with you. At most, you give someone a gracious nod of your head, as if you were a princess." He gave a little laugh. "Yes, that's it exactly. You are like a princess expecting everyone to do everything for you, and you just command them all."

Chapter Twelve

Isa recoiled. He didn't... no, no, he couldn't *know*, could he? Had he looked inside of her journal? No, she didn't think it said as much there. Could he have spoken to Herr Mueller's men? If he had, wouldn't he have simply handed her over?

No, if he had spoken with them—even if he had decided not to force her to return to school with them—he would not be going so far out of their way to trick the men into going in the wrong direction.

He couldn't know the truth. He just couldn't!

"It's quite all right, Miss Günter," Mrs. Brompton said, reaching out and patting her hand. "I don't mind at all. My lady treated me in exactly the same way. And shame on you, my lord, for upsetting the girl in this way. Why look at her! She is as pale as a sheet." The woman gave Isa's hand another pat. "It's quite all right, miss. Don't you mind a word of what he says."

Isa pulled herself together and, just out of an odd quirk of curiosity, she asked, "And what do you know of royalty, Lord Ranleigh?"

"Admittedly not much," he began.

"Have you ever met a princess—or a prince for that matter?" she pressed.

"I've met the Prince Regent a number of times," his lordship said. "Have you?"

"No, I have not met the Prince Regent." That was true. She left out the small fact that she *had* met royalty... that she *was* royalty.

"Well, I'll tell you that he, at least, says thank you when someone does something for him." He paused and thought about it for a moment. "Not all the time, granted, but frequently."

Isa just looked at him and tried not to laugh. He was undercutting his own argument.

"And he is much more thoughtful of others. I'm certain all royalty are. I'm sure they know how to treat other people with kindness and respect."

"Do you really believe so?" Isa asked, thinking about it. "Why would they? I mean, if they are royalty—"

"Even royalty know they need the support of their people. If they behave rudely or in a high-handed manner as you have been doing, they are going to lose that support. They will lose the good will of those they govern."

Isa thought about it. She could never remember her father using anything beyond commands, but Nik certainly did—and he was much better liked than their father. People were more scared or in awe of the prince. Nik they actually liked.

Isa wanted to be liked as well. In fact, she wanted it more than anything. It was the one thing she'd never had—friends. She hated to admit this, even silently to herself, but maybe... could that be *why* she'd never had any friends? Maybe she needed to be more like Nik and less like her father.

"You are very quiet, Miss Günter," Lord Ranleigh said after a moment while Isa was thinking this through. "Have I hit a nerve?"

She opened her mouth immediately to say that he had done no such thing, then changed her mind. "Yes, actually, I believe you may have just answered something that has been nagging at me for some time. I... I thank you, Lord Ranleigh, for pointing this out to me and will endeavor to do better in the future."

The man's mouth dropped open. Well, that was a great deal more satisfying than anticipated. Isa laughed but just turned toward the window to continue contemplating this.

-Day 19: In Which Our Hero Has a Bit of Fun-

Sam sighed as he sat back with his ale. The women had gone up to sleep, but he simply wasn't tired. How was it that it was both exhausting and not tiring at all just sitting in a carriage all day? He would have loved to go for a good long ride, but he hadn't a horse. He'd taken a walk about the village with Miss Günter after they'd arrived—she'd been feeling eager for some exercise as well—but there hadn't been anything of interest to see, not even a bookshop.

He had been impressed with her at dinner, however. She had definitely made more of an effort to be polite after his little lecture that afternoon in the coach. He was rather shocked. He'd felt bad for lecturing her in that way, but honestly, someone had to tell the girl she wasn't behaving appropriately. It didn't seem as if anyone ever had.

As he had done so often since he'd met her, he wondered about her background. Did she have any family beyond this brother she was chasing after? Did she had a mother or chaperone who was, even now, tearing her hair out over the missing girl—one who'd clearly never taught her to be polite. She said she'd come from school, but how had she managed to just leave to go find her brother? Surely, there was a headmistress who was in charge of the girls at the school. Perhaps it was she who was, even now, beside herself with worry over her missing student.

A group of three young men came into the inn laughing and looking like they were ready to kick up a lark. Sam watched them with envy. They weren't much younger than him and looked like they might be university students. He wondered what they were doing here instead of at school.

"A bottle of port, Mr. Hencher," one of them called out to the innkeeper before they turned to look for a table. The room was nearly empty, so they didn't take long settling themselves. But one of the young men spied Sam sitting there by himself.

"I say, aren't you Hilsop's brother, what's his name?" one of the men asked, approaching him.

Sam smiled. "Lord Anson? No, I'm Ranleigh."

"Oh, right! Er, well, I mean, it's very nice to meet you, Lord Ranleigh," the young man said, remembering his manners. "I'm Marron. Over there are my friends, Sumerton and Newly."

"Is there a school holiday I wasn't aware of?" Sam asked, standing and shaking Lord Marron's hand.

"Newly and Sumerton were sent down," he informed. "I'm just, er, seeing they reach their respective homes safely," Marron said with a little giggle.

Clearly, they'd already been imbibing for some time.

"Ah, how good of you," Sam said with a laugh.

"Say, you aren't here by yourself, are you?"

"Escorting a, er, cousin south. She's gone up to bed," Ranleigh explained.

"Oh. Well then, you must join us!" Marron turned back to his friends. "Lord Ranleigh here is going to join us. Any of you chaps mind?"

"No! Not at all," Newly said.

"We could use a fourth!" Sumerton added, pulling out a deck of cards.

Lord Newly spilled a purse of coins onto the table in front of him and began stacking them up.

Now, this was much more like it! Maybe he'd even be able to recoup some of the funds he'd dropped on this venture so far.

Four bottles of brandy and many hours later, Sam pulled the large pile of coins from the center of the table and attempted to fit them all into his purse. They wouldn't fit, so he stuffed them into his pockets. He, like his new friends, had had a great deal to drink, but he had inherited one thing from his father—the ability to play cards and win even while drunk. The gentlemen around the table, sadly, were not so capable.

He stood up on wobbly legs. "Gentlemen, it has been a pleasure." He bowed but nearly lost his balance.

"What? Going so soon? But..." Marron started.

"Of course, now that he's cheated us of all our money, he wants to call it a night," Somerton slurred. He stood and gave Sam's shoulder a shove, making him back away from the table into the center of the room. "Give it back. Give it all back!"

"I didn't cheat, you idiot. You're drunk and couldn't tell a queen from a knave," Sam told him.

"Hey, now. I may be drunk, but I know my cards. And I know when I've been cheated." Somerton gave Sam another shove, but this time Sam wasn't taking it. He shoved him back. The man nearly lost his balance but came back at him, leading with his shoulder.

He caught Sam right in the solar plexus, knocking the wind out of him with an *oof*! And then they really started going at it. He'd just taken an upper cut to his chin when suddenly Somerton was pulled back. Finally, one of the other men—

He turned just as Somerton did, but the other man grabbed hold of Miss Günter and raised his fist. At the same moment, Sam registered who it was Somerton was holding and what he was about to do. A fury he'd never known existed spiked within him. He took hold of Somerton's throat, growling, "You harm her and you're a dead man."

Somerton let go, raising his hands in defeat. "I didn't know who—"

"Leave. Now!" Sam snapped, shoving the other man away from him and toward his friends.

"A misunderstanding, Ranleigh. Truly, an honest misunderstanding," Newly said, steadying Somerton on his feet.

"Absolutely. Three sheets to wind, you know," Marron agreed.

Somerton wisely stayed silent while his friends bundled him out of the inn.

"A good night to you, Ranleigh, miss," Newly said on his way out the door.

Sam could feel his heart continuing to pound in his chest as the men left. He licked at the corner of his mouth and tasted blood. "Just what the—" he started, turning toward Miss Günter. "What are you doing down here?"

"I heard the scuffle and came down to see what it was," she said, wiping at his mouth with her thumb.

He pulled his handkerchief out and pressed it to his lip. "And so, you just thought it would be a good idea to get involved?"

"I've punched a man before," she said in her defense. "My brother and I—"

"Your brother would never hurt you. Somerton would have! That was honestly the stupidest thing—"

"Oh, and you fighting with him was intelligent?" she snapped, interrupting him.

She had him there. He opened his mouth but had no excuse. "No, it wasn't. I've also had too much to drink," he admitted.

"I think we had both better return to our beds," she said.

The image of her climbing into a bed did something unspeakable to his body, but he quickly shook the idea out of his mind and focused on what was important, her safety and well-being. Sadly, his tired, overstimulated brain could barely form a coherent thought anymore. He would think this through tomorrow.

"After you, Miss Günter," he said, indicating the stairs. She nodded and preceded up him up.

-Day 20: A Little Excitement on the Side-

Isa sat back in her chair and continued to pet the cat that had settled into her lap. When the innkeeper's wife had seen the animal in the common room, she apologized before beginning to screech at the animal to scare it away. But Isa had stopped the woman immediately, claiming that she liked cats and was happy to have its company.

The woman apologized again. "I just don't know how it keeps gettin' in here, miss. I keep throwin' it out!"

"It's quite all right. I'm very happy to have her in my lap," Isa had told her. And she was. She liked animals and cats in particular.

"It scares the customers," the woman commented, looking down at the cat.

"Well, I am not frightened of a black cat, I assure you." She'd then ordered another pot of tea while she calmed the cat by petting and cooing at her. That had been over half an hour ago. The animal was still in her lap, and the cup of tea in front of her was growing cold, but she really had no appetite for it. "When do you think we'll hear from Lord Ranleigh?" she asked Mrs. Brompton who was staring out the window.

"I only wish I knew. It would be nice if Mr. Davies would give us an update," Mrs. Brompton said, turning toward her.

"If we had any more information, we would know if we had time to go for a walk," Isa grumbled.

"I have a feeling we may have time. Is there some place in particular you'd like to go? A shop you'd like to see?"

"No, not really. Is there anything you need?" Isa shifted her eyes to look at her companion while continuing to scratch gently between the cat's ears.

"No, I can't say there is." Mrs. Brompton took a sip of her tea, gave a little grimace, and put it back down.

They sat in silence for another few minutes.

"Good morning, ladies. You both look like you're having a lovely day so far." Mr. Davies with his ever-present good cheer slid into the chair next to Mrs. Brompton.

"We're bored," Isa said, not mincing her words.

"Is there any news of his lordship?" Mrs. Brompton asked.

Mr. Davies laughed and shook his head. "Snoring away."

Chapter Thirteen

"For heaven's sake!" Mrs. Brompton exclaimed.

"Had a late night, he did," Mr. Davies said, a broad smile lighting up his face.

"What? Here?" Mrs. Brompton was clearly baffled. Isa hadn't said a word about the previous night to her, unsure whether his lordship wanted to keep it quiet. Clearly, Mr. Davies had no such concerns.

"Met up with some other..." he paused and made eye contact with Isa. "Er, gentlemen. They had quite a night of it, drinking and playing cards."

Isa nodded.

Mr. Davies looked at her oddly.

"I came down just before the gentlemen left," she told him.

"You did?" Mrs. Brompton's eyes widened. "You didn't say anything."

Isa shrugged. "I didn't think Lord Ranleigh would want it discussed."

"Oh, well..." Mr. Davies said with a shrug and a smile covering his face. He clearly found the whole thing quite amusing. "He didn't say not to."

"So, he is upstairs sleeping off the effects of all the liquor he drank last night?" Mrs. Brompton asked in a coldly disapproving manner.

"Precisely," Mr. Davies agreed, the smile not wavering from his face.

Isa carefully placed the cat onto the floor and started to stand. "Well, I think he's slept quite enough. I am not going to waste my time while—"

Mr. Davies stood and blocked her way. "Now, now, miss, you wouldn't be so hasty if you knew how much money he won, er, you *don't* know, do you?"

Isa sat back down. "What do you mean? What money?"

The man took his seat again. "He and the other gentlemen were playing some pretty deep cards. Came up stairs with his purse and pockets full of coin, cash, and IOUs."

"Really?" Mrs. Brompton said, becoming very interested as well.

Mr. Davies nodded. "More than enough there to pay for this entire journey and then some."

"I didn't realize..." Isa hedged.

"In that case, maybe he deserves his rest," Mrs. Brompton agreed.

"You ever play cards, Mrs. Brompton?" Mr. Davies asked, turning toward her with a smile that could melt any woman's heart.

"Oh, Mr. Davies," the woman giggled. "Of course not!"

"Oh, come now, surely you've played something innocent-like? Or perhaps you prefer to spend your time with your friends in other ways?" he asked.

Isa just laughed inwardly as she watched this man turn on the charm. It was funny to see older people flirt. She only felt a little awkward being witness to it. She allowed her gaze to wander around the room.

The cat had slipped under the table of a gentleman and lady seated across from them against the opposite wall. It was sniffing around, clearly looking for some food while the couple above her was clearly enjoying a nice tête-à-tête with their heads so close they were nearly touching across the table. They seemed to be completely oblivious to the animal at their feet. Farther down the room were a couple ladies enjoying their tea, and beyond them, two men sharing a couple of pints of ale.

Isa's eyes stopped at the two men and the quickly turned back to Mrs. Brompton and Mr. Davies still flirting away right in front of her. The two men were staring at her! Not only that, but they could very well be the same two men who'd been following them since Wendover. She cursed herself for not getting a better look at them then.

She shifted her eyes ever so slightly, so she could see them again without obviously looking at them. The man with his back to her had turned away, but the other man was still watching her. Her heartbeat kicked up a notch.

What was she going to do? Lord Ranleigh was fast asleep upstairs. They couldn't very well leave. Even if she sent Mr. Davies up to wake him, it would be at least an hour before the man was awake, dressed, and ready to go. No, she had to do something... now.

What was it that Lord Ranleigh had said about a red fish? Red carp? Red herring? Something like that. He'd said he wanted to lure the men in one direction while they took another. That was why they'd come here to Frimley. He wanted the men to think they were on their way to Portsmouth. Well, maybe they needed a bit of a nudge.

"Excuse me," Isa said quietly so as to not disturb Mrs. Brompton and Mr. Davies, who were still so deep in their own conversation they'd probably completely forgot she was even there.

She slipped upstairs to her room and quickly changed into her riding clothes, leaving her gown on the bed just in case Mrs. Brompton came up looking for her. The older woman would see her dress there and know Isa was coming back. She then grabbed her saddle bag and went back downstairs where she deliberately stood for a moment in a spot where the men would be able to see her, and Mrs. Brompton, in the window seat on the opposite side of the room, would not.

As soon as she saw the one man facing the door catch sight of her, she went out the door and straight to the stable.

"I need to borrow a mount for an hour or so. I am staying at the inn with my cousin, Lord Ranleigh," she told the groom.

The man nodded. "Yer coachman is Jones, is that right?"

"No, Mr. Davies," she corrected him.

He smiled. "Right. Ye said ye needed to borrow a horse?"

"Yes, quickly, if you would?"

"Very good, er, sir," the groom said, looking at her oddly.

She frowned at him. He knew full-well she was not a boy. She honestly didn't care what he thought so long as he got her a saddled horse to ride.

He managed to do so just as the men from inside had come out the door. As she mounted, she could see them looking around for her. She would be spotted the minute she rode out. "Which way to Portsmouth?" she asked the groom loud enough for the men to hear.

The groom pointed. "That a-way. But if yer wantin' to go that far—"

"Don't worry, you'll get your horse back." She set out in the direction he had pointed.

Her first instinct was to kick the horse into a gallop straight away, but she held back, knowing she had to wait for the men so they could see her heading in this direction.

Goodness, but it felt good to be back on a horse! It had been much, much too long. In fact, she couldn't think of another time when she'd gone for longer than a couple of days without going out for a ride. The last time was... when she'd been ill with influenza, and even then, she'd wanted to go riding. Only her father absolutely forbidding her kept her from doing so.

She glanced back and saw the men had begun the chase. Perfect.

She kicked the horse into a gallop and rode for all she was worth. The area was long with meadows and the occasional farm. She came upon another coach and passed it. After nearly a mile, the horse began to flag. She looked behind her but didn't see the men. Up ahead, there were some tall hedgerows. It must have been some estate that was either too close to the road, or the road had shifted too close to the estate. Either way, they'd planted the trees to provide themselves some privacy. It was perfect. Isa would take advantage of it.

She pulled the horse to a stop, dismounted, and walked him through the trees. They were so closely planted, the horse barely fit. There was a nice little country home on the other side. Luckily, it wasn't as close to the road as she'd feared. She did pause to inspect the trees she'd come between to make sure they had sprung back into place well enough it wouldn't be obvious a horse had just walked through. Then she stood back and watched.

She didn't have very long to wait before she saw the two men gallop past. They were clearly in a tearing hurry, trying to catch up to her. She gave a little smile, waiting another few minutes until they were well past, and then walked the horse back out onto the road.

The ride back to the inn was done in a much more leisurely fashion.

-Day 20: Honesty-

The groom looked very confused when she returned the horse to him. "Thought you was headed to Portsmouth," he said as he took the horse.

"I changed my mind," she told him with a smile. Now, to sneak back up to her room without being seen by Mrs. Brompton.

She went in the front door and peeked around the corner. The table was empty. She wondered if they'd gone for a walk. Well, at least they wouldn't see her come back in.

In her room, she quickly washed off the smell of horse and changed back into her gown, carefully folding her riding clothes and placing them back into her saddle bag.

"Oh! There you are," Mrs. Brompton said, coming into the room.

Isa gave the woman a little smile. "Yes, here I am."

"We thought perhaps you had gone for a walk, so we went out looking for you," her companion said.

"I actually went for a ride. I much prefer riding to walking," she said with a little laugh.

The woman nodded in a slightly confused way. "That would explain your gown on the bed."

"Yes."

"Well, we were thinking of having a bite to eat if you'd like to come down."

"Most definitely. Riding always gives me an appetite," Isa said, following the woman out the door.

Mr. Davies was back at the same table in the window. "Ah, you found 'er."

"Yes," Mrs. Brompton started.

Isa had a thought. "Mr. Davies, you said Lord Ranleigh had come upstairs last night with his purse filled with coins?"

"That's right," the man nodded.

"Do you think you could fetch a few for me? I borrowed a horse to go for a ride, and I would rather Lord Ranleigh not learn about it. I thought if I paid for it now before he comes down..."

"Why don't you want him to know?" Mrs. Brompton asked.

"Oh, just because of the extra expense. Honestly, he has been so kind and generous..." Isa started. In truth, she didn't want to worry either Mrs. Brompton or Lord Ranleigh about the men showing up again. Hopefully, her little trick will have taken care of them—for a short time, at least.

"Don't you worry, miss, I'll take care of it for you. His lordship won't hear a peep about it," Mr. Davies said, giving her a wink. "So that's where you went. Out riding?"

"Yes. I love to ride, and with this journey taking so long... well, it's been some time since I was in the saddle. I truly miss it."

"You miss what?" Lord Ranleigh asked, slipping into the chair across from her.

"Oh!" She gave a little laugh. "You startled me, my lord. I did not see you come down."

He gave her a hesitant smile. He did not look well. His face was pale and his eyes bloodshot. His hair barely looked as if he'd pulled a comb through it. "I do beg your pardon."

"I was just saying that I miss riding, that is all."

"Ah, I see."

Isa just couldn't get over how awful he looked. She'd never seen him not be immaculately dressed. Considering they'd been traveling together for some days, that was quite a feat. However, today, he most definitely made up for that.

"Please stop staring so loudly, Miss Günter," he croaked.

Isa laughed. "How does one stare loudly, Lord Ranleigh? How is that even possible?"

"I don't know. I can only tell you what I feel, and right now my head is splitting, and everything is ten times louder than it should be," he said.

"Well, I suppose then you are getting just what you deserve," she informed him. "You had quite a night last night."

"That I did. And I seem to recall you were there at the end? Or was I just dreaming that?" he asked, looking at her.

"No, I was there. I saw you upstairs after your fight with one of the men," she told him.

"Ah, yes, that's right." He fingered his split lip before shaking his head. "I can't believe you got yourself involved—"

"How much money did you win?" Isa asked, determined to distract him from scolding her once again. He seemed to enjoy doing so, but she was getting tired of it.

"I haven't counted it," the man admitted, one side of his lips quirking up. It must have hurt because he grimaced slightly.

"I can't believe you walked away with anything," Mr. Davies said, sounding a bit in awe.

"Oh, I always win when I'm drunk. Never when I'm sober, though. It's some strange thing I inherited from my father," Lord Ranleigh said, shaking his head and then wincing again.

A cup of coffee appeared on the table in front of him.

"Aaah, thank you, angel from above," he said, looking up at the serving maid.

"Can you stomach any food, my lord?" she asked with a smirk.

"No, just coffee. Thank you."

"We'd like some cold meats and cheeses if you would, darlin'," Mr. Davies told her, displaying his charming smile.

She gave a little giggle and went off to fetch their food, leaving Isa just shaking her head in wonder.

Chapter Fourteen

His lordship then looked to Mr. Davies in expectation. "Well?"

The man looked confused. "Well what, sir?"

"Well, what is your secret recipe for *after* an evening of drinking?" Lord Ranleigh asked.

"Oh! I don't have one," Mr. Davies admitted.

Lord Ranleigh just sighed. "And that is why you'll never become a valet, Mr. Davies. A good valet always has a recipe."

"Or possibly a good gentleman does not turn away from the promise he made himself to stop getting drunk and gambling," Isa said sweetly with a smile on her face.

Lord Ranleigh sighed again. "Touché, Miss Günter."

"Do correct me if I'm wrong, but I distinctly remember you telling me you were turning over a new leaf?" Maybe it was time she turned the tables on him.

His lordship looked rather shamefacedly into his coffee.

"And then at the first opportunity presented to you—"

"Yes, yes, you are right. I cannot say otherwise. You are right, and I… I am embarrassed and as guilty as one can be. I should not have indulged. I should not have played cards with those chaps."

"And you most certainly should not have got into a fight with one of them afterward," she persisted.

He closed his eyes briefly.

"It was irresponsible, my lord," she pointed out.

He nodded. "That was beyond the pale." He looked up at her. "Please believe me, Miss Günter, that is truly out of the ordinary for me—the fight, I mean. And I would never, ever put you at risk of physical harm. If I'd realized you were there..."

"Of course, you did not. That was my fault, I fully admit. But you should not have been in the situation in the first place," she told him straight out.

"No, I should not have," he agreed.

"Then why did you?" she asked earnestly.

"Because it looked like fun, and I haven't done so for some time—even before I left London. And I thought perhaps I might be able to win a few quid," he admitted in a rather shamefaced way. "The fight—"

"Was extraordinary, I understand," she said.

"And you did win, my lord. I have to admit that, while you were sleeping, I went into your room—since you were so kind as to give me the key—and counted your winnings," Mr. Davies interrupted.

"Did you? And how much was it?" his lordship asked.

"Four hundred and ninety-two pounds if you count the two IOUs from Lord Marron and Lord Newly."

Lord Ranleigh smiled. "Just under a monkey, then. Not bad. I'll have to see about getting those IOUs cashed in. It might need to wait until I return to London, though."

"Is that a lot of money?" Isa asked. She honestly had no idea.

"Is it—" Mr. Davies gave a little laugh and a shake of his head. "Well, let's just say it's more than I'll probably ever earn in my life."

"Oh!"

"It's a good amount of money," Mrs. Brompton confirmed.

"Well then, how about 'congratulations,' and please do not do that again?" Isa told Lord Ranleigh with a smile.

He just laughed and then winced. "Yes, I think that's the right of it. Very delicately put, Miss Günter."

"But I should reserve the right to tease you about this and remind you of how you went back on your word, at least once or twice more before we reach Margate," she added.

He smiled at her. "Considering all the scolding and lecturing I've done to you, I believe you absolutely are entitled to that."

Isa nodded. If she wasn't mistaken, she and Lord Ranleigh had become friends. She liked that. She liked that a great deal.

"I must also say, in a more serious and less friendly way, my lord, that we have now lost another day thanks to your little bit of fun last night," Isa pointed out, becoming more serious.

"What? Why? We can continue on today, it's only..." he pulled out his watch and looked at it. He blinked a few times, then gave his watch a shake. "That can't be right."

Mr. Davies looked over at the watch in his lordship's hand. "Yep, that's right. It's going on four. Miss Günter is right. There's no point in setting out now. We wouldn't get very far."

"I am sorry, Miss Günter. Well, perhaps tomorrow we can leave bright and early. On the other hand, if I'm not mistaken, we were going to take our time to ensure we don't meet up with those men again, so truly this is just as well," Lord Ranleigh pointed out.

Isa bit her lip to force herself to keep quiet.

Lord Ranleigh must have taken her silence for disapproval for he said, "If you remember, we discussed it yesterday morning. I may be nursing a splitting head, but I remember perfectly our discussion at breakfast. We agreed your brother would still most likely be wherever he is for at least a little while, so there is no need to push ourselves to go any faster."

She had to admit to herself that it had felt good sharing some truths with Lord Ranleigh, but she still didn't know if he was right in his assumption that, if Nik was in Margate, he would stay there. Why would he? On the other hand, if he were going to go home to Aachen-Düren, or return to school, he would have done it already. So, she may not find him there, anyway.

She hated not knowing where Nik was!

-Day 21: Rain!-

Rain was falling from the sky in sheets when Isa woke the following morning. She stood at the window of her room and just groaned.

"Oh, it's not too bad," Mrs. Brompton said from behind her. "I'm sure it'll let up soon."

Sadly, it didn't.

As they joined the men at breakfast, Isa asked, "What are we to do? Can we continue on?"

"Of course!" Lord Ranleigh said immediately.

"I don't know," Mr. Davies said dubiously at the same time.

They looked at each other.

"It will stop soon," his lordship said.

"Might. But it might not, and we're heading into Surrey Hills. Could be difficult going," Mr. Davies pointed out.

"Surrey Hills?" Isa asked.

"It's a very beautiful area. From the top of Leith Hill, you can see for miles," Mrs. Brompton said. "We traveled this way after visiting Ankerwyke Yew with my lady," she explained to Lord Ranleigh's curious look. "I think this is a rather common route," she added.

He nodded. "Yes, I suppose it is."

"There are an awful lot of lakes if I remember right," Mr. Davies said.

"They call them water meadows," Mrs. Brompton said with a smile. "They're lovely."

"Not in the rain, they ain't," Mr. Davies pointed out.

Mrs. Brompton lost her smile. "Oh, well no, I don't suppose so."

"Will we need to lose another day?" Isa couldn't help but ask. She could feel a tightness in her chest at the worry.

"No. No, we won't," Lord Ranleigh said, as if coming to a decision. "We'll set out and see how far we can get—and hopefully it will ease up."

They all separated to prepare themselves for the journey. An hour later when Mr. Davies pulled the coach in front, he had somehow found himself an oilskin coat to keep the worst of the rain off.

"Good man," Lord Ranleigh said, slapping him on the shoulder before climbing into the coach.

About ten minutes into the journey, just as they were leaving the edges of the town, Isa happened to look down. Staring at her from under the seat across from her were two bright yellow eyes. Her mouth dropped open. It was the cat she'd been petting the day before at the inn!

She looked up at Lord Ranleigh sitting above the cat, completely unaware of its presence. He was staring out the window with a worried look on his face. The weather hadn't cleared; it seemed to be getting worse.

Isa cleared her throat. "Er, my lord, how do you feel about cats?"

He turned toward her with a confused expression. "Cats?"

"Yes. Small, furry animals..."

He frowned at her. "I know what a cat is. I'm just confused as to why you would ask."

"Oh, because there's one under your seat," she said, adding a smile for good measure.

As if the cat had realized they were talking about it, it came out from its hiding place, jumped into Isa's lap, and made herself comfortable.

Lord Ranleigh's mouth dropped open. "Where did that come from?"

"Oh, is that the cat you were petting at the inn?" Mrs. Brompton asked, reaching out a hand for the cat to sniff. When the cat was satisfied the hand posed no threat, she allowed Mrs. Brompton to scratch her between her ears.

"I think it is. How she managed to get into our coach, I have absolutely no idea."

"How odd!" Lord Ranleigh said. "Well, we should stop and let it out," he said, sitting back as if the cat was about to attack him.

"Don't you like cats?" she asked with a tilt of her head.

"I don't dislike them, but, er, I don't particularly like them either," he said.

"She's very pretty," Mrs. Brompton said, moving to rub under the cat's chin. The kitty began to purr loudly.

"But surely, someone is going to be missing it," Lord Ranleigh said.

"I don't believe so. The innkeeper's wife was trying to scare her away yesterday. I don't imagine she has a home or an owner," Isa told him.

"But we can't care for an animal on the road," Lord Ranleigh protested.

"I don't believe she'll require much caring for. Cats are quite independent. They can really care for themselves. Don't worry, my lord, I'll keep you safe from her," Isa said, trying to hold back her giggles at his obvious uncertainty about the cat.

He *harumphed* and went back to his book.

"What will you call her?" Mrs. Brompton asked, pulling her hand back.

Isa considered the cat for a moment. She was entirely black with slightly longer fur and big bright yellow eyes. "I think I'll call her Luna. She has yellow moon eyes, doesn't she?"

Mrs. Brompton nodded. "It's a good name."

"What do you think, Luna?" Isa asked the cat. In answer, she continued to purr and rubbed her face against Isa's hand.

She giggled. "I think she likes it."

Chapter Fifteen

As Isa watched the wet world go by, she did have to admit it was very pretty. They climbed hills and, even at one point, seemed to be going along a road that fell off sharply to either side. She could only imagine if the coach slipped. It would be a horrible tumble all the way down. With a nervous swallow, she sat back from the window.

"It truly is lovely in nice weather," Mrs. Brompton said. She too had been watching out the window.

"I'm sure it is," Isa said. "It just makes me a little nervous in the rain. The hills."

"Don't worry. We'll make it through just fine," Lord Ranleigh said, giving her a reassuring smile. "And the rain will stop soon."

"You've been saying that for the past hour, my lord," Isa pointed out.

"And if anything, it's got harder," Mrs. Brompton finished for her.

Isa agreed.

As they made their way down the hill they'd climbed, Isa could feel the wheels slip, making her worry for the horses. Even Lord Ranleigh looked nervous at that. Once they were back on flat land, the going seemed to be even slower, however. There were a great many lakes as Mr. Davies had said, and some of them came right up to the roadway.

The horses slowed to a walk and then eventually stopped altogether. The coach sank ever so slightly.

"Oh dear," Mrs. Brompton whispered.

"I'd better see what's happening," his lordship said, turning his coat collar up. He opened the door and let down the step carefully so as to not splash into the water that nearly surrounded the coach.

Isa could hear him call out to Mr. Davies. "What seems to be the trouble?" After that, there was merely the sound of the pouring rain on the roof of the coach, drowning out any other sound.

"Maybe I should go and see as well," Isa said. She looked out the window but couldn't really see to the front of the coach.

"Oh no, Miss Günter, you'll get soaking wet! And your gown!" Mrs. Brompton protested.

Isa looked down at her pretty pale-blue dress. "Yes, you're right. I'd better change into my riding clothes." She pulled her saddlebag from the floor and found her breeches, shirt, and coat.

"What in heaven's name...?" Mrs. Brompton exclaimed.

"I always ride in breeches, Mrs. Brompton. It's just much more practical," Isa said, shimmying them on under her dress. With Mrs. Brompton's assistance, she took off her gown. As the lady was folding it carefully, Isa slipped her shirt on over her head, tucked it in, and put on her coat, collar up just as Lord Ranleigh had done. As she'd been wearing her riding boots under her gown—she'd forgot to bring any other shoes—she felt ready to face the weather.

She carefully climbed down the steps as Lord Ranleigh had done so as not to cause too much of a splash. She was completely soaked within the minute it took her to walk to the front of the coach to see what the men were up to.

"Miss Günter! What are you doing? And what are you wearing?" Lord Ranleigh exclaimed from the horses' heads.

"My riding clothes," she explained shortly. She'd practically had to shout over the noise of the rain. "What is the problem?"

"There's too much mud," Mr. Davies explained.

"The coach is sinking into it, and the horses can barely manage to pull their own hooves out of it to move forward," Lord Ranleigh explained.

Isa wasn't surprised. Just walking from the door of the coach to the front, her own feet had stuck fast into the mud, and it had taken great effort to move one foot in front of the other. "Can we try pushing the coach? It looks like it is mostly this area in front of the lake that is the worst," she suggested.

"We were just discussing that," Lord Ranleigh shouted back to her.

"I think it may be too great a distance, but we'll give it a try. Otherwise, we'll just be stuck here," Mr. Davies said.

Isa looked forward. It would have been a good brisk fifteen-minute walk in good weather to where the lake ended, and the road looked more passable. In this weather, pushing the coach as the horses pulled, it might take them an hour or more if they were lucky.

"You urge the horses forward, Miss Günter, and Davies and I will push from the back," Lord Ranleigh suggested.

She nodded and went to the horses' heads, taking hold of the rig. "Ready?" she shouted back to the men as they disappeared behind the back of the coach.

"Ready!" Lord Ranleigh called back.

She watched, waiting for the coach to rock forward, but there was nothing. At the slightest movement forward, she encouraged the horses to pull, but the coach didn't budge. After a few more tries, the men came back.

"It's no use. It's completely bogged down," Mr. Davies said, wiping his face with a soaking wet handkerchief.

Lord Ranleigh was wiping his hands together, shaking his head. "We'll have to walk. Hopefully, the next town won't be too far."

"But what about Mrs. Brompton?" Isa asked. "Do you think she could walk a mile or more?"

The men just looked at each other with worried expressions. "We can sit her on one of the horses," Mr. Davies suggested.

"Excellent idea," Lord Ranleigh agreed. He headed back to the coach door as Mr. Davies began unhitching the team. Isa helped, taking charge of one of the horses and walking it around the vehicle so Mrs. Brompton could go straight from the coach and onto the animal's back. There were no saddles, so she would have to manage bareback.

Of course, her transition from coach to horse was not as easy as Isa had hoped and involved Lord Ranleigh having to actually carry her just a step or two to see her settled on the animal. Once there, the poor woman held on to the horse's mane for dear life.

"I don't ride," she cried.

"You don't need to really ride, Mrs. Brompton. Just sit there and keep your balance, that's all," Isa told her. Even that seemed to be a little difficult for the poor woman, but she did her best.

They loaded up the other horse with their luggage, and Isa tucked Luna, the cat, under her coat to keep her as dry as possible. They left the coach stuck fast in the mud.

-Day 21: An Inn and a Cold-

It was a very long, wet trudge to the next town, but thankfully there were no major hills to climb up or slide down—merely a mile or so of squelching through the mud and rain.

"How are you doing, Mrs. Brompton?" Sam asked, looking up at the woman who couldn't have looked more miserable trying to keep her balance atop the horse. Her hair was hanging in her face, half-fallen down from its simple bun despite her hat, and she was clearly flagging, her shoulders rounded. She attempted to give him a bit of a smile, though, and for that, he was grateful.

"As well as can be expected, my lord," she called through the rain.

He nodded and looked over at Miss Günter. She, too, looked the worse for wear, but at least, she wasn't quite as soaking wet as the rest of them. Davies had given her his oilskin as soon as it was clear they'd have to walk. It was too long for her and dragged along the ground, but he was grateful to Davies for having given it up to her.

She wasn't wearing a hat, but her hair had still managed to stay up. It was merely plastered to her head like a straw-colored cap. He did worry, though, because her cheeks were unusually pale, and she walked with her arms crossed in front of her, holding that damned cat under her coat. "Miss Günter?"

She didn't respond.

He called out again. "Miss Günter, are you doing all right?"

She snapped to life and turned toward him.

"Do you want to ride behind Mrs. Brompton for a while?" he asked.

"No, that's fine," she said. "I am well. I would ask you to carry the cat…"

Sam recoiled at the thought. He wasn't normally a superstitious man, but was it really all right to be traveling with a black cat? Might the rain have stopped, otherwise? Might they have not got bogged down? He didn't know.

His mother had never allowed animals into the house—not even a dog—when he'd been growing up, so he was unused to their presence. He knew nothing of cats and had never had the desire to learn about them.

"I imagine she would be much more wet with you, though," Miss Günter finished. She readjusted the animal in her arms and continued on.

He wished he could offer her some sort of protection or another layer, but he had nothing but the coat on his back. It was plastered to him and soaking wet, so it probably wouldn't do her much good. She, at least, was mostly dry underneath the oilskin.

They were a sorry lot that slogged into the Plough Inn.

"Oy, Margery!" the innkeeper called out the moment he saw them.

A large woman bustled up *tsking*. "Oh, you poor dears! Got caught out, did ye? Come on, come on over to the fire." She ushered them straight to the large blaze at the far end of the common room. She started to take the oilskin from Miss Günter, but the young woman first bent down to release the cat she'd been carrying. The innkeeper's wife nearly screeched when she saw the animal. She took a step back.

"It's all right, ma'am. She's harmless and will likely take care of herself and possibly any mice you might have," Miss Günter said, giving the woman a smile and the cat a pet.

The woman stiffened for a moment. "We have no mice. And I have a perfectly good mouser of my own."

"Oh, of course you do," Miss Günter agreed.

"Ye'll be spending the night, I presume?" she asked, eyeing the cat.

"Yes. Two rooms, please," Sam told her.

She gave a nod and hurried away to see them readied.

They all just stood there in silence, warming their hands and heaving a sigh of relief—until Mrs. Brompton sneezed.

Chapter Sixteen

"Oh! I do beg your pardon," she said, pulling a handkerchief out from her sleeve. Before she had even unfolded it, she sneezed again and again.

"Oh, dear," Miss Günter said. She went straight over to the bar where the innkeeper was cleaning some glasses. When she returned, she said, "They're bringing you some tea with honey."

"That is so kind of you, miss," Mrs. Brompton said, giving her arms a rub. "What I think we all need is to get out of these wet clothes, though."

"You are right. I'll go see if—" Sam started. He didn't get to finish his sentence when the innkeeper's wife came back and ushered them all upstairs. "Nice fires going now," she said as she led the way.

"I just ordered tea," Miss Günter told her.

The woman nodded and said, "I'll have it sent up."

They went their separate ways, Sam and Davies into one room, the women and the cat into the other, but Sam was worried about Mrs. Brompton.

-Day 22: The Sick Room-

Isa was woken in the middle of the night by strange moaning and muttering noises. She sat up, realizing they were coming from Mrs. Brompton who was asleep in a cot near the window. Getting up, she went over to the woman who had started tossing and turning. If she wasn't careful, she was going to roll herself right out of the little bed, Isa worried.

"Mrs. Brompton, Mrs. Brompton," Isa whispered. She put a hand on the woman's arm but pulled it away again almost immediately. A hand to the woman's forehead confirmed what she'd thought—the woman was burning up with fever. "Oh, dear."

She stood up and retrieved the basin and a cloth, dipping it into the cool water as she brought it back over. She laid it over the woman's forehead, but even as she sat there on the floor hoping it would cool the fever, she could feel a cold breeze coming from the window. This would not do!

"All right, Mrs. Brompton, let's see if we can't get you over to the bed," Isa announced. First, she wiped the woman's face and neck with the cool cloth and spoke to her gently as she did so. "You need to get up, Mrs. Brompton. I need you to wake up, just for a short time, I promise."

The woman groaned.

"Come on, now. You need to wake up," Isa said sternly.

It must have been the tone of voice because the woman blinked open her eyes.

"Well done! Now, let's get you up." Isa stood and took Mrs. Brompton's hands and pulled her to sitting.

"Oh, my lady, you need me. Of course, I will be right there, my lady, never you fear," Mrs. Brompton mumbled.

"Yes, yes, I need you to get up." Isa helped her swing her legs over the side of the cot and then pulled her to standing. The woman swayed but Isa caught her, throwing the woman's arm across her shoulders. Half dragging her, half walking on her own, Isa managed to get her over to the bed and then into it.

"There!" she said with a huff.

"You need me, my lady? I'll get up," Mrs. Brompton said in her delirium.

"No, no. I don't need you any longer. You just rest. Go back to sleep," Isa told her.

"Oh, are you sure?" Mrs. Brompton looked up at her with glazed eyes.

"Absolutely." Isa fetched the basin and cloth once again and went back to bathing the woman's face and neck.

She moaned. "Oh, that feels so good, b-but I'm so cold. Is it cold?"

Isa looked at the blanket covering her and then went and got the other one still on the cot. With both blankets tucked firmly around her, the older woman's teeth still chattered, so Isa built up the fire some more. After that, there was nothing else she could do for the poor woman but bathe her face and try to keep her comfortable.

Isa must have dozed off because the next thing she knew there was a knock on the door, and the sun had risen. She found herself lying at the foot of the bed. There was another knock.

"I got hot water for you," a maid called out from the other side of the door.

Isa got up and opened the door to let the maid in. "I would like the hot water, but my companion is ill. Bring up some fresh cold water for her and inform Lord Ranleigh should you see him."

The maid nodded, placed the basin of hot water on the stand, and took the bowl by the bed before going off to do as requested. Isa quickly washed herself and got dressed. She was just checking on Mrs. Brompton, who was beginning to twist about again, when there was another knock.

She called out, "Enter," thinking it would be the maid with the fresh water, but Lord Ranleigh came in.

"I heard Mrs. Brompton... oh, dear!" he said, taking a look at the fever-flushed woman in the bed.

Isa picked up the cloth covering the woman's forehead and wiped it down her face. "She's been like this most of the night."

"And you've been caring for her?"

Isa gave a nod.

"All night?"

"I slept some," she admitted.

"Why don't you go down and get some breakfast. I'll sit with her while you do so." He started to pull up the chair from the dressing table.

"It's all right. I do not mind staying if you would have a tray sent up," Isa said.

"But—"

The maid came in just then with the basin of fresh water. "Here you are, miss. We don't have a doctor in town, but I could call for the druggist and see if he can do anythin' for her."

"Yes, do that," Lord Ranleigh said immediately.

"I'm not sure what he could do," Isa said.

"I don't know, but I feel we should do something for the poor woman," Lord Ranleigh admitted.

She nodded and went back to bathing Mrs. Brompton's forehead.

"Thank you for taking such good care of her," he said before leaving. "I'll have a tray sent up."

Isa watched him go, certain that there was really nothing anyone could do. She hadn't had a lot of experience with illness, but she did remember being sick a few times herself. She knew tea with ginger and honey was good for the throat, and she knew there really wasn't anything to be done for a fever aside from bathing the forehead. So, she would do what she could.

As she sat there watching the woman sleep, she had the oddest sensation. What was it? Fear? No, not really that. Worry, she supposed. She was worried for her brother—where he might be, what he was doing. But why would she feel that for Mrs. Brompton who she'd only known for a week now? It didn't make any sense.

The woman began to swing her head back and forth with the effects of her dream. Isa jumped up and took away the cloth, rinsing it out before wiping the woman's face and neck once again, making calming noises. "Why do I care about you?" she asked the woman, keeping her voice low and gentle. "I don't know you well. You aren't *my* servant even though you've been acting as such for this journey. And yet, I do care. How very odd. I suppose it is because you are so kind and thoughtful. You have been more than generous with both your time and your money. You were there when I needed you and I… I thank you for that."

The woman stopped moving and sighed back into sleep. Had she heard her? Isa had no idea. She went back to her vigil. After all Mrs. Brompton had done for her, the least she could do in return was to watch over her as she suffered through a fever. Isa spent the morning alternately bathing the woman's forehead and writing in her journal, catching Nik up on all that happened.

-Day 22: Fetching the Coach-

Davies was extremely upset to hear that Mrs. Brompton was unwell. He even went up to her room and sat with her for a while, giving Miss Günter a break. Sam felt slightly guilty about that, but truly he would be completely useless in a sick room. He had no idea what he might need to do.

Instead, he saw that Miss Günter was fed and entertained while Davies sat with Mrs. Brompton. Before she headed back up to the sick room, he stopped her with a light hand on her arm. "I have to say, Miss Günter, I am very pleasantly surprised at how much care you are taking with Mrs. Brompton. I don't believe even a few days ago I would have thought you capable."

She frowned at him, then shook her head. "To be completely honest, Lord Ranleigh, I have never cared for anyone outside of my family, but Mrs. Brompton… well, she has been exceedingly kind and patient with me as I muddle my way through the journey. I believe she deserves all the care I can give her." With that, she turned and went back upstairs, and Sam turned away, admiring Miss Günter in a way he wouldn't have thought possible just a few days ago.

Early in the afternoon, the rain finally stopped, and the sun broke through the cloud cover. Davies found Sam sitting in the common room with a book.

"I've gathered together some men, and we're going to see about getting the coach free and brought here."

Sam jumped to his feet. "I'll come with you."

"You, my lord?"

"Yes, me. I am eager to *do* something, and some physical labor sounds just the thing."

Davies gave a little laugh, shook his head. His gaze fell to Sam's boots. "I guess that'll mean I'll be spending another few hours cleanin' your boots again."

"I'll clean them tonight—I am *that* eager to get out of here."

"Oh! Well then, come along!" Davies led the way out to the stable where four strong men were waiting by a cart. There were two strong work horses hitched to it, and the horses which had pulled Sam's coach tied to the back. The men and Sam all climbed in, and they went off to find his traveling coach.

Happily, it was right where they'd left it. With the sun shining, the water had receded, and the mud was already beginning to dry up.

"Just in time," one of the men said.

"Aye, ye don't want the mud too wet or it won't move, and ye don't want it hardened up around the wheels either," another man explained.

They hitched up the work horses, and the men surrounded the coach. Sam joined in the back ready to shove the vehicle forward.

It took quite a bit of rocking it back and forth to get it unstuck, but with their combined strength and that of the horses, they finally managed it.

Once it was free, they swapped out the horses and headed back to Godalming.

"I have to admit I have been feeling a bit guilty for getting us into this predicament," Sam admitted to Davies as they drove along. He was sitting up on the bench next to the man since he thought it would be silly to ride inside.

"Why's that, my lord? You didn't cause the rain."

"No, but if I hadn't got drunk in Frimley, we would have been past this low area when the rain began."

Davies nodded. "Don't know that we mightn't have got bogged down somewhere else."

"That's true," Sam admitted.

"Miss Günter doin' all right? She's awfully anxious to get to her brother."

"Yes, she is. I don't know why it is, but she seems to feel her brother is in some sort of trouble. At least, that's what I've been able to gather from the little bits she's let slip," Sam said.

Davies gave a dry laugh. "And what's a little thing like her going to do to help him if he is? I'm assuming he's older than her?"

"Yes. She said he was a student at Oxford."

The man nodded and gave a chuckle. "In that case, it's almost certain he's in some sort of trouble. And equally certain she won't be able to do a thing for him."

Sam gave a little laugh as he thought back to his days at university. He'd got into a good deal of trouble, and Davies was right. There was nothing she could do. In fact, she might be more of a hindrance than a help, depending on just what sort of trouble her brother had got into. Sam wondered if he wasn't going to have to help the brother out as well.

Chapter Seventeen

-Day 24: A Lovely Day for a Picnic-

Another full day of rain passed with nothing but nursing before Isa was woken by the sun streaming in through the window. She was in the little cot meant for a servant while her companion was sleeping in her bed. She spent a moment in wonder at this fact and then shoved it off remembering how sick Mrs. Brompton had been the day before. She also wondered how the woman had spent the night.

Isa hadn't been woken by her moans or mumbles, so hopefully she had slept well. Getting up, she checked on the woman. Her forehead was much cooler to Isa's great relief. Before she even lifted her hand from Mrs. Brompton's forehead, the woman's eyelids fluttered open.

"Oh, Miss Günter," she croaked.

"How are you feeling?" Isa asked with concern.

The woman opened her mouth to speak and tried to lick her lips, but clearly her mouth was too dry. Isa quickly got her a glass of water and then helped her to sit up enough to drink some.

Sinking back down, Mrs. Brompton whispered, "Thank you. Oh, I am as weak as a kitten."

"Of course you are, you were feverish all day yesterday," Isa told her.

"Oh, but I'm in your bed!" Mrs. Brompton exclaimed, suddenly realizing where she was.

"Don't worry about that. You just sleep and get better." Isa smoothed back Mrs. Brompton's hair and ran her hand over the woman's eyes forcing her to close them again. With a sigh, she did so.

As quietly as she could, Isa got dressed and then left to run downstairs to order some breakfast to be brought up to her. She spied Lord Ranleigh sitting at a table in the common room.

"Good morning," she said, approaching the table.

He stood. "Good morning. How is Mrs. Brompton?"

"Much better. She slept the whole night and no longer has a fever. She is very weak, though. I left her sleeping just now, but I don't want to leave her alone for long."

"I'll send Davies up to sit with her while you eat, then," he offered.

"No, that's all right. I'll eat upstairs. And I want to bring a little food for her, as well, if she can stomach it."

"Very well, but then you and I will go out later this morning. I'm having the kitchen prepare us a picnic."

"What? But I can't leave—"

"Yes, you can! You have been sitting in that room taking care of Mrs. Brompton for long enough. She is on the mend, thanks to your care, and you deserve a break," he told her sternly.

She couldn't disagree. "Mr. Davies will stay with her, then?"

"I'll do what?" the man himself asked, joining them.

"You will look after Mrs. Brompton while I take Miss Günter for a picnic this afternoon," Lord Ranleigh informed him.

Mr. Davies nodded vigorously. "Be more than happy to! Shall I go up to her now?"

"No need. I'm going, but I would appreciate the time this afternoon."

"No worries. No worries at all," Mr. Davies said with more enthusiasm than Isa expected.

She gave them both a smile and returned to her sick duty.

A few hours later, Mr. Davies came in and relieved her.

"She's woken up every so often needing water, and there's broth for her the next time she wakes," she told him as he settled into the chair Isa had occupied.

"Very good, miss," he said.

As Isa reached the door, he whispered to her loudly, "Oh, and... thank you, Miss Günter, for takin' such good care of her."

She just gave him a little smile. She blinked, her eyes adjusting as she went out into the bright sunshine of the day.

Lord Ranleigh had borrowed a gig from the stable, and they drove out to explore the beautiful Surrey Hills. There were miles of farmland to be seen from the top of the hills and lovely woods to tramp through. Isa was sorry she hadn't worn her breeches, but she hadn't felt that to be appropriate.

Lord Ranleigh was an extremely considerate gentleman, though, helping her over fallen trees and through thicker vegetation. At some point, he'd taken her hand to assist her and then just hadn't let go. Isa didn't mind. Oh no, she didn't mind at all.

"Goodness," she said as they were returning to the gig to collect their picnic basket, "I don't think I've felt this happy and carefree for the longest time!"

He smiled at her. "Well, I'm glad. You deserve this after spending all day nursing poor Mrs. Brompton."

"Well, it's not difficult nursing someone. There are long stretches when you just sit there while they sleep, but I did borrow her book, so at least I had that."

"And was it a good book?"

"You wouldn't believe! *I* could hardly believe it. I thought she'd be reading something improving or sermons or tips on how to get out stains or something like that," Isa told him.

He laughed. "And what was she reading?"

"A novel called *Waverly* by an anonymous author!"

"Really? Oh, I think I've heard of that. My mother read it and recommended it to me," he said as they walked back to the trees to sit in the shade and enjoy their repast.

"It's quite good. Not at all what I'm used to reading but enjoyable, nonetheless."

"What is it you like to read?" he asked, handing her one edge of the blanket the kitchen had thoughtfully provided.

"I like more lurid tales. My favorite is *The Necromancer* by Ludwig Flammenberg, but I don't know if it's been translated into English, so you may not have heard of it."

"You read it in German?"

She nodded and began pulling food out of the basket.

"So where are you from?"

She looked up at him and just smiled, asking, "What sort of books do you like to read, my lord? Do you read novels or more improving works?" It was a good try on his part, but she wasn't ready to give that information up to him. Not yet.

He huffed out a little laugh. "I generally prefer history. There are some very exciting adventures to be found in the pages of history books."

"*Waverly* is just like that. It's about Scotland and their monarchy."

"Really? All my mother told me about was some romance," he said, laughing.

"There is some of that too..." she admitted.

"Well, it does sound as if I'll need to borrow it as soon as you're done with it."

They ate in silence for a little while with Isa glancing around at the lovely wood. She listened to the birdsong, and enjoyed the fresh, scented air now lightly perfumed by their meal. Truly, she could not think of a more perfect day. A bottle of wine had been provided, and she was happily sipping at her second glass when Lord Ranleigh said, "You know, I was thinking about your brother."

She perked up at that.

"You were worrying about why he left school," Lord Ranleigh continued. "But the answer seems pretty obvious to me."

"Oh?" She tried not to laugh—what could this man know of her brother or his situation?

"He probably just got himself into a spot of trouble and thought it best to make himself scarce for a little while, that's all. It happens all the time at university."

"Trouble? What sort of trouble?"

"Oh, you know, the sort that all young men get into—drinking, playing a jest on someone he shouldn't have... that sort of thing."

"I see." She frowned, thinking about it. She supposed it was possible, but Nik was usually such a studious sort. She couldn't imagine him getting into that sort of trouble. On the other hand, he had been telling her about the friends he'd made and did say they were a merry group. Perhaps that merriment got a little out of hand. "That would explain why he didn't tell me he was leaving," she said, allowing some of her thoughts to be voiced.

"Exactly! You're not about to tell your younger sister you've got into trouble, just like you won't mention it to your parents, either. No, you disappear for a week or so until it's blown over, return to university, and no one's the wiser." He finished off the wine in his glass and stood up after putting his empty glass back into the basket with the rest of the remains of their meal. "Mark my words, if we don't find him in Margate, he's probably already headed back to Oxford."

Isa did the same and started to shake out and fold the cloth they'd been sitting on. "I suppose it's possible."

"Not only possible, but entirely—"

A gun shot rang out, and Isa suddenly found herself shoved to the ground underneath Lord Ranleigh's weight. With barely a glance down to see if she was all right, he was up and running after a quickly retreating man.

Isa jumped to her own feet, hiked up her skirts, and headed after him. She arrived at Lord Ranleigh's side just in time to see the man leap onto a horse and gallop away.

Sam watched in frustration as the man disappeared down the road. He very briefly glanced to the gig, but they'd unhitched the horse and tied him to a nearby tree to graze. It would take too long to hitch him up again. The man would be long gone.

He turned and found Isa standing next to him also looking after the man. My God, but she must be terrified. His own heart was pounding at the close call. He enveloped her in his arms, grateful she was all right.

Oh, but she felt so good. She was so small and delicate, and she *was* shaking. He could feel her tremors even as he held her even closer, trying to reassure her, to calm her.

"It's all right. He's gone. It's all right," he whispered into her hair. It smelled good. She smelled good—much better than she had a right to after a week of traveling and spending all the previous day in a sick room.

She felt good in his arms, too. So soft, so feminine. He released her enough to look down into her eyes as she tilted her head to look up at him with her beautiful, nervous blue eyes. All thought slid from his mind, everything but those succulent pink lips. He had to taste them. He had to see if she tasted as good as she smelled, if her lips felt as good as they looked.

He lowered his head and kissed her gently, testing, tasting. When she kissed him back, he allowed himself to deepen the kiss, to run his tongue along the seam of her lips and then delve inside the sweetness of her mouth when they parted for him. Oh, yes, she did taste as delicious as he had thought. So sweet with just a hint of the wine she'd just been drinking.

Heat stirred as his blood rushed through him. She felt so good. He held her even closer, wanting to feel each and every curve of her lovely, slim body. She had such lovely curves. Soft and delicate just like the rest of her. He could feel her hands around his back, holding on to him and pulling him closer even as he did the same to her. She needed his warmth, his strength, his comfort, and he was more than willing to give it.

Sadly, reason returned to his mind much too quickly. He was standing at the edge of a wood kissing the most beautiful woman who he hardly knew and who'd just been shot at.

Shot at!

Chapter Eighteen

Why?

They both pulled back at the same time. Perhaps she'd felt the shift in him, or maybe reason had come back to her as well. Either way, he lifted his head and put a hand to her cheek.

"Are you all right?"

She nodded.

"Any idea who that might have been, or why he wanted to kill you?"

She shook her head. "Are you sure he was aiming at me and not at us? Maybe this is his land, and he wanted to scare us off."

Sam sighed. "If we were, he would have said so, not just shot at us and then ridden off. And I saw him a moment before he pulled the trigger. He was definitely aiming at you."

She looked worried but said nothing.

"Isa, you must have some idea. People don't just shoot at others for no reason."

She pursed her lovely lips—lips he'd love to taste again, but now wasn't the time. She was clearly thinking of something, and he wanted to finally get to the bottom of this. He stepped back, away from her. "There is something more you're not telling me, and now it's gone beyond a silly little game. Lives are in danger—mine, yours, perhaps those of Mrs. Brompton and Davies. And you are not going to tell me why, are you?"

"If I knew I would! I swear it to you, my lord," she cried.

"Samuel. Call me by my name when you lie to me."

She dropped her face into her hands, and he wondered if she was crying. He paused and waited, but he couldn't stand seeing her this way. When she didn't immediately lift her face up again, he enclosed her into his arms once more and just held her. She was trembling again. This time he did believe her. He believed she did not, in fact, know why someone wanted her dead.

That was some consolation, he supposed.

She gave a sniff and he let her go, watching as she wiped her hands across her wet cheeks, brushing away the tears. He was about to offer her his handkerchief when she lifted her chin, pulling herself together with such strength Sam was impressed despite himself.

"I truly do not know who or why anyone would shoot at me or try t-to kill me. But perhaps it isn't just me. Perhaps that is why my brother ran from Oxford as well. Perhaps that's why he's hiding out in Margate."

"You think someone tried to kill him as well?"

"It would explain why he's disappeared," she said with a nod.

It actually would make sense. If someone had tried to kill him, he would do his best to disappear as well, and he certainly wouldn't tell anyone. "But why would someone be trying to kill him? A gambling debt? A woman? I beg your pardon, that was indelicate of me, but I'm just trying to think—"

"If I knew..."

"Of course, you wouldn't. But if it were either of those things, or really anything else, why would they then go after you? It's one thing to get back at someone, but something very different to go after their family as well," Sam pointed out.

Isa just shook her head. She didn't know, of course. How could she? "If they couldn't locate him?"

"It still doesn't answer the question as to why they would come after you. And you haven't exactly made yourself easy to find with our constant travels over the past week. No, someone has been deliberately searching for you, following us, and now..." He stopped, noticing she was only becoming more upset as he spelled things out. "Right. Well, I think it's time we left. We don't know where that man went or if he'll be back to try again. I'd rather not be here just in case he does."

-Day 24: On the Run Again-

They both went up to Isa's room when they got back to the inn.

"Davies, I need you to go and get the coach. We need to leave, now," Sam said upon entering the room.

Isa turned and gave him an unpleasant look. "Now, who is being rude?" she asked quietly as she turned back toward the bed. Mrs. Brompton, luckily, was sitting up and looking so much better. "I'm so sorry to rouse you from your sickbed, Mrs. Brompton, but we need to leave as soon as may be," Isa told her.

"Why? What's happened?" Mr. Davies asked, standing and turning toward them.

"Someone just shot at us," Sam told them.

"But it must have been an accident," Mrs. Brompton exclaimed, clearly upset.

"No, he was aiming at Miss Günter," Sam said.

"But... why?" Mrs. Brompton asked, turning to Isa. Mr. Davies looked very much like he would like to know the answer as well.

"I have absolutely no idea, honestly," she told them. "The man rode off the moment Lord Ranleigh began chasing after him, and we had no way of following—we had unhitched the horse from the vehicle we'd borrowed."

"We thought it would be best if we simply came back here as quickly as possible and continued on," Sam finished.

"But surely, the man is watching us and will follow," Mr. Davies pointed out.

Sam nodded. "He might be, but we'll keep an eye out, and I've got an idea."

"Do you?" Isa turned to him.

"We'll discuss it on our way. For now, I just want to be off as soon as possible," he answered, then motioned for Mr. Davies to leave the room with him so Mrs. Brompton could get up and prepared to go.

As soon as the men were gone, Isa helped the older lady to get dressed. The poor thing was still weak and unsteady on her feet, but they managed. They were downstairs within the half hour. Mr. Davies was just pulling the coach up to the front when they arrived in the common room.

Sam appeared from the other side of the room. "Ready?"

Upon their nods, they all got into the coach after Sam took a good look around to be sure no one was watching or following them.

"The cat! We forgot Luna," Isa screamed as they began pulling away.

"Damn the cat," Lord Ranleigh started, but just as he said it, a little black head emerged from under the seat and jumped into Isa's lap.

With a sigh of relief, she hugged the little puss and began petting her. "Oh, you clever thing, you!" She buried her face in the animal's soft fur. A bump made her look up. Lord Ranleigh had reached down under his seat and pulled out a case. He placed it carefully on his lap and opened it.

"What is that?" Isa asked. She couldn't see around the open lid.

"My pistols. I brought them just in case."

Isa moved the cat off her lap and switched seats so she was next to him and could see. It was a beautiful set. She picked one up.

"It's not loaded," he told her, probably noticing how carefully she was handling the gun.

She nodded, examining the piece. "It's beautiful work."

He smiled at her. "Do you know about guns?"

"I do. I have a set of my own that my father had made for me. They are lighter, naturally, but quite good, nonetheless."

Sam frowned at her. "Why—"

"I enjoy shooting and hunting," she answered before he even had a chance to finish his question.

"Really?"

"Really," she said. She reached for the powder and began to load the gun as Sam finished loading the one in his hand.

He watched her expertise in handling the weapon, clearly impressed. When she finished, she carefully placed it back in the case next to its mate.

"It's a good thing you brought them, although I do hope we won't need to use them.

"I couldn't agree more." He snapped the case shut and tucked it back under the seat.

It was nearly six in the evening when they finally reached Crawley. It was a much larger town than many of the others they'd been through recently. Mr. Davies pulled up to a bustling posting house.

"Just one moment. Please stay here, and I'll see to rooms for us," Sam said as the coach pulled to a halt.

"Why should we not go in with you?" Isa asked.

"Because I would rather you not be seen if possible. If that man comes around asking for you, I don't want anyone to be able to say they saw you enter." With that, Sam got down and closed the door behind him.

Isa immediately pulled out her saddle bag and began quickly changing into her breeches.

"What are you doing?" Mrs. Brompton asked.

"If we want to be certain no one can say they've seen a young lady matching my description, we'd better make certain that one hasn't entered the inn. The only thing I'm missing is a hat. Could you see if Mr. Davies has one I could borrow?"

Mrs. Brompton gave a little giggle and got down while Isa finished changing. She came back a few minutes later with a soft cap which was precisely right. It covered Isa's hair, and she could pull it low over her face so that no one would be able to get a good look at her.

She had just finished tucking her hair up into the cap when Sam opened the door again. He did a double take at the young lad sitting across from Mrs. Brompton, and then a grin covered his face. "Perfect. Just keep your head down," he told her.

"Naturally," Isa said as she jumped down from the coach before turning to assist Mrs. Brompton.

"I've ordered dinner to be brought up to your room, and I'll call for you in the morning."

"You don't think we should risk even having dinner or breakfast together?" Isa asked.

"It would be safer if we did not. I'll see you back in the coach first thing tomorrow morning."

They gave a nod, headed into the inn, and straight up to the room that had been assigned to them. Isa did her best not to look around too much for fear someone might see her. It was a little nerve-racking, but she knew her disguise was a good one so long as she kept her head down.

Chapter Nineteen

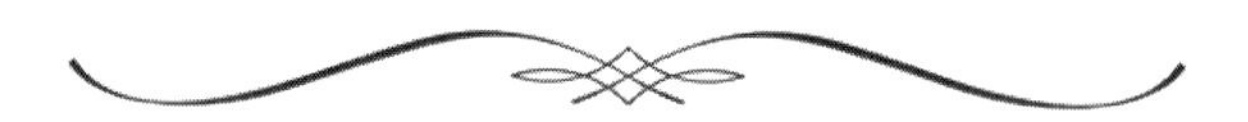

-Day 24: Extra Precautions-

Sam just shook his head in wonder as he joined Davies on the bench of the coach after seeing the women safely to their room.

"She is a one, isn't she, my lord?" Davies said with a laugh as he drove the coach from the town.

"She is most definitely unique," Sam agreed with a laugh.

"Never quite seen her like. One minute lookin' down her nose at us, the next caring for Mrs. Brompton, as if she was her own mother," the man commented.

"I have to admit I can't quite figure her out, either. There's most definitely a much deeper story here that I know nothing about."

"Oh, you can be sure of that, my lord, you can be sure of that," Davies said with a laugh. He sobered quickly though. "No idea who shot at her or why, though?"

"None. And she didn't know, either. She was truly upset by that, I must say. She was trembling like a leaf and nearly in tears."

"Well, any ordinary woman would be in strong hysterics after that, I would imagine."

"Yes. Miss Günter is made of sterner stuff, but she is not completely immune to the fright of being shot at," Sam said.

"I'm sure she was grateful to you for bein' there for her."

"Well, I..." Sam was about to admit to his heroics but decided to keep that to himself. "I imagine so," he said instead.

"Didn't show her appreciation?" Davies asked.

Sam thought back to the kiss. "Oh no, she did. She most definitely did." He couldn't keep the smile from spreading across his face as his blood raced, remembering the feel of her against him.

Davies gave a little chuckle, and Sam could only imagine what he must be thinking. Well, he wouldn't disabuse him of those thoughts since they were probably much closer to the truth than a gentleman would admit to out loud.

"She is a beauty," Davies commented.

"That she is, despite the trouble she has brought me. She has also made my life a great deal more interesting and, oddly enough, happier." He thought about it for a moment. "It's very strange, but I hadn't realized I wasn't truly happy until I was. Is that unusual?"

"No. Sounds perfectly reasonable to me, sir. Know the feelin' myself."

"Mrs. Brompton?" Sam asked.

The man's cheeks pinkened. "She is a lovely woman, my lord. Never met anyone so sweet and gentle."

"She most definitely is. Not bad looking, either," Sam ventured.

"Oh, she's a looker all right," Davies agreed. "Shame she's relocating to Dover. Awfully far from Wendover."

"Hmm, yes. I'm sorry about that."

"We'll have to have a think on it, my lord, and see what plays out. Maybe the miss can convince her not to retire quite yet. Still a vital woman, Mrs. Brompton."

"Indeed. Now, let's turn our minds to this coach, shall we?"

When they pulled up in front of Tilgate Manor, Sam's traveling carriage was much the worse for wear. It had hurt poor Davies to damage the vehicle, but he agreed it would be for the best, and they hadn't inflicted any damage that couldn't be fixed easily enough.

The door to the manor was opened before Sam could even knock.

Someone must have heard them pull up, which wasn't surprising since something was scraping against one wheel of the coach and making an awful racket.

He handed over his card to the footman who'd answered the door. "Lord Ranleigh here to see Lord Newly if he is at home."

The man bowed him into the house. "Yes, my lord, please, come this way."

He was shown into a large, very nice, if old-fashioned, drawing room with a deep blue sofa and matching chairs gathered around a fireplace at the closer end of the room. The farther end held a small round table surrounded by chairs.

He stood looking out onto the lovely manicured lawn as he waited.

"Ranleigh, this is a surprise," Lord Newly said, coming into the room. He was dressed in a sporting coat, buckskin breeches, and boots that shined as Sam's had once done—before he'd begun on this incredible journey.

Sam came forward and shook the hand Newly had extended. "I am so sorry to drop in like this," he said. "I thought, if you wouldn't mind, I might call in that chip you owe me."

"Of course," Newly said, frowning, probably trying to remember how much he owed him or perhaps the fight that broke out after their game. Sam, himself, wasn't proud of his behavior that night. "I was, er, rather hoping you wouldn't ask until next quarter's allowance," he said awkwardly.

"Oh, no! I don't mean money. Actually, here." Sam handed over the IOU Newly had written out for him at the end of the game they'd played. "I was wondering if I might take this in kind."

Newly took the paper and then cocked his head. "In what way?"

"You know I'm on my way to Dover," Sam started.

Newly nodded.

"Well, my coach must have hit a rock or something. The springs are shot, and there's some awful noise going on. Need to get the thing repaired. I was wondering if I might borrow yours. In a bit of a hurry, you see," Sam explained.

"Oh! Yes. I—" the man was interrupted by another, older man

coming into the room. He turned and said, "Father, this is, er, a friend of mine, Lord Ranleigh."

"How do you do, sir," Sam said, giving Lord Duncombe a small bow.

"Ranleigh? Ah, er, sorry to hear about your father," the older man said.

"Thank you, my lord."

"I do hope you are not following in his footsteps?" Lord Duncombe asked with a lift of one eyebrow.

"Er, no, my lord. In fact, I am planning on taking my seat in Parliament next session. I need to see to my estate first—I'm afraid my father didn't quite keep things as he should have."

Lord Duncombe frowned. "No, I don't suppose he did."

"I am just on my way to Dover to see some people about that, in fact, when my coach... well, broke," Sam said with an apologetic smile. "Luckily, I remembered that Tilgate was close by and thought I might drop in to ask a favor."

"He wants to borrow our traveling coach," Newly added.

"Oh, I was going to use it—leaving for London next week—but I suppose I could take the barouche up to Town. Lady Duncombe had asked for it to be brought in. I was going to send a groom with it, but I can take it and lend you the coach."

"I would be so grateful, my lord," Sam said.

"Yes, of course. Not a problem. Er, you'll stay the night, of course," his lordship added.

"Oh, that is very good of you, but I've already got a room in Crawley. Perhaps my man can stay and bring your coach 'round first thing in the morning, though?" Sam asked. It was so tempting to take Lord Duncombe up on his offer to spend the night in a good bed, but he didn't want to leave the women alone for the entire night. So long as they stayed in their room, they were safe, but he didn't want to take any chances.

"Yes, that would be fine. But you will join us for dinner. We were just about to sit down when you arrived," Lord Duncombe said.

"That is very kind. I shall be happy to do so."

-JOURNAL #4-

Nik,

Someone is trying to KILL me! A man shot at me and Lord Ranleigh today while we were out picnicking. Either one of us could have been killed!

I'm now beginning to understand why you ran. Why you are hiding. Why you faked your death. It was all to get whoever is trying to kill us off your back. I completely understand this now. Only... now they are after me! Now that they think you are dead, they are trying to put me in the ground as well.

It's strange, but if I was alone, I don't think I would be quite as scared as I am now. I would know I would be able to avoid these men, whoever they are. But I'm not alone. I've got Lord Ranleigh, Mrs. Brompton, and Mr. Davies, our coachman. They are all in danger now because of me. I would be devastated if anything were to happen to them. My only hope is these men are only out for me and so will leave the others alone—that they will do nothing to truly endanger any of the people I'm traveling with. And perhaps there is safety in numbers. I can pray that in their effort not to hurt anyone else, they will have a harder time trying to kill me.

Lord Ranleigh asked me who might be wanting me dead. I was relieved to finally be able to tell him the complete and honest truth: I don't know! I am going through my mind trying to figure out an answer to this. Who would want us dead?

If someone were after the throne, you would think they would go after Papa first. The last I heard—granted, it was about a month ago—he was perfectly well and safe. Why else would someone want us dead but for the throne? And who would do so? Who stands to gain?

I know Uncle Kottenfurst would become Papa's heir were you and I out of the picture, but would he truly go to such lengths? I remember him fondly as a sweet, kind, laughing man. Surely, he wouldn't kill us! But if it's not him, then who? Are there any others who would inherit Papa's throne were we dead? Is Uncle Kottenfurst in danger as well?

The only other idea I can think of—and it is absolutely unbelievable to my mind—is that Herr Mueller's men either misunderstood his instructions and thinks he wants me returned to him alive or dead. Or perhaps they are trying to scare me into returning to school. I have to admit, if that were the case, they don't know me very well. As you very well know, once I get an idea in my head, I am going to carry it through to the end no matter what. You have frequently complained about how stubborn I am!

In a way, I do hope it is Herr Mueller's man who was shooting at me, for I cannot think of who might want me dead, otherwise. The man was also a bad shot. I was sitting quite still and provided quite an open target.

I am still thinking of you daily and hoping you are well. Wherever you are, I pray, also, that you are safe. I don't know how, and I don't know when, but I will find you, my dearest brother. I can only hope you, too, are praying for my safety. I fear I may need it.

-Day 25: Anxiety-

The following morning, Miss Günter once again slinked out of the inn dressed as a boy. Keeping her head down and loping like one would expect of a boy of fourteen or so, it was unlikely anyone looked twice at her. Sam caught himself doing a double take when she came out of the inn and leapt into the coach after Mrs. Brompton. If she hadn't been immediately followed by that blasted cat, he would have thought some stranger had just climbed into their borrowed carriage.

When Sam climbed in, after settling the bill and giving instructions to Davies, he noticed Miss Günter and Mrs. Brompton looking around the well-appointed coach.

"Keep your head down, please, Miss Günter," he snapped. "You don't want anyone peering in and noticing you."

She corrected herself immediately, slouching back against the seat with her arms crossed over her chest, keeping her chin down, hat lowered. Anyone peering in through the window would only have seen the figure of the boy they expected to see.

"You do that very well," Mrs. Brompton commented with a laugh as they rolled out of Crawley.

Miss Günter looked up at her with a grin. "I've watched my brother for years—and I used to get scolded for mimicking the way he sat and the way he walked when he was younger.

Once they were cleared of the town, she sat up again and removed her hat. Her long, dark blond hair tumbled out, and Sam had the hardest time not reaching forward to run his fingers through its soft waves. He wanted so much to brush it away from her lovely face, maybe glide a finger down her soft cheek, over those beautiful high cheekbones and that cute little nose of hers. Instead, he did nothing but clear his throat in an effort to hide his sigh of disappointment.

Chapter Twenty

"Where did this coach come from?" Miss Günter asked.

"It belongs to Lord Duncombe. He's Newly's father," he answered.

She still looked at him quizzically, so he explained further. "Lord Newly is one of the men I gambled with the other night. Duncombe's estate is not far from Crawley, so I cashed in the IOU he gave me in exchange for borrowing his coach. Lord Duncombe was very good about it."

"Oh! That *was* nice of him," Mrs. Brompton commented.

"And that was clever of you to change vehicles since yours has your coat of arms on it, and this one doesn't," Miss Günter added.

"Exactly. No one will be looking for a coach with the Duncombe coat of arms nor associate me with it." Sam gave the women a smile.

"And will we be going straight on to Margate today?" Miss Günter asked.

"No, we are going to continue with our plan to take our time. I am still convinced that is the best strategy."

"But, my lord," Miss Günter said, leaning forward. "A man tried to kill me yesterday. Surely, you don't want to give him another opportunity?"

Mrs. Brompton's eyes took on a worried expression as she looked from him to Miss Günter and back again. He didn't want to worry either woman, but he was certain he was doing the right thing.

"Going straight on to Margate—not that we could get there within a day even if we tried—is just what those men are expecting us to do," Sam explained. "We are therefore going to take our time and go as slowly as we possibly can."

"But if we got to Margate quickly—" Miss Günter started to argue.

"Then they would find us that much faster. Please, Miss Günter, leave this up to me," he said, cutting her off. "You entrusted this journey into my hands. Now, let me carry this out as I believe is best."

He could just hear a soft growl coming from her as she threw herself back onto the seat. She took up her earlier position with her arms crossed. Only this time, she wasn't pretending to be a boy. She was just angry. He could see that, but he wasn't going to change his mind no matter how much she sulked or complained.

-Day 26: Taking a Break-

"This is such a lovely area," Mrs. Brompton said in a bright voice as the four of them strolled slowly down a wooded lane through a wood. "And it feels so good to be out in the fresh air and getting some exercise. I am not used to being cooped up in a coach for so very long. I'm certain that's why I got sick, for I can assure you that when I am busy, I am never ill."

Isa could hear Mr. Davies make some noncommittal noises of agreement. He was walking with Mrs. Brompton on his arm just behind Isa and Lord Ranleigh. She was having a slightly difficult time walking so slowly, but if they hadn't, they would have lost the older couple long ago.

The trees thinned out to their left and snatches of a meadow could be seen.

"Oh, would you just look at that!" Mrs. Brompton exclaimed in delight.

They all stopped to look at the meadow filled with bluebells.

"Isn't that just a sight," Mr. Davies said with some awe to his voice.

"Very pretty," Isa agreed.

"Surely you can do better than that," Lord Ranleigh protested. "I know you're unhappy at taking the day and not traveling forward, but honestly, have you ever seen anything so lovely?"

Isa grudgingly agreed, "Yes, the flowers are very pretty."

"And a whole field of them!" Mrs. Brompton said happily.

"A whole field of them," Isa agreed. It was pretty, but she was still feeling frustrated. She tried her best to shake it off. Indeed, she had been trying the whole morning. So far, she still had this odd sensation in the pit of her stomach, and she didn't like it. "And the sun shining does feel good," she added for good measure.

"It quite lifts the spirits. Does it not, Mr. Davies?" Mrs. Brompton asked.

"Indeed, it does, Mrs. Brompton. Indeed, it does," the older man agreed heartily.

They continued walking slowly with Isa trying her best to relax. The trees grew thick once again, and Lord Ranleigh picked up their pace a touch, creating a wider distance between them and the older couple.

"I am sorry you're so unhappy at the delay," he said quietly.

Isa sighed. "I'm trying, my lord, I'm trying."

"And what happened to you calling me by my name?" he asked, looking over at her.

Her mouth dropped open a touch. "Oh! I, er, forgot. Samuel," she added.

He nodded. "Thank you. You could call me Sam if you prefer. It's what my friends call me."

She smiled for the first time that day. "Am I your friend?"

"Are you not?" he countered.

"I don't know. I don't think I've ever had any friends aside from my brother," she admitted.

He looked at her oddly. "Well, I would be honored if you'd considered me one."

"No, I believe the honor is mine," she said.

He nodded, giving a little chuckle. "Well, that's settled. We're friends. You'll call me Sam, and I'll call you Isabelle."

"Isa," she corrected. She'd almost forgot the fake name she'd given him, and she was certain she would never remember to answer to it.

"Isa," he agreed. He glanced behind them. "Such a shame we aren't alone."

Isa, too, looked back. Mrs. Brompton and Mr. Davies were quite a way behind them now, but still within view. She looked up at Sam.

He smiled slyly down at her. "I would so like… well… but we're not, so it will have to wait for a more appropriate time."

Isa had a feeling she knew what he was not saying. He wanted to kiss her again. She could feel her cheeks heat as she thought of the kiss they'd shared. It had been incredible.

She had never been kissed before but had always wondered what it would be like. Now that she knew, she wanted to do it again. It had been so odd. They'd only touched lips, but she'd been able to feel it through her entire body. She'd grown so warm and contented and yet wanting so much more… only she didn't exactly know what it was she'd wanted. She was certain Sam would have shown her if they'd had the opportunity.

It would have to come at another time. And judging from the expression on his face, he was thinking the same thing.

She giggled. "This is definitely not the time."

He laughed, too. "Your cheeks are bright red."

"Oh dear!" She put a hand to her cheek. "Please do change the subject! Mrs. Brompton would know what we were talking about should she see me flushed like this. She is a clever one!"

He laughed again. "That she is. And I'm sure Davies wouldn't mind showing her if she didn't."

"Really? Are there feelings there?" Isa asked, deliberately turning her mind to the couple behind them.

"Absolutely. I have a suspicion they are on both sides as well," he said.

"Goodness." Isa laughed. "Well, I suppose you're never too old."

"No. I just hope I don't lose my coachman when we reach Dover and Mrs. Brompton leaves us."

"Oh dear! I hope not. Although I haven't given it much thought, I wonder if Mrs. Brompton can be convinced to put off her retirement for a little while. I have so enjoyed having her with me."

"You don't have a maid or companion of your own?"

"I have a companion but not a maid, and I can't say I like Frau Schmitz very much. She is... cold."

"I'm sorry to hear that. Cold is definitely not a word one could use to describe Mrs. Brompton," he said, slowing down his pace a bit so they wouldn't completely lose the other couple behind them.

"Absolutely not. Just the opposite. And my father hired Schmitz, so I sometimes wonder where her loyalties lie," Isa admitted.

"Do you think she is spying on you?" he asked.

"I wouldn't be surprised," Isa said with a nod.

"You don't think she has anything to do with those—"

"The men after me? No! Absolutely not," she said quickly. "I don't know who they might be, nor who might have sent them. That completely confuses me."

Sam nodded and sighed. "Well, hopefully we won't be bothered by them anymore."

"Hopefully!"

When they got back to the inn, the innkeeper stopped them. "I beg your pardon, miss, my lord."

"Yes?" Sam said, turning toward the man.

"There were some nasty looking men askin' after the young lady," he told them, nodding to Isa.

She widened her eyes. "What did you tell them?"

"I have to say, I didn't like the look o' them. I said you weren't here. That you'd stopped and then gone on."

Isa let out her breath. "Thank you, sir."

"Now, you all look like respectable people, but I don't want any trouble," the man started.

"And you will not have any now that you've sent those men on their way," Sam reassured him. "We don't know who they are, but we think they have mistaken my cousin for someone else. They've been following us, and we don't like it."

The man nodded. "Well, so long as you are who you say you are..."

"I assure you we have not lied to you," Isa said quickly.

"And we will be gone tomorrow, so you may rest peacefully. We do not want to bring you any problems," Sam added.

The man looked relieved to hear this.

As they walked away, Sam smiled down at Isa. "See, I told you it was a good idea to stop here for the day."

She had to agree. If they'd been on the road, they would certainly have met up with those men. "Hopefully, they'll continue on thinking we're ahead of them."

"I'm certain they will," Sam said with confidence.

-Day 27: Talking to the Coachman-

Sam was certain they'd tricked the men following them. When they prepared to leave the following morning, he suggested to Isa that she might like to sit up on the bench next to Mr. Davies. She must have mentioned to him at least two or three times the previous day how good it felt to be out in the fresh air and getting some exercise, so now his suggestion was both thoughtful and welcome.

Isa had been on good relations with her groom at home in Aachen-Düren, so she figured speaking with a coachman wouldn't be too different. Still, she wasn't precisely sure what to speak to him about, but she did feel it incumbent upon herself to strike up some sort of conversation. "It is a lovely day," she began as they headed out of town.

"Aye. The spring is really upon us now, eh?" Mr. Davies agreed, turning a bright smile toward her. "The flowers are bloomin', the birds a-singin', and love is all around us."

"Love?" That conversation changed a lot faster than she expected.

The man laughed. "It's a sayin', that's all, miss. Although, yes, I believe that love is in the air amongst us, don't you?"

"I'm sure I don't know what you mean," she said, straightening her back. She wasn't about to divulge her innermost feelings to this man.

"Oh, I don't mean you, miss. Although, if there was something between you and his lordship, I would be the last one to say a thing I can assure ye."

She relaxed a touch. "Then who were you speaking of?"

"Why me and Mrs. Brompton, o' course! Had a lovely time of it yesterday walkin' through the woods. Chatting like old friends, we were. You and his lordship were way ahead of us, which I, for one, really appreciated. It gave us a chance to be alone without really being alone, you know? Made it more easy-like on Mrs. Brompton, so she could feel comfortable knowing you was nearby, but not quite so close as to overhear our conversation."

"Oh! I'm so happy you were able to converse and enjoy the day together," Isa said. She turned and gave him a smile. "So, there *is* something growing between the two of you. I thought there might be when you were so quick to offer to sit with Mrs. Brompton when she was just recovering from her cold."

"Indeed, miss. Mighty observant of you." He nodded happily. "We also had a nice time together in Frimley that day when his lordship was nursin' that hangover. You disappeared on us, and we went out walkin' through the town lookin' for you. Now, granted, the missus was a little distracted that day, wonderin' where you might have got off to, but on the whole, it was a pleasant afternoon."

"I'm sorry I was a cause for concern. I didn't mean to make Mrs. Brompton worry, although I am glad you had some time to yourselves."

"I don't think she was all that worried. You'd left a dress out, she said, as if to tell her you'd be back," he pointed out.

"Yes, precisely! I did that so she would *not* worry," Isa agreed quickly.

"Right. She got it. So yeah, we've had a very nice time gettin' to know each other. She's a special woman I have to say. Much better than anyone else I've had a fancy for," he told her.

"She *is* special. I don't know if you have noticed this, Mr. Davies, but I'm afraid I've never given much thought to the people who've waited on me. Somehow, though—whether it is the unique nature of this journey or Mrs. Brompton herself—I've found myself growing quite attached to her," Isa admitted.

Mr. Davies chuckled. "I have to admit, it's pretty clear yer not used to hobnobbing with us lower folk."

Chapter Twenty-One

Isa took a moment to decipher his words. His accent seemed to be getting stronger the more he spoke with her, but she thought she understood his meaning. "I was friendly with my groom at home," she said, defending herself.

"Oh, yeah?"

"Yes. I was never allowed to go anywhere without him, and I am afraid there was more than one occasion when I snuck out of the... er, house to go riding. He always followed, no matter what time of day or night, and he always made sure I was safe." She'd nearly said *palace* but caught herself just in time. She also gave herself a moment to think about Gustov who, she had to admit, she had hardly given a thought to since she'd come to England. "He would ride with me for hours, sometimes trailing behind, sometimes next to me, listening to me as I talked about this or that."

Mr. Davies laughed. "Probably ranted to him about yer parents or yer teachers, did ye?"

"Oh, most definitely!" Isa giggled. "He got quite a full ear of all my complaints."

"Yep, that's what grooms are good for, to be certain."

They lapsed into silence for a little while before Isa said, "I cannot tell you how happy I am to be back on the road." She was just speaking what was at the forefront of her mind and only realized afterward she might be opening the doors for some awkward conversation.

"I could tell you were a bit anxious yesterday not movin' forward," the coachman observed.

"I am just worried for my brother," she admitted.

He nodded. "His lordship and I had all but decided he was probably just involved in some schoolboy lark until you were shot at."

"I know his lordship thought so. In fact, I believe he was saying as much to me just before he jumped forward, knocking me to the ground to protect from me being shot."

"Did he now? Saved yer hide. Well, ye must be awfully grateful to his lordship for that," Mr. Davies said, clearly impressed.

"I am! Although, might I admit to you that when he was hitching the horse up to the gig we had borrowed, I looked to see if I would have been hit?" She leaned toward the man a bit to explain. "I was sitting in front of a tree when the gunman shot at me. If he would have hit me, the bullet should have embedded into the tree."

"Aah, but it weren't there, is that what yer tellin' me?" Mr. Davies asked, getting it immediately.

"No, it wasn't. His shot went wide. I actually found it in the tree off to my right a few feet away. Lord Ranleigh was sitting to my left."

"Goodness! But that means he might have almost pushed you into the line of shot by accident," Mr. Davies exclaimed.

"Luckily, he not only pushed me to the right, but down to the ground as well so below the trajectory of the bullet," she told him.

The man shook his head in wonder. "Good thing!"

"Yes. It was a very brave thing to do. If the gunman had been a better shot, his lordship might have been hit." Isa gave an involuntary shudder at the thought. She would have been horribly upset if anything had happened to Sam because of her.

"Well, it's a good thing we've lost them, and may they stay as far from us as possible." He turned away from her and spit off the side.

"I could not agree more."

"But it was awfully romantic of his lordship to protect ye like that, weren't it?" Mr. Davies asked, leaning toward her a bit and giving her a grin.

She just laughed. "Yes, I suppose it was. He is a very kind and considerate man."

"And not too shabby lookin', neither."

"Not shabby at all! He is handsome and well-dressed," Isa agreed.

"Uh-huh. So, do ye like him?" He turned and wiggled his eyebrows at her.

Isa laughed. "As I say, he is a kind and considerate man." She became more serious as she thought about all he had done for her. "I will owe him a huge debt when this is all over."

"Oh, he won't think like that. Probably won't accept anythin' from ye, neither. He's a true gentleman."

"I believe you are right. I shall endeavor to repay him in some way, however. And I'm certain my brother will have a great deal to say on the matter once we find him."

-Day 27: Another Town, Another Day-

"Where are we now?" Isa asked as she was assisted down from the coach by Mr. Davies. It had been lovely sitting up on the bench getting the fresh air. After so many days of traveling for only a few hours a day, they were finally making some true progress.

"Hawkhurst," he answered as he went to open the coach door to allow Sam and Mrs. Brompton to descend.

Isa stopped to look around. The town was pretty with its white, half-timber buildings. There had been some pretty houses with thatched roofs as well just outside of the town. It was all quite idyllic, and she could only hope it remained equally quiet. Boring would be lovely.

"Oh, what a pretty town," Mrs. Brompton commented, coming to stand next to Isa. "Shall we go for a walk? I certainly could use a spell to stretch my legs."

"As could I," Isa agreed.

Mrs. Brompton smiled at her. "Well, at least your cheeks have some color to them now after sitting up on the bench all morning."

Isa smiled at her before turning to inform Sam of their plans. He was seeing that their belongings were carried inside the inn. "If you wait just a moment, I'll be happy to join you," he told her.

"That would be very nice," Mrs. Brompton said before Isa even had a chance to respond.

The gentleman popped into the inn to see about their rooms and then joined them just a few minutes later. He clapped his hands together, giving them a rub. "So, let's see what we have here. Shall we, ladies?" He stepped in between them and held out an elbow for each of them to take.

Mrs. Brompton gave a little giggle, and Isa happily took the proffered arm.

They thoroughly inspected the main street of the town and found there to be a rather fine bookstore as well as a general store. Sam purchased a few personal essentials—some shaving soap and a new strop for his blade—since he'd somehow left his behind in Crawley and his razor was getting quite dull. Isa felt embarrassed by such evidence of his masculinity and waited for him outside with Mrs. Brompton.

At dinner, Isa looked at Sam eagerly and asked, "So, are we going to continue on tomorrow, or do you want to take another day to confound the men?"

"No, no. I think it's best we move forward now. We're getting close. Another few days and we should arrive in Margate."

Isa's breath caught in her throat. "Really? That would be incredible!"

"Now, don't get your hopes up, miss. You never know what we may run into along the way. We still have another day of this forested area. It's very pretty, but should it rain again..." Mr. Davies just left the threat hanging in the air.

"But it was a beautiful day today," she pointed out.

"Indeed, it was. But this is England where the weather can turn in a moment," Sam told her.

"Oh." Isa slumped back into her chair.

"Don't get discouraged," Mrs. Brompton said. "We will be there soon enough."

Isa did her best to give the woman a grateful smile. "Of course."

-Day 28: Mrs. Brompton in Peril-

"Shoo! Shoo, now," Mrs. Brompton said, trying to coax Luna off Isa's gown. She had carefully laid it out on the bed, and the cat had promptly walked over and sat on it.

Isa finished drying her hands and dropped the towel onto the washstand. She laughed as the cat just looked up at Mrs. Brompton in complete innocence. Going over to the bed, she reached down to move the cat, but the animal simply stretched out and turned over so Isa could rub her belly.

"Oh, you adorable little thing you," Isa laughed, complying with the cat's wishes before scooping her up into her arms.

Mrs. Brompton immediately snatched the gown up and tried shaking it out. "It is completely covered in cat hair now," the woman complained.

"Oh, that is all right. There is no one who I need to impress," Isa said. She snuggled with Luna a moment more and then released her onto the floor in order to finish getting dressed.

Mrs. Brompton had just completed buttoning her when there was a light knock on their door.

"I wonder if Lord Ranleigh sent breakfast up to us," Mrs. Brompton said, going to open the door. "Good morning, I—oh!" She was suddenly shoved back into the room. She stumbled back nearly losing her balance. Isa started forward to assist her.

"Where's the girl?" a man asked, forcing his way in and closing the door behind him without a backward glance. He was tall and very large with an ordinary brown workman's coat and a black cap on. His deep-set eyes peered out from under the brim with malice, but more importantly, he was holding a long, wicked-looking blade to Mrs. Brompton's neck, point first.

The woman threw her hands up into the air, letting out a terrified squeak. The knife was right in the hollow of her throat. One wrong move and he would be drawing blood.

Isa stepped forward. “What do you want with us?” she asked with a great deal more bravado than she felt. Her heart was racing, and a cold sweat chilled her to the bone.

“Nothin’ with her, it’s you I want,” the man growled.

“How dare you come in here and—” Mrs. Brompton started, but her words were suddenly cut short by the man shoving a handkerchief into her mouth. He grabbed her roughly and threw her into the only straight-backed chair in the room, the one that had been sitting in front of the small dressing table. He pulled a rope out of his pocket. “I’d brought this for the girl just in case, but now she’s just going to have to come quietly,” he said, giving her a glare as if daring her to say anything.

He quickly tied Mrs. Brompton’s hands together behind her back and then grabbed Isa’s arm and started dragging her toward the door. She could hardly believe she’d just stood there, watching him while he’d tied up poor Mrs. Brompton. Her wits must be addled, she scolded herself. There had to be a way out of this. Isa started going through options in her mind.

The last thing she saw before the man shoved her out the door, the point of his knife digging into her back, was Mrs. Brompton’s wide, terrified eyes. The man closed the door behind him, leaving the woman sitting in the middle of the room unable to move or even scream for help.

Chapter Twenty-Two

"You will go down quietly," the man said in a low, threatening voice. "One sound and I'll be carving your kidneys out of your back, get that?"

Isa nodded.

"Good girl."

He directed her down the stairs and out the back, much to Isa's dismay. She'd been hoping he would take her out the front door, and then she might have been able to catch sight of Sam. Clearly, the man had thought of that, though.

Could she slam her foot down on his instep? He was certainly holding her close enough, and she did have her boots on. Before she could act, he shifted her next to him, so he had his arm around her shoulders. He was taller than her and so had a good, strong grip on her. She couldn't maneuver, except to walk forward as he directed. Anyone seeing them might have thought them awfully intimate but wouldn't have thought anything more.

They walked down the path toward the outhouse and the back gate, which Isa thought might lead toward the stable. If he took her there, surely she could appeal for help from one of the grooms, or perhaps Mr. Davies would be in there readying the coach.

Her eyes took in everything around them, searching for a weapon of some sort. Something, anything she could use to get herself away from this man. Unfortunately, one of her shoulders was pressed against his chest, and he had a strong grip on the other. She could barely move her arms.

He bent his head down toward her ear. "One sound, one false move and I will be returning you in pieces."

"So you have already said," she ground out.

"Just want to—want to—" He sneezed. And then sneezed again. "I just want you to remem—*achoo*!" He stopped walking when he'd let out the enormous sneeze. He shoved his knife into his coat pocket in order to rub at his eyes, but he still managed to keep hold of Isa's shoulder.

She looked up at him. His eyes were turning red and puffy. He sneezed again. Just as he'd straightened up, a cat screeched and Luna threw herself from a nearby tree, claws first, straight at the man's face.

He screamed and let go of Isa, batting the cat away. Isa jumped back and was about to sprint away when Sam appeared out of nowhere and threw a punch at the man, catching him right across the jaw. The man went down and didn't move.

Isa didn't wait a moment, but immediately turned, hiked up her skirts, and ran at full speed back into the inn. She could hear Sam screaming at her from behind, but she didn't even slow down to hear what he was saying. She had to rescue Mrs. Brompton.

-Day 28: Thanks for Nothing-

Sam was just buttoning his breeches in the outhouse when he heard a cat screech, immediately followed by a man's scream. What the hell was Isa's cat doing now?

He bolted out the door to find a man letting go of Isa as he batted the cat away from his face. It was immediately clear the man had been trying to remove Isa against her will. As the man was off balance after dealing with the cat, Sam didn't even stop to think but just called on all his training from Gentleman Jackson's Boxing Saloon to land a facer on the fellow. He went down like a stone.

Sam turned to see if Isa was all right, but she was already sprinting back toward the inn. Well, wasn't that gratitude for you! Fury spiked within him. He'd just saved the girl, and she didn't even stop to say thank you? And where was she going like a fox being chased by a pack of hounds?

"Isa, stop!" he called after her. "Who is this man? What's..." There was no point in screaming at an empty garden; she was gone. He didn't know what to do with the fellow, but he figured the man wasn't going to be moving anytime soon, so he ran after her. He caught sight of her just as she reached the top of the stairs and turned toward her room. What could be so important? He sprinted up after her.

When he reached her room, he found Mrs. Brompton in strong hysterics sitting in a chair. Isa was behind her, working on untying a rope holding the woman's hands together. She said something in German that didn't sound very polite and looked up. "Do you have a knife? He tied this too tightly," she asked him.

"No! Wait, I'll get one." He ran to his own room where his portmanteau was still sitting on his bed where he'd left it. He grabbed his razor and went back to Mrs. Brompton. He'd just sharpened the blade, so it sliced quickly through the rope.

Isa immediately gathered the sobbing woman into her arms. "It's all right, now. It's all right. Shhh..." she said soothingly.

"Oh, th-thank-thank God! You-you're all right," Mrs. Brompton cried, clutching on to Isa.

"I'm fine. It's all right now. Between Luna and Lord Ranleigh, the man was left unconscious in the garden."

"I should go down and see that he doesn't get away," Sam said, otherwise feeling useless as the two women held each other.

As he made his way down the stairs, he realized all his anger at Isa and all his fear for her had dissipated, only to be replaced with respect and pride in her quick action to escape from a bad situation and run to Mrs. Brompton's rescue.

When he got back to the garden, he found the man trying to sit up but, somehow, was forced back down by the cat. It was standing next to him, hissing and swiping a clawed paw at him. The man cowered in fear, sneezing and wiping at red, swollen eyes.

"Good girl, Luna," Sam said, reaching down and pulling the man to his feet.

"Get that"—*achoo*!—"bloody"—*achoo*!—"cat away"—*achoo*!—"from me!" the man said or perhaps sneezed.

"Yes, I'll get *it* away from you, and *you* straight to the magistrate!" Sam said, shoving the man into the inn.

It took the better part of an hour to see the man into the hands of the law. When he finally returned to the inn, he found Isa and Mrs. Brompton sitting in a far corner of the common room having some tea.

Isa stood up as soon as she saw him come in and waved to him. "Where have you been?"

"Taking care of that ruffian who tried to kidnap you," Sam told her. "He won't be bothering us again. The local magistrate is having him sent up to London to face a judge."

She smiled at him. "Well-done." She sat back down and motioned for him to take the seat next to Mrs. Brompton.

"You are looking much better," he commented to the lady.

She gave him a tremulous smile. "I will be fine, thank you, my lord. I was just..." Her lips began to quiver, and her eyes filled with tears. "I was never so scared..."

He patted her hand soothingly. "It's all right. Of course, you were terrified. And I am so sorry for it."

She sniffed, dabbing at her nose and eyes with a damp handkerchief. "Thank you."

"The magistrate tried to get the man to say who hired him to kidnap you, but either he didn't know, or he wouldn't say," Sam told Isa.

She sighed and shook her head. "I just wish I knew who would want to cause me such harm."

"You truly have no idea?" he asked.

"None," she assured him. Sadly, he believed her.

"I think we should stay here the night so you can recover, Mrs. Brompton," Sam said.

"Are you certain?" Isa asked. She looked from Mrs. Brompton to

Sam and back again. The woman was not looking her best. She was still teary-eyed, and he thought she might even be shaking ever so slightly.

"Yes, I am certain. That man is in the custody of the magistrate. He won't be bothering us anymore," he told Isa. "And I believe Mrs. Brompton could use some time to recover."

Mrs. Brompton reached out and put a hand on Isa's arm. "I know you want to reach your brother just as quickly as can be, but please, let's just stay here the night. Lord Ranleigh is right. I would appreciate a little time."

Isa nodded. "Of course."

It was a quiet afternoon and evening. First thing the following morning when he went to settle the bill, he found the innkeeper so apologetic for the incident the previous day, as if he could have done anything to stop it. He dismissed Sam's efforts to pay for their rooms and dinner. Sam could do nothing but thank the man kindly and join the women in the coach.

-Day 29: Shot Dead-

As they continued on their way, Isa was thrilled to be able to take out the book Mrs. Brompton had lent her. The woman had finished reading her novel, then purchased another book by the same author for herself at the bookstore they'd found at the last town. Isa had asked to borrow *Waverly* since she'd begun reading it while Mrs. Brompton had been ill and was curious to see how it continued.

It was such a relief to be able to entertain herself as they drove for hours on end—until she actually opened the book and began reading. It started mildly enough, but much too quickly, Isa remembered why she never read in a moving carriage—she got motion sick. She leaned her head against the window glass, staring out at the passing scenery.

"Is the book not to your liking?" Sam asked.

"No, it is. It is very good. I am just feeling a little sick. I forgot I get sick in a moving vehicle if I do not look out."

He gave her a sympathetic look. "My father was the same way. He claimed it was why he never ventured to the Continent for fear of being seasick in the same way."

"Oh, my goodness, yes! It was an awful, awful journey!" Isa shook her head, remembering how ill she had been from the moment she'd stepped aboard the ship to cross what the English called the Channel. It was also why she hoped with all her might that her brother, Nik, had not boarded a ship to go home. She did not want to have to follow him across the water.

"Are you feeling ill now? Do we need to stop?" Sam asked, so thoughtful as always.

"It is all right," she told him. "I will just look out the window. The feeling will pass."

After another hour, Isa began to hear the thundering of a horse galloping. It sounded like it was catching up fast. Both out of boredom and curiosity, she let down the glass in the window and stuck her head out to look behind them.

A lone riding was advancing on them quickly and, much to her surprise, was holding out his arm toward her. With the crack of the pistol, she realized almost too late that it was a gun he was pointing at her.

She ducked back into the carriage.

"Miss Günter!" Mrs. Brompton screeched.

She dove under the seat for Sam's dueling pistols they'd loaded the other day.

"What are you doing?" he asked, grabbing hold of the case and stopping her.

"I am going to protect us!" she told him and yanked the case out of his hand.

"How? We're moving too fast." He paused to look out the window. "I think that shot spooked the horses."

"It is all right." Isa moved to the rear-facing seat next to Sam and fit the upper half of her body out the window. It was a good thing she was a small person, and the window was of a good size. She just fit.

"Hold them steady, Mr. Davies," she screamed up to the coachman.

"I'm doin' the best I can," he called back. "What the... what do you think..."

"Just drive!" she shouted up to him. She wasn't taking her eyes off the man following them. He was reaching back into his saddle bag for his other pistol. She waited for him to sit straight back up again, aiming as she did so. The moment she had the full width of his torso facing her and she was about to pull the trigger, the coach hit a hole in the road. She nearly lost her balance.

She could feel someone inside the coach grab on to her waist to make sure she didn't fall. "Hold them steady, Mr. Davies, and keep from the holes!" she screamed.

"I'm trying!" he called back. "I'm trying," he said a second time more quietly.

The gunman was now aiming at her. He, too, had to contend with holes in the road and trying to ride his horse while steadying and aiming a pistol. It clearly wasn't easy, and Isa was grateful for his difficulties. It gave her the time she needed to aim once again. This time she got her shot off before they hit another rut.

She bounced with the jolting of the coach, her ribs hitting painfully against the window ledge, and grateful she was being held from inside. When she looked back again, the gunman was gone. His horse, however, was still coming toward them, riderless.

Chapter Twenty-Three

"Wait! Stop!" she called to Mr. Davies.

"Whoa!" she heard him call out to the horses. "Whoa, now." He slowed and then brought the coach to a halt as she ducked back inside.

"Well? What happened?" Sam asked, the moment he could see her face.

"I think I might have hit him."

"Oh, mercy!" Mrs. Brompton said, placing a hand to her bosom.

The coach had nearly come to a complete stop when Sam opened up the door and jumped out. Isa followed, also ignoring the steps that could have been let down. Sam started toward the fallen man, lying in the middle of the road. Isa gave a whistle and the horse, which had slowed to a walk, came toward her.

She made soothing noises toward the nervous animal. He was lathered and blowing from being ridden so hard. "Shhh, it's all right. It's all right, now," she told him. She approached the animal slowly and carefully. The horse calmed at her soothing words and came closer to her. Once she felt it safe, she took a hold of the bridle and stroked the horse's nose, continuing her soothing sounds.

Sam appeared next to her, making the horse shy a little away. "It's all right. It's all right now," she said to the horse and pet his nose some more. It calmed him.

"I don't know how you did it, but you hit him squarely in the chest. He's dead," Sam said quietly.

Isa turned toward him. She couldn't help the small smile that twitched on her lips. But then she became serious once again as she reminded herself that she'd just killed a man. "I am a very good shot," she told Sam and then added, "but I have never killed a person before." The enormity of what she'd done hadn't hit her, but she was certain it would before too long.

"I would not have expected so. But we'll need to report this to the local authorities. We can't just leave him here."

"Goodness, no!" And then, she thought about it. "Oh, Sam, I am so sorry! I am causing you so much trouble."

"It's not your fault someone is trying to kill you. And I'm grateful it was you who shot him, rather than the other way around," he said, pulling her into his arms.

Isa loosely held the reins of the horse as she sank into Sam's protection. He felt so good. So strong and sturdy. "I am so glad you are here with me. I do not know what I would do were I alone. I... I do not think I could manage," she told him, feeling a hollowness suddenly open up within her.

"It's all right," he said, mimicking the words she'd just said to the horse. Just as the animal had, she found them calming, soothing. Having Sam's strength surrounding her helped as well. She looked up at him, wishing he would kiss her. "Thank you," she whispered.

"Is he... is he...?" Mrs. Brompton's voice asked from the coach. She hadn't even had the nerve to let down the steps and get out onto the road.

At the reminder that they weren't alone, Isa took a step back from the comfort Sam was providing her. She supposed she should be grateful he hadn't done as she'd wanted. That would have been extremely awkward and embarrassing.

"He is," Sam called back. "Davies, I'll need some assistance."

The coachman was standing at the heads of the coach horses, but he gave them a pat and left them. Isa was certain they wouldn't go anywhere without him.

The two men took the horse Isa had calmed and retrieved the body, laying it over the saddle and tying it down so it wouldn't fall off, then tied the horse to the back of the coach. It was a slow walk to the next town.

Mrs. Brompton was suspiciously silent the whole way. Isa was simply exhausted from the excitement and managed to close her eyes. The moment she did so, however, the vision of the man riding after them, aiming his gun at her, invaded her peace, and her eyes popped open again.

"What's wrong?" Sam asked. He must have been watching her.

"Nothing. I... I just keep seeing that man chasing after us," she admitted.

He looked like he wanted to take her into his arms again, but with Mrs. Brompton sitting right there next to her, he could do no such thing. "I'm so sorry," he finally whispered.

Isa just nodded and rested her head against the side of the coach and stared out the window, unwilling and unable to close her eyes.

-JOURNAL ENTRY #5-

I killed a man.

Isa couldn't believe the words she'd just written. She read them and re-read them, brushed the tear from her eyes before it could fall on her page, and then wrote the words again.

My dearest Nik, I killed a man. He was trying to kill me, but Lord Ranleigh had his dueling pistols. I took one, squeezed out of the window of the coach, and killed the man aiming his gun at me.

I still can't quite believe it, but he truly would have killed me if I hadn't... if I hadn't done that to him. Mr. Davies—the coachman—stopped the carriage. I calmed the man's horse, which was understandably terrified. (I'm surprised he hadn't bolted the minute his rider fell from his back.) Lord

Ranleigh and Mr. Davies put the man's body onto his horse, and we took him to the next town.

His lordship is meeting with the magistrate now to explain what happened. I just hope I won't have to stand before the man. I would probably have to reveal my real name. And I don't know what the laws are in this country for killing someone. Will I have to go to court? Will I be tried and have to go to gaol? If I tell the truth of my real name and position, I'm sure none of that would happen, but it couldn't lead to anything good. It might strain relations between Aachen-Düren and England. And Sam... oh goodness, what would he say if he learned who I truly was and how I've been lying to him this whole time?

Oh, Nik, I wish this had never happened!

And of course, I just keep wondering... thinking... if they are shooting and seriously trying to kill me, what did they do to you? I know you are safe. I can feel it. I know that they didn't succeed. You are too clever for that. Too smart. You would have got away. I'm now certain you escaped from whoever it was who was trying to kill you and then faked your own death to get them to stop coming after you. I'm certain of it. As certain as I am that the sun will rise tomorrow.

The only problem, my dearest Nik, is that when they thought they'd succeeded in killing you, they then started coming after me. And if they succeed in killing me, who will they go after next? Papa? Uncle Kottenfurst?

I still don't believe it was our uncle who sent the men. I don't know who might have, but how could it be our dear, sweet, laughing uncle? The only thing is—he's a soldier. He would know how to kill someone—not that he's doing it himself. But still, sending men after us... And he is the only one who would stand to gain anything from our deaths. Without us in the way, he becomes the heir to Papa's throne. Who else could it be?

Well, I shall leave such useless speculation for now. I have no idea how I'm going to sleep tonight. Every time I close my eyes, I see that man coming after me, shooting at me. My dear, sweet brother, I pray he didn't actually shoot you. No. No, he couldn't have. You made it out. You made it away. You must be in Margate, and I will be with you soon. Please be there waiting for me.

-Day 29: Taking the Blame-

The magistrate, Baron Baining, lived not too far out of town. After seeing the women settled, Sam borrowed a horse and took the body of the gunman to his estate.

When the butler finally answered the door, he handed over his card. "The Marquess of Ranleigh to see Baron Baining," he said, using formal language so the man would know this was a matter of business not pleasure.

The man bowed Sam into the house, but as he did so, he caught sight of the horse tied up just outside the door with the body draped over it. The man did a double take and then proceeded to move much faster.

"If you would please come this way, my lord."

After a brief knock, he led Sam into a well-appointed study. "My lord, the Marquess of Ranleigh on official business."

"Oh?" A rotund man looked up from where he'd been pouring over some book in his hand. "Oh! He's here," he said, clearly surprised to see Sam standing right there. "Er, how do you do?"

"How do you do, Baron? I'm afraid I bring disturbing news," Sam started.

"And a dead body," the butler added.

Sam turned and gave him a quizzical look. Clearly the baron ran his household on more relaxed terms.

"I beg your pardon? A dead body?" the baron asked.

"Er, yes. I was planning on passing through this area on my way to Dover when a thief waylaid me. He shot above my coachman's head and called for my vehicle to stop. I am traveling with my young cousin, who is a sensitive girl, and her chaperone. I never travel without my pistols and was able to lean out the window and shoot the man before he had the opportunity to rob us. I hadn't actually intended to kill him, but well, I was in a moving carriage and he on his galloping horse." Sam paused and smiled. "It was a lucky shot."

"Goodness, I imagine so!"

"But then I knew I couldn't just leave him there in the road, and my cousin was quite distraught as you can imagine. I have brought him here to explain the situation to you."

"Quite so, quite so," the baron nodded. He narrowed his eyes at Sam. "Seems to me you're a great deal more responsible and honest than your father ever was. He would have just left him and gone on with his journey—most likely a race for some astronomical wager, knowing him." The man frowned his disapproval. "But I am extremely pleased to see you are a man of a different stamp."

Sam sighed. It didn't seem as if he would ever be able to get away from his father's reputation, no matter where he went. "Yes. You could say that I learned precisely how *not* to behave from him."

"Although from what I've heard, you did run wild in your younger days?" the man asked, with a lift of his eyebrow.

"As any young man does. Since inheriting the title, I have changed my ways," Sam told him.

"Grown up," the man corrected him with a nod. "Something your father never seemed to have done. Well, I am pleased to see it."

"Thank you." Society was entirely too small, Sam thought with an inner grimace. "And about the man?" he gestured toward the front of the house.

"Oh, that! Well, clearly this was an accidental killing in self-defense. Don't think another thing of it. I'll take care of everything. We will, of course, have to hold an inquisition, but it should be a pretty open and shut case."

"And will I need to be present for this?" Sam asked.

"Of course!"

"Then if it could be held at all possible haste, I would greatly appreciate it."

"I do understand. Would the day after tomorrow do? Are you staying in the area?" the man asked.

Sam frowned. "Could you not put something together by tomorrow?"

The gentleman came forward and patted Sam on his back in a condescending way. "Just like your father after all. A little patience, my lord. I'll see you on Thursday."

Sam hated being treated like a child and, even more so, as if he were his father. He clenched his teeth together and then took in a deep breath. He didn't seem to have a choice in the matter. He might as well accept this delay. Isa was not going to be happy, but at least she wasn't going to have to face any consequences.

"Very well, then. I am staying at the inn in town with my cousin."

"Excellent. I will see you here in the morning a few days hence."

The baron bowed, and Sam acknowledged him before turning toward the door.

"Er, you don't need my cousin's presence, do you?" Sam asked before leaving.

"Oh, no! No, no, I would not want to cause unnecessary distress to the young lady."

"Very good. Thank you."

He left the dead man and his horse where they were and returned to the inn.

Chapter Twenty-Four

He found Isa pacing in her room, clearly still agitated.

"Mrs. Brompton, could I please send you downstairs for some tea for Miss Günter? She seems to be in need of something restorative," Sam said after entering the room.

Mrs. Brompton was clearly torn between her duty as chaperone and Isa's obvious need for tea. She sighed in resignation. "Very well, I will trust you to behave yourselves, but I shall return promptly."

"Of course," Sam said, giving her an innocent smile.

The moment she was gone, Isa was in his arms holding him so tightly he feared she wouldn't ever let go. "It's all right," he said, soothing his hands up and down her back. "It's all perfectly all right. I met with the magistrate, and I'll have to appear for an inquiry, but you shall not."

"No?" Isa asked, pulling back slightly so she could look up at him.

"No. I told him I was the one who shot the man, and it was a fluke I actually hit and killed him. I explained it was all in self-defense. If anyone needs to appear as a witness, it will be Davies. I explained you were a sensitive girl and quite distraught at the whole thing."

Isa's hand flew to her mouth as she tried to hide her laughter. She took another step back. "Me? Sensitive?"

"Well, you have been rather distraught," Sam pointed out.

"Yes, because I thought I might be tried and sentenced to gaol or to hang or, or... I did not know what!" she told him.

He smiled and cupped her face in his hand. "None of that will happen. It was an act of self-defense against a thief trying to waylay us on the highway. No one will miss the man, and no one will question his death."

"That is incredible." Isa shook her head in wonder.

Sam shrugged. "I'm a nobleman. My word is good enough." He paused, then added because he had to tell her the truth, "Unfortunately, this inquiry can't happen until the day after tomorrow. When I protested—and I assure you, I did—I was told to be patient. So, I'm afraid I'm going to have to ask you to be the same."

Isa crossed her arms in front of her and stared at him long and hard, then seemed to deflate as she accepted there was nothing they could do but wait.

Isa sighed and looked like she was about to step forward into Sam's arms again when Mrs. Brompton reentered the room.

"Tea is on its way up," the woman said, looking critically from one to the other.

"Sam told the magistrate he was the one who shot the man, and they are just going to forget it. I will not get into trouble," Isa told her. "But we have to wait two days before the matter can be handled."

Mrs. Brompton's mouth opened in surprise, but she closed it quickly and nodded. "I knew you'd do the right thing, my lord."

-Day 31: Fight Between Men-

Isa thought it best if she just stayed in her room while Sam went to the inquisition. Both he and Mrs. Brompton agreed it was the safest thing. The previous day had been a study in boredom. She had ventured out but had stayed close to the inn. Thank goodness, Mrs. Brompton had finished her new book and passed it on to Isa, or else she certainly would have been tempted to retrieve Sam's pistols and gone searching for that magistrate.

"Don't worry, I'm sure this won't take very long, and then we'll be on our way," Sam told her as she was waiting for her breakfast to be delivered to her room.

Isa nodded, and while he was standing there looking at her expectantly, she realized she should thank him. She was still getting used to this! She gave him a sweet smile. "Thank you, Sam, I appreciate that you are handling this."

He bowed and gave her a bright smile in return. "It is entirely my pleasure." With that, he turned and left.

"Goodness, I never know when I am supposed to be grateful for someone doing something, and when I do not need to be," she commented to Mrs. Brompton.

The woman chuckled. "It's always safest to say thank you and be told that you needn't. If you don't and you should have, the person you should have thanked will be upset."

"Yes. I suppose that is a good idea. Always thank someone, and then I cannot get into trouble for not having done so," Isa agreed. She shook her head. "It was easier..." She caught herself as she was about to say, "When it was known she was a princess."

"When you were a child? I'm sure it was, but you're an adult now and really should have been taught this years ago," Mrs. Brompton said. "I'm quite surprised you weren't."

Isa was spared from answering her by the maid arriving with their breakfast.

They waited for nearly an hour after Sam had left, then Isa began to get worried. She stood up and put her book away. "I'll need to go for a walk if I'm going to have to wait much longer," she informed Mrs. Brompton.

"Surely, they'll be finished soon, and then we'll be on our way," her chaperone pointed out.

"Well then, I won't be out for long. But I do need some exercise. Let's take our things downstairs to Mr. Davies and be ready to go as soon as his lordship is done."

Mrs. Brompton agreed, and they went down, followed by Luna,

who had been allowing Isa to mindlessly pet her as she sat reading and waiting.

Isa stopped in the common room to make sure Sam wasn't there. He wasn't, but the moment she popped her head in the door, a pair of men sitting at a far table stood up. They didn't look like farmers or gentlemen, and they were staring straight at her. Isa ducked back out quickly.

Mrs. Brompton was speaking with the innkeeper's wife near the front door when two more men walked into the inn. They stopped immediately upon seeing Isa. She wasn't entirely certain, but she thought she heard one of them say, "There she is!" They came straight toward her.

The two men from the common room came out just at that moment, noticing the men who'd just come in the door.

Isa backed away toward Mrs. Brompton.

"We saw 'er first," one of the men from the common room told the others.

"I couldn't care less. We're 'ere for 'er," one of the men by the door said.

"Well, I don't care what you want. We been hired to take 'er out," said the other man from the common room.

"And we're 'ere to protect the princess," the other man by the door said.

As the four men came together in a flurry of flying fists, Isa grabbed Mrs. Brompton and headed out the back. There were a lot of *oofs* and grunts, but Isa didn't stay to watch. She and Mrs. Brompton ran through the back and found their way to the stable.

Mr. Davies was sitting on a bench just outside.

"Let's go. We need to hitch up the horses now," Isa told him.

He jumped to his feet. "Is his lordship back?"

"No. I don't know, but there are four men inside fighting over which one gets to take me," Isa told him.

"Isa, what is going on inside—" Sam said, running up to them.

"Oh, good! Let's go," Isa said, following Mr. Davies into the stable. She ran to where Mr. Davies was preparing the coach to hitch up the horses. A groom was taking his time bringing the horses out, but Isa couldn't wait. She grabbed one and guided him over and into position while the groom protested. She ignored the man and started back for the second horse, but Sam was ahead of her. He guided the other horse into his place and tossed a coin to the groom before turning back to Isa. "Do you have your saddlebags?"

"Yes," she told him.

"Good. I brought my portmanteau down this morning and settled everything. Let's go." He gave the horse a pat, and they all piled into the coach and were gone within minutes.

As Mr. Davies sprinted the horses to get them out of the area as quickly as possible, Sam turned to Isa. "Who were those men, and why are there now four of them?"

Isa used the excuse of settling the cat on her lap to try to think of what she could possibly tell him. Goodness knew it couldn't be the truth. She wondered if Mrs. Brompton had heard that one man refer to her as princess. She could only hope she hadn't.

Keeping her gaze down on the animal in her lap, she said, "I, er, I think—from what I overheard them say—one pair of men were sent to retrieve me and, I suppose, bring me back to school. The other was there to..." Isa faltered, trying to remember the words the man had used.

"Take her out, I believe, were his exact words," Mrs. Brompton said.

Isa looked up at her, silently pleading for her not to say anything more.

The woman gave her a reassuring smile and an almost imperceptible nod. It relieved Isa so much she could feel the tightness in her chest easing right away.

"Take her out?" Sam repeated. "So, one pair were trying to take you home and the other to kill you?"

She looked over at him. "I guess so."

"But why..."

"Would someone want to kill me? We've been over this, Sam, and I still have absolutely no idea. I didn't exactly have a chance to ask the men," she told him. She was getting tired of having to explain something she didn't have the answer to.

He just frowned at her before sighing. “Of course you don’t know. But now it looks as if there are two sets of men after you, and we don’t know which is which.”

“We’ll just have to avoid them all,” Isa agreed.

“And find your brother,” Mrs. Brompton added.

“Yes. He must have some answers for us,” Isa said. She looked at Sam, hoping he would understand.

He just nodded and sat back.

“How did the inquiry go?” she asked him.

“Fine. The magistrate asked me to explain the events of the day once again in front of witnesses. I did so, and that was that. The vicar said he would see the man buried in the local cemetery.”

“Even though we don’t know who he was?” Mrs. Brompton asked.

“Yes. I suppose they’ll just leave off the marker or leave it blank,” Sam said. “I didn’t ask.”

“Well, I’m glad it wasn’t a problem. Thank you, once again, for taking the blame,” Isa told him. She got a nod of approval from Mrs. Brompton and a smile from Sam.

“I couldn’t let you take responsibility. It was completely self-defense. I only wish we knew who and why—” He paused and shook his head. “Well, it’s over. We’ll be in Canterbury tonight. It’s a much bigger, busier town, so it’ll be harder for these men—all these men—to find you.” He thought about it for a moment and then smiled. “My friend, Dev, has an estate not too far from there. We’ll head there instead of into town.”

“He won’t mind?” Isa asked.

“No. I’m sure he’s still in London, and I know his housekeeper—a very sweet woman. She’ll let us stay for as long as we want,” he told them.

“Well, hopefully, it’ll just be for one night,” Isa pointed.

“Yes, but if we want to put off these men, we might do well to stay another day. You know they’ll be searching for us in both Margate and Dover tomorrow.”

“I suppose...” Isa said. She didn’t like waiting, but they’d already taken so long to get this far that she supposed one more day couldn’t hurt.

Chapter Twenty-Five

-Day 31: Chased by Friends-

"Do we dare go inside?" Sam asked Isa. They had stopped to change horses and were standing outside an inn, waiting for that to be completed.

Her stomach growled in her response. She was so embarrassed! She placed a hand on it, as if that would quiet it.

Sam just laughed. "Well, I think that answers that."

"As my stomach noted, I am hungry," she admitted with a little laugh.

"I could do with a bite myself," Mrs. Brompton added.

"As could I," Sam agreed. "So, it's settled." He strode over to Mr. Davies, who was overseeing the change in horses, and spoke to him for a moment. The man smiled and nodded before returning to his work.

"He'll join us in a few minutes, but we'll need to eat quickly. He doesn't want to leave the horses standing for long."

Isa was followed by Mrs. Brompton and Sam into the common room. She stood for a moment in the doorway, looking around the room. It had almost become second nature to her now, to pause when entering an inn to look out for any men who might be after her. She was about to continue on to an empty table when two men stood from a corner where they'd been eating. They were staring straight at her and coming toward her.

She immediately turned around and pushed Mrs. Brompton and Sam back out the door. "Let's go. I don't think I'm all that hungry, anyway."

"Is there someone—" Mrs. Brompton started.

"Yes, please, let us leave now. They're coming this way," Isa said, pushing them out the front door and toward the coach.

Sam waylaid Mr. Davies, and they were all in the coach and heading off before anyone could catch up to them.

"I can't believe there are already more men after you," Sam said. "They must have posted men at every inn in every little town between Crawley and Margate!"

"I don't know. I don't know," Isa said. She didn't realize she was wringing her hands until Sam reached across and laid a calming hand on hers.

"It's all right, Isa. We'll figure this out. And we won't even be going into Canterbury but staying at my friend's estate tonight. You'll be safe."

She looked up into his deep green eyes and felt a reassurance she never would have expected before. Just feeling his warm hand on hers, seeing his strong confidence—it was what she really needed right now, and she was so incredibly grateful he was there. She was about to say so when she heard Mr. Davies give a "hiyah!" and the coach suddenly started going much faster. She paused to listen. It was difficult to discern over the sudden pounding of the horses, but she thought she could hear another horse galloping up from behind them. Just to be sure, she put down the window and leaned out.

"No, not again!" Mrs. Brompton cried.

Sam was already reaching beneath his seat for his pistols. "What is it?" he asked Isa when she pulled her head back in.

"There's a carriage. A tall fancy one, what are they called?"

"A phaeton?" Sam asked.

"Yes, that's it. There's a phaeton with two men—the two from the inn—and it definitely looks as if they're chasing us," she told him.

"In a phaeton?" Sam was clearly confused.

"Oh dear, oh dear," Mrs. Brompton said. She was practically shaking with nerves.

Isa took her hand for a moment. "It's all right, Mrs. Brompton. We'll take care of these men just as we did the others. You don't need to fear." If only she could believe her own words! She was astounded they'd come out sounding as self-assured as they did when she was feeling anything but.

She reached for Sam's pistols as he stuck his head out the window. She'd shot a man once; she could do so again. She could, she could do this, she told herself. She took a deep breath and was preparing herself to take Sam's place at the window when he turned to face the other way and called out to Mr. Davies, "Stop! Stop the coach! It's all right."

He pulled his head back into the carriage. Seeing the gun in Isa's hand, he reached out and took it from her, firmly placing it back into its case.

"But…" Isa started to protest.

"It's all right. Those are my friends. What they're doing here or why, I have no idea, but I'd recognize that phaeton and horse anywhere," he told her with a smile.

Mr. Davies brought the coach to a slow stop to ensure the horses weren't hurt, and the carriage behind them had time to slow and stop safely as well. Before the coach had even come to a complete halt, Sam opened the door and jumped out. Isa followed, lowering the step this time for herself and Mrs. Brompton.

"What in the devil are you doing here?" Isa could hear Sam ask the men in the phaeton.

They both jumped down and took his hand, one of them giving him a slap on his shoulder. They were smiling and laughing.

"We were looking for you! Heard from Newly you were in this area on your way to Dover in his father's coach. You just disappeared! For over two weeks!" the man with dark hair said.

"We expected you back in two days with my mother's necklace," the lighter haired gentleman added.

"Where have you been? What rig and roll are you up to?" the darker man asked with a laugh. He peered behind Sam, noticing Isa standing there listening to their conversation. “Er, and who’s the beauty?”

“Oh-ho! Well, that certainly answers a lot of questions,” the lighter-haired man said with a laugh, catching sight of Isa. He slapped Sam’s shoulder again.

“No, no, it’s not what you think,” Sam said quickly. He turned and beckoned Isa to join them. “This is Miss Günter. She was in a fix and needed a ride. I’m just escorting her to her brother. It’s all on the up and up,” he added.

Mrs. Brompton made her appearance just then as if to emphasize his words.

The two gentlemen widened their eyes at the sight of her.

“It looks like there is a good deal of explaining to be done,” the dark-haired man said. “Shall we meet up at Blean?”

“Yes. That’s just where we were heading anyway—hoping to impose on your hospitality,” Sam said.

“Ha! Whether I was there or not?” the man asked with a laugh.

“Well… yes,” Sam admitted.

“Sounds like an excellent plan,” the lighter-haired man said. He turned back to their vehicle. “Come along, let’s get going. I didn’t get to eat my meal, and I’m famished. It’s at least another three hours from here.”

“At least you got to start yours! I didn’t even get that,” Sam answered with a laugh.

He turned and guided Isa and Mrs. Brompton back to their coach. Davies was standing next to the horses, awaiting orders.

“Continue on, Davies. My friends will follow,” Sam told him.

The man gave a nod and climbed back up onto the bench.

Once they were on their way again, Sam explained, “Those are my two closest friends,” he told them. “The Earl of Devereaux and Viscount Wythe. It’s Dev—Devereaux’s—home we’re going to.”

“Oh!” Mrs. Brompton said. She seemed quite pleased with the idea they would be staying at the home of an earl.

Isa wasn’t so sure. She wasn’t particularly keen on the idea that Sam would most likely be sharing her story with more people—even his closest friends. Clearly, someone was already in London telling tales of where Sam was and where he was going. Thank goodness, the men hadn't known he wasn't alone. She didn't want word to get out to anyone regarding her possible whereabouts. It was bad enough Herr Mueller's men had already found her at least twice in the past week, and whoever was trying to kill her had done so even more than that. She couldn't imagine what would happen if even more people knew! Goodness, even her father would probably learn of this escapade!

The thought left her shuddering at the possible consequences.

"Isa, are you all right? You're suddenly looking very pale and upset," Sam said. He reached out and took her hand. "It's fine, you know. Dev and Wythe won't say a word to anyone, I promise you. They're bang-up chaps."

She tried to give him a smile. "I believe you, but... well, clearly someone is already telling everyone where you are and where you're heading. It's how your friends found us."

"That's true," Sam agreed with a nod. "But Newly doesn't know that you and Mrs. Brompton are with me."

"Yes, I am grateful for that," Isa said.

"So, don't worry. It's going to be fine. And maybe my friends can help us... I don't know, search for your brother," Sam offered.

Isa widened her eyes at that. She hadn't even thought about how she was going to find Nik once they got to Margate. With a nod, she agreed. "Yes, that's true. That would be very helpful," she managed to say. Her chest was still tight with worry, but she tried to keep in mind that Sam's friends would be helpful and not give her away. There was no one to get her into even more trouble than she had already done on her own, and she could only hope Nik would know how to get her out of this scrape.

But first they had to find him.

-Day 31: Friends-

A huge grin spread across Sam's face as he greeted Mrs. MacDonald. The plump housekeeper had seen him and Dev through so many childhood escapades, and she'd still always managed to sneak him some biscuits or cake. She had been a firm believer that boys will always get into trouble, and a few sweets never hurt anyone.

"Oh, Master Samuel, how good it is to see you again!" the woman exclaimed while bustling up to the group standing just inside the door. "Ah, but you are Lord Ranleigh now, aren't you, my lord? Oh, how times do change," she said, looking up at him fondly.

"But some things never do, Mrs. MacDonald," Sam said. "Like you! How in the world do you look exactly the same as you did fifteen years ago?"

"Oh!" The woman burst out laughing. "You were always a charmer. Now, there is to be none of that. You'll get your biscuits and cake all the same. I've got cook busy in the kitchen even now."

"You are too good to me, madam. I'm certain I don't deserve you," Sam told her.

"No, you don't, and you can't have her either," Dev said, putting a possessive arm around the woman. "You will spare some of those sweets for me, won't you, Mrs. MacDonald?"

"Of course, my lord, there will be enough for everyone—even you, Lord Wythe," the woman said with a fond smile for the third of their trio. Sam and Wythe had spent many happy school holidays with Dev's family, and Mrs. MacDonald had always been there.

Sam turned to Isa. "Miss Günter, may I present Mrs. MacDonald, Dev's housekeeper. And Mrs. MacDonald, this is Mrs. Brompton, Miss Günter's chaperone."

Isa nodded to the woman but looked a little overwhelmed. Perhaps it was the familiarity with which Sam had been speaking to her. Of course, she didn't know how long he'd known the housekeeper.

"I am pleased to meet you both. Welcome to Blean," Mrs. MacDonald said, curtsying to Isa and nodding to Mrs. Brompton.

"Please allow me to show you into the drawing room. I'm afraid rooms aren't made up just yet since we weren't expecting such a party, but everything will be ready in a trice," the woman said as she led them upstairs.

"That is very good of you, Mrs. MacDonald. We are terribly sorry to put you to so much trouble," Mrs. Brompton said.

"Oh no, not at all. Lord Devereaux does this sort of thing quite often, coming with friends or sending notes saying this one or that will be stopping by for a night. We're always at the ready," Mrs. MacDonald said with a laugh.

"How difficult that must be," the chaperone said with a cluck of her tongue.

"Oh, you get used to it." She swept open the doors to a large room with a round table in the center under a grand chandelier. Beyond that were sofas and chairs in gold damask arranged around the fireplace with a mantel edged in gold and a large painting of Dev's father above it in a matching gold frame. There was a good deal of space for more seating arrangements if they were needed, but for now, there was plenty for the number of people.

"Oh, Mrs. MacDonald, let us retire to the family drawing room. It is so much cozier," Dev said.

"Of course, my lord, as you wish." She led the way through a door on the left and into a smaller room with a less formal atmosphere. The sofa and chairs were a deep blue, and there was a pretty little escritoire in one corner.

"Much better, thank you," Dev said approvingly.

"I shall have tea brought up momentarily," the woman said as she pulled open the drapes to let in the remaining light of the day.

"Thank you," Isa said, watching the woman bustle about.

"She never does stand still for more than a minute or two," Sam told her with a broad smile.

Isa gave him a hesitant smile. "So I see."

Mrs. MacDonald gave a little laugh as she scuttled out the door to see to their tea.

Chapter Twenty-Six

"You are very familiar with this house?" Isa asked, turning and looking around.

"Not this house in particular," Sam started.

"I only inherited this estate when I was twenty-one," Dev told her. "It was a part of my maternal grandfather's holdings, but he left it to me."

"He didn't like his son much so only left him what was entailed," Sam explained.

Isa looked a little confused at that but nodded, anyway.

"My main holding is in the north," Dev explained.

"But this is convenient since it's so close to London," Wythe added from the sofa where he'd made himself comfortable. He looked at the odd expression on Dev's face and then said, "What? I didn't think we were being formal here, are we?"

"I do apologize for my friend's atrocious manners, Miss Günter," Dev said, turning to Isa. "Would you care to sit down?"

"Oh, thank you, no. I have been sitting for far too long. I'd like to stand, so please, Lord Wythe is absolutely correct," Isa said, giving Wythe a smile.

The man looked smugly at Dev as if to say, "I told you so."

Dev just shook his head slowly before turning back to Isa and giving her a smile. “So, have you been traveling long? Where did you and Ranleigh meet up?”

“Yes, Ran, tell us the story,” Wythe said, sitting up eagerly.

Sam sat on a chair and told them the entire story from the time he met Isa in Oxford straight through to the fight between the two sets of men that morning as they were leaving the inn. In the middle of it, Mrs. MacDonald came back in with their tea, complete with still warm biscuits and cake just as she’d promised. Mrs. Brompton poured tea for everyone.

When he finished, Wythe gave a whistle and Dev exclaimed, “My word!” He turned toward Isa. “And you have no idea who any of these men are?”

“I think one pair might have been sent to bring me back to school,” Isa admitted. “The others, the ones who are trying to kill me, I do not know.”

“Nor why anyone would want you dead?” Wythe asked.

Isa just shook her head before reaching for another biscuit.

“Do you figure it has something to do with your brother?” Dev asked.

Isa shrugged. “That is all I can imagine it could be, although why anyone would want him dead is equally baffling.”

“Naturally. It sounds like it might be related to his reason for leaving Oxford,” Dev pointed out.

Isa nodded. “I have thought of that. But until I can find him, I won’t know for certain.”

“Yes, of course.”

“So, you’ll just stay the night and try to get on to Margate as quickly as possible?” Dev asked.

“I was actually thinking we might spend two nights here, just to throw these men off our trail a bit. It’s worked for the most part, taking our time,” Sam told them.

His friends both nodded.

Dev turned a smile on Isa. “Well, I am more than happy to have you spend as long as you need here.”

“That is very good of you, my lord. I appreciate your generosity,”

Isa said a little stiffly. It was clear she wasn't completely comfortable but was trying her best. As she said this, there was suddenly a great deal of barking, and Sam just barely caught sight of Isa's cat flash by before two large, beautiful golden retrievers came running into the room. Isa gasped. She clearly had seen the cat, too. She jumped to her feet. "*Genug! Stoppt den Lärm*!" She clapped her hands.

Both dogs stopped and turned toward her.

She pointed to the ground in front her. "Here. Now!"

The two animals immediately sat at her feet, looking up at her expectantly.

"How did you do that?" Dev asked, stunned.

Isa squatted down and started scratching both dogs under their chins simultaneously. She murmured to them quietly in German, in what sounded like praising words; although, Sam couldn't understand what she was actually saying. She turned and looked at Dev over her shoulder briefly. "It is all in your tone of voice."

One of the dogs started to move toward the cat that was now hiding under the sofa.

"Ah-ah," Isa told him and grabbed on to his head to turn it back toward her. "You may not chase the cat. I know it is great fun, and she is an intruder in your territory, but she is a guest, and you must treat her kindly," she told the animal.

The dog lowered himself to the floor, looking for all the world as if he were sulking.

"I know. You are a very good boy," she told the one dog. She turned to the other and added, "And you, too." She then turned back to Dev. "What are their names?"

"Loki and Dionysus, or Dio for short," Dev told her.

She smiled and looked back between the dogs. "Let's see. You must be Loki?" she asked the dog lying down. He lifted his head and allowed his tongue to hang out of his mouth as he panted a little doggy smile at her. She laughed. "I figured as much."

"Oh, yes. Loki is always getting into trouble," Dev laughed. "Dio is a bit better behaved but not much."

The cat slowly emerged from under the sofa.

"It's all right, Luna," Isa cooed to her. "Loki and Dio won't hurt you." She turned and gave the dogs a look of warning.

Loki didn't move his body but extended his head to sniff at the cat. Dio stepped over his brother to smell her. The cat hesitantly smelled the two dogs as well.

"There, we're all friends now," Isa said happily.

"That's amazing," Wythe said. "You're really good with animals."

"Much better than I am with people, I'm afraid," Isa agreed with a laugh as she stood up and took her seat again.

Wythe smiled and nodded.

"You aren't supposed to agree with her, you dolt," Dev scolded him.

"Well, I'm sure she knows herself," Wythe said, defending himself.

"Miss Günter takes a little time to warm up to people, but then she's very friendly," Sam said, giving her a smile.

She nodded her agreement. "You will please be patient with me."

"Naturally," Dev said.

By the time Mrs. MacDonald came to inform them their rooms were ready, the cat had settled herself in between the two dogs, and the three of them were fast asleep.

-Day 31: Problems-

Isa was in heaven. The very first thing she did when she was shown up to her room was to request a bath. Mrs. Brompton oversaw the placement of the tub in front of the fire that had been built up, and then no fewer than three footmen came in, each bearing two buckets of steaming, hot water.

She quickly shucked her gown with Mrs. Brompton's assistance and then sank into the water with a sigh of contentment. After a moment of simply enjoying the warmth, she ducked her head down to wet her hair. Mrs. Brompton then took to washing it, scrubbing her scalp in the most intensely satisfying way.

Isa couldn't help but moan in happiness.

"Am I rubbing too hard?" Mrs. Brompton asked, her hands pausing their delicious action.

"No, no! It feels wonderful," Isa said quickly.

The woman resumed her work.

"This is so much nicer than dunking my head in a bucket of ice-cold water," Isa commented as she sat up a bit so the woman could reach the back of her head.

Mrs. Brompton chuckled. "I have to admit, I am looking forward to doing the very same thing. I asked the housekeeper, and she told me that, while they don't normally provide hot baths for servants, she would make an exception in my case since we've been traveling for so long."

"That is good of her," Isa said as she tilted her head back so Mrs. Brompton could rinse the soap from her hair. Once she was done and had squeezed out some of the excess water, Isa picked up the lovely rose-scented soap the housekeeper had provided and took to scrubbing her arms and legs.

"Miss Günter," Mrs. Brompton began hesitantly.

"Hmmm?"

"I may be wrong, but I could have sworn one of the men we witnessed fighting today referred to you as the princess."

Isa stopped soaping herself. She turned toward Mrs. Brompton, widening her eyes in surprise. "Really? How very odd, indeed! My father always called me his little princess, but well, you know fathers." She forced a smile onto her lips. "Perhaps the man was just repeating what he'd heard my father call me?"

"Of course, that must be it," the woman said, nodding. "You would certainly tell me if you were actually royalty."

Isa returned to her scrubbing, facing forward again with her back toward the woman and kept quiet.

-Day 31: Playing Games-

Isa was happy to stay quiet through a good portion of dinner. Mrs. Brompton wasn't there to act as a buffer between her and the gentlemen. She knew she didn't need such support when she was alone with Sam. She always felt comfortable and secure with him, but his friends were another matter.

She just didn't know why she couldn't feel comfortable with Lords Devereaux and Wythe. They seemed to be very nice people, and they were Sam's closest friends. But she just didn't feel at ease with them. And she knew it wasn't the men per se, it was her. Sam was right, she didn't feel at ease with anyone until she got to know them better. She supposed it was being raised in a palace as a princess. She learned not to trust people straight away. They always wanted something from you, and if they didn't, that was suspicious, too.

Nik had somehow learned how to be warm and open and personable, but that was just his way. Isa was quieter, more wary.

"Miss Günter?" Lord Devereaux's voice cut into Isa's thoughts.

"I beg your pardon?" she asked, noticing that the three men were all looking at her.

"Woolgathering?" Sam asked with a smile.

"Er, yes. I am sorry. What did you say, my lord?" she asked.

"I asked where you were from. You clearly have an accent. Is it German?" Lord Devereaux asked with a smile.

"Er, yes. I am from a small principality which I am sure you have never heard of," she told him. She was pretty sure she had shared that with Sam as well. She couldn't quite remember what she'd told him of her background.

"There are quite a few, aren't there?" Wythe asked. From the expression on his face, she gathered he was not entirely confident in his knowledge of the German-speaking states.

"Yes, there are," she told him with a smile. "It is hard to keep track of them all, I'm certain. I had to learn of all of them in some detail, and even then, I get some confused and can't quite remember which are grand duchies, which are duchies, and which are principalities."

"What's the difference?" Lord Wythe asked.

"Just the title of the person who rules the area, really," she said.

"And so… who rules where you live?" he asked.

"The prince, Prince Heinrich. I live in a principality," she explained, carefully leaving out that he was her father.

Chapter Twenty-Seven

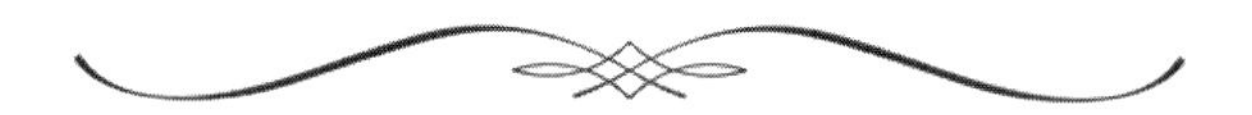

"Oh, I see," he nodded.

"And you say it is one of the smaller principalities?" Lord Devereaux asked.

"Yes." She wasn't about to get more specific than that. Already, she'd probably said more than necessary. They seemed to be expecting her to go on, however. "Er, it's quite pretty. We have lots of forests, some excellent farms, and one major city, which is the capital."

"Do you miss it?" Sam asked.

A vision of her father's castle came to her mind's eye. The palace was incredibly beautiful, quite grand, really. It had been their family's home for over ten generations, being renovated and enlarged with each successive generation as needed. "I miss it very much."

"What do you miss most, aside from your parents, I suppose?" Lord Devereaux asked.

"The forests, of course," Isa answered quickly.

"Of course?" Sam asked.

Isa laughed. "You wouldn't know this from just having met me as we traveled from Oxford, but I hunt and ride a great deal. In fact, if you were to ask anyone I know how often they'd seen me on my feet and how often on horseback, they would tell you straight away that I am more often on my horse than anywhere else."

"Really?" Lord Wythe asked.

"The loss of your horse must have been especially devastating, then," Sam said quickly.

A sharp pain stabbed at her. "You cannot imagine," she said.

"I'm so sorry, I didn't mean to cause you more distress," he said quickly.

She shook it off and managed to dredge up a smile. "It is all right. I shall… I shall replace her, I suppose. But it will take a great deal of time to train a new horse. I have had my Lilli for five years. We understood each other. We could communicate and anticipate one another's moves."

Lord Devereaux nodded. "I had a horse like that once. Sam, do you remember Apollo?"

Sam smiled and nodded. "How could I forget him?" He turned to Isa. "He was enormous. Dev had him through our last years at school and straight through university, didn't you?" he asked, turning back to his friend.

Lord Devereaux nodded. "He's still at Devault Abbey enjoying his retirement," he told Isa.

She smiled. "I am sure he is happy to see you when you visit."

"Oh yes! Goodness, he practically runs me down each time I'm up there, just in his eagerness to greet me," Lord Devereaux laughed. "His joints just aren't up to carrying a rider for very long, but we'll go for a slow walk together when I see him."

"You do not want to…" She didn't quite know how to phrase the words nicely in English.

"Put him down? No! I couldn't," Lord Devereaux said quickly.

Isa nodded. "I hope I will be able to find another as intrepid as my Lilli. She was strong and had no fear. She could take any jump I set her to."

"That's a good horse," Sam agreed.

"She was."

The footmen came forward and cleared away their plates. Isa wasn't certain if she should retire by herself or what the proper etiquette should be when it was just the four of them. In her father's palace, if the courtiers dined with the family, they followed the strict rules which dictated that the ladies leave the gentlemen to their wine after dinner. But if it was just her, Nik, and her father, they were more relaxed and all retired together, usually to her father's library for a game of chess, cards, or just to read.

"Er, how about if we take our port up in the drawing room?" Lord Devereaux suggested.

Sam gave his friend a grateful smile. "An excellent idea."

"Shall we play some cards?" Lord Wythe asked as he stood.

"Do you play whist?" Isa asked.

The three men turned toward her. "Er, yes," Lord Wythe said, giving her a smile. "Do you play?"

"I do. I have not played for a little while, but it is a favorite game of my family's," she said.

"How much do you—" Lord Wythe started.

"I think it might be better if we didn't play for anything more than empty points, Wythe," Sam said, cutting his friend off.

"What? But where's the fun—" Lord Wythe began to protest.

"The fun is in the play. Not the gambling," Sam said sternly.

"Did you suffer a head injury along your way?" Lord Wythe asked, frowning at his friend. "Is this the same Ranleigh I've known for..."

"If you'll remember, I told you I was giving up the, er, folly of my youth," Sam started.

"Ah, yes, becoming responsible," Lord Devereaux said with a broad smile. "Still committed to that, are you?"

"More so than ever," Sam told him, sounding a little less tense than when he'd been speaking with Lord Wythe.

"Well then, I think we could manage to play for empty points, don't you, Wythe?" Lord Devereaux said, slapping his friend's back as they started up the stairs.

Lord Wythe grumbled something Isa couldn't catch but figured it was just as well. She gave Sam a smile and said to him quietly as they headed up after the two men, "Good for you, Sam. I am certain it cannot be easy to turn down your friends like that. But you truly have changed and are being responsible. I appreciate that."

He nodded but didn't look entirely pleased with either himself or her words. This must be more difficult than she imagined. She could only hope he stuck to his good intentions.

After a game of whist and another which Lord Wythe taught her called vingt-et-un, Isa decided to retire for the night. It was clear the gentlemen wanted to talk and drink, and she was tired.

"You will please excuse me, gentlemen?" she asked, standing.

They all stood. "Of course," Lord Wythe said first. Sam gave her a smile, which sent a rush of warmth through her even as she returned it.

"Good night," she said to them all.

Just as she closed the door behind her, she remembered her shawl which she'd left on the back of her chair. She started to open the door again to retrieve it when she heard Lord Devereaux. "Well, Ranleigh, old man, you've certainly caught a looker. She's a diamond if I ever saw one." The man laughed, and she could hear what sounded like a slap to Sam's back.

"She is not only beautiful but sweet and kind as well. And I worry she may be in more trouble than we know."

"You really think someone was trying to kill her?" Lord Devereaux asked.

"I know so. I was shot at as well if you remember," Sam said.

"What sort of trouble could that brother of hers have got into that they would come after his family?" Lord Wythe asked.

"I don't know, but I am determined to find out," Sam said. There was silence for a moment, and then she heard him say, "I think I'm going to bed as well."

"What? It's only eleven," Lord Wythe protested. "The night is young."

"Yes, but I was up early this morning," Sam said.

"You poor chap. She's not only got your leading strings measured out but has attached them firmly, hasn't she?" Wythe said.

There was a silence for a minute, and then she could hear Sam's voice saying coldly, "I've told you I was not going to follow in my father's footsteps, that I was making a change for better. You can believe whatever you want, but I'm for bed."

Isa beat a hasty retreat, not wanting to be found eavesdropping.

-JOURNAL ENTRY #6-

Back in her room, Isa pulled out her journal. She'd discovered a very pretty lap desk in the bottom of the wardrobe complete with ink, a couple of quills, and a pen knife. She now pulled it forward toward her crossed legs as she sat on her bed. She carefully sharpened a quill, then dipped it into the ink.

You would not believe, my dearest Nik, that we are at the home of the Earl of Devereaux, one of Lord Ranleigh's friends. We met them on the road after we left the last town. I thought, at first, they were two of the men following us and couldn't tell you how relieved I was that they were not.

We met the men following us and discovered that there is not one pair but two. I'm not entirely surprised. I was sure Herr Mueller had sent men after me, and then there are those who are actually trying to kill me. The four men intercepted each other when we stopped to eat something around midday. They engaged in fisticuffs in the inn with me and Mrs. Brompton standing right there. And unfortunately, one of the men—most likely Herr Mueller's man—referred to me as the princess! When Mrs. Brompton questioned me about it earlier today when we were alone in my room, I fobbed her off with a slight fib. I do hope she forgets about it!

We are very comfortable here. Even more incredible than finally staying in a room all by myself—my new chaperone has been sharing a room with me—and having a bed I know is clean and oh-so-comfortable, is that Lord Ranleigh has truly changed! He used to be quite a reprobate! He would drink and gamble and has even done so while we were on the road. But this evening, his friends invited him to join them in revelry, and he turned them down! I was never so proud of him. He truly is becoming more responsible.

I am greatly looking forward to tomorrow. We will take the day to relax and then after that continue onward to Margate, at last! Secretly, I am wondering if Lord Devereaux has horses he could lend us to go riding. I would not venture beyond his land for fear of being found by the men chasing me, but I don't see why I shouldn't enjoy a good ride here. We'll see. I won't hold my breath since it is quite likely that he wouldn't have so many horses in his stable.

Soon, my dearest, soon I pray I will be able to hand you this letter so you may read of my adventures.

Until then, Brother, I hope you are safe... wherever you are.

Chapter Twenty-Eight

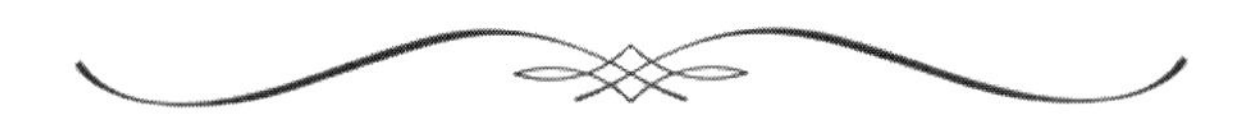

-Day 32: A Beautiful Day-

The following morning Isa was enjoying a good breakfast alone in the breakfast room when Sam joined her, looking very smart in a bottle-green coat with a deeper green brocade waistcoat. He wore buckskin breeches, and his boots shined in a way they hadn't since they began their journey.

She smiled her welcome. "I suppose Lord Devereaux and Lord Wythe are not used to rising early in the morning."

He gave a little laugh as he went over to the sideboard where there was an impressive array of dishes laid out. "No, I don't think so. I don't imagine we'll be seeing them until this afternoon. Sadly for me, that's just as well since I've got some letters to respond to."

"How have you received mail?" she asked, after swallowing a mouthful of egg.

Sam frowned at her. "Dev was kind enough to bring me the pile of letters sitting on my desk. He and I live very close to one another in London, and he stopped by my home."

"He also brought you some clothes, I see," she commented.

"Er, yes," Sam said, shifting self-consciously. "I'm sorry we have nothing to offer you."

"That is all right. My boots were cleaned last night as were my riding clothes—neither of which have received proper care since I left school."

"Well, I'm glad to hear that. I'm sure we can go out riding this afternoon with Dev and Wythe if you'd like," Sam offered.

Isa's heartbeat kicked up a notch at the prospect of being back in the saddle, but before she could say anything, Lord Devereaux joined them.

"What's that I hear? You're planning to go riding?" he asked by way of greeting.

"Good morning, my lord," Isa said. "Yes. Sam was just saying as much."

"Sam? Really? Sam?" Lord Devereaux asked. One side of his lips twitched up into a smile.

Sam frowned at his friend. "Yes, Dev, I did say that, and yes, Miss Günter calls me by my given name, and I use hers. Don't pretend as if you've never called me Sam before because it's what you've called me ever since we met."

"Well, yes, but now you're Ranleigh, and so that's what we call you," Lord Devereaux commented as he went about filling a plate with food.

"Oh! Should I not call you by your given name here? I do beg your pardon," Isa said, worrying how much of a faux pas she'd made.

"Yes, you should call me by my name. It's perfectly fine. Dev just enjoys teasing his friends," Sam told her before giving Lord Devereaux another glaring look.

"Ah." Isa took a sip of her tea and then turned to Lord Devereaux. "Might that mean you consider me to be one of your friends, my lord?"

Lord Devereaux stopped as he was just about to sit down at the head of the table. He gave Isa a kind smile. "I would be honored if you'd consider me one of yours, Miss Günter. But then you'd have to call me Dev instead of Lord Devereaux." He took his seat.

She smiled. "Now I will have three, no perhaps four!" The thought made her oddly giddy.

"Four what?" Sam asked.

"Friends." She ticked them off on her fingers. "My brother, of course, you, Mrs. Brompton—I think I can count her as a friend, don't you?—and now Dev."

Sam exchanged an odd look with Dev that Isa couldn't decipher, but she didn't think it was one of happiness. "Er, yes, I do believe you could count Mrs. Brompton as a friend. You've certainly been extraordinarily kind to her, and I'm sure she likes you a great deal," Sam told her.

"Surely, you have friends at school, Miss Günter?" Dev asked.

"Please call me Isa. And no. I tried to make friends, but I am just not very good at it, I'm afraid," she told him.

"Or at home?" he asked.

She shook her head. "Not really." She certainly didn't count the courtiers, who had no other choice but to spend time with her, as her friends. She didn't particularly like them and didn't think they liked her. "Perhaps my groom at home, but he is paid to accompany me wherever I go."

"Oh." Dev began eating so didn't say anything more.

"So, riding this afternoon, Dev?" Sam asked, changing the topic.

"Absolutely," he said around a mouthful of food.

As Sam predicted, Lord Wythe didn't put in an appearance until they'd gathered for the midday meal. He did come down dressed to go riding, though, so Isa supposed someone must have informed him of their plans.

After she'd finished eating, Isa excused herself to go change for their afternoon excursion. She rejoined the gentlemen in the dining room where they were still sitting around the table.

She walked back into the room, and immediately, Lord Wythe started choking on whatever it was he'd just swallowed. The other gentlemen stood at the entrance—Sam smiling and Dev with his eyes widened and mouth hanging open a touch. As soon as he'd regained control of himself, Lord Wythe, too, stood.

"I beg your pardon, Miss Günter, but what... what..." Lord Wythe started.

"What?" Isa asked.

"Dev and Wythe aren't used to your riding clothes," Sam said, giving his friends a broad smile.

"Oh! I do hope you are not offended. I prefer riding in breeches. It is so much easier than skirts," she said.

"I'm sure it is," Dev said, nodding. "Er, I'll have to send amended instructions to the stable. I requested one of the horses be saddled with a sidesaddle, but clearly you won't be needing that." He gave a nod to a footman standing in the corner of the room. The man nodded back and left presumably to deliver the message to the stable.

"That was very thoughtful, Dev, but no. A regular saddle would be fine," Isa told him.

"Well then, Wythe, if you're finished?" Dev asked, looking at Lord Wythe.

He picked up his wine glass and drained it in one gulp. "I am now."

They all walked out to the stable where Isa inspected the mount chosen for her, a horse named Artemis, and tightened the girth on the saddle.

"Do you approve, Isa?" Dev asked with a laugh after she'd finished her inspection.

"Oh, yes. She's lovely," Isa told him. The mare wasn't nearly as well appointed as Lilli had been, but she looked strong. "How does she take a fence?"

"Quite well, actually," he told her. "I've only ridden her a few times, but I was pleased with the way she acquitted herself."

"Have you not had her long?" Isa asked as she accepted assistance from a groom to mount.

"No. Actually, I am thinking of starting to breed horses up at my estate near York. I purchased her for that purpose but haven't yet sent her up," he told her as they rode out.

"Well, she looks like she would do quite well. Will you use your favorite horse, what was his name, Apollo? As stud?"

"Yes, as a matter of fact. That's precisely what I was thinking." He gave her a smile, adding, "Shall we put them through their paces and let them shake out any excess energy? Gentlemen?" He turned toward Sam and Lord Wythe who were following.

"Yes," Sam answered immediately.

"I'm game," Lord Wythe agreed.

They kicked their horses into a trot and soon were at a full gallop, riding across the fields of Dev's estate. Isa felt her heart lift and, for the first time in weeks, could finally breathe. She was laughing and a trifle winded when they eventually slowed. "Oh, but that felt good! And you are right, Artemis is a very sweet goer."

They rode the boundaries of the estate before heading back across the fields. Isa caught sight of a fence separating one field from another. "Who will race me to the next field?"

"I'm in!" Sam said immediately. Dev echoed him.

"Is there money on this?" Lord Wythe asked.

"I am afraid not, my lord. Just your pride," Isa answered, and with that, she kicked Artemis into motion. Just as she expected, the horse was fast. Sam was on a larger gelding, and they quickly caught up. Dev and Lord Wythe were just behind. Artemis took the fence with ease, much to Isa's delight. She pulled up after they had all cleared it.

"I think it was a tie," Sam said, laughing.

"Sadly, I think you beat me by a nose," she answered right back.

"All right," he agreed.

"It's not fair. You had a head start," Lord Wythe complained. "You're supposed to give the rest of us notice."

"But where would the fun in that be?" Isa laughed.

Dev and Sam laughed along with her, but Lord Wythe just scowled at her. "Fine. Let's see how you do on the next one." He took off, heading for the next fence at the far end of the field.

Isa spurred her horse into another gallop and managed to pass him just before he reached the fence. This time she was the first over, followed by Sam, then Lord Wythe, and finally, Dev.

"There you are, my lord. I won fairly that time," she told him. He didn't seem happy.

Sam just laughed. "Well done, Isa. You take those fences without a moment's hesitation."

"You're a regular female Corinthian," Dev agreed.

"I take it that is good?" she asked.

"It's very good," Sam agreed, moving his horse alongside hers. He reached out his right hand toward her. "Well done."

She took it with her left, giving him a happy smile.

"Well, I'm done," Lord Wythe said, frowning at them. "My pride can only take so much beating."

"Oh, come now, Wythe," Sam protested, letting go of Isa's hand.

"No, I know when to cut my losses." He turned his horse around and headed for the house at a slow trot.

"I hope I did not offend him," Isa said, now feeling bad for saying it was only his pride for which they were racing.

"He's been in a foul mood all day, for some reason. But I'll go and see if I can't cheer him up," Dev said. He then gave Sam a sly smile. "You two might want some time alone as well." Before either she or Sam could answer, he wheeled his horse around and went chasing after Lord Wythe.

"I do hope I did not do anything wrong," Isa told Sam as they watched him ride off.

"No. Wythe can be a little... childish sometimes. Don't worry about it. Come. I do believe there is a pretty little stream not too far where we can water the horses." He continued onward toward some trees.

Isa kicked her mare into a gentle trot and rode beside him. It was, indeed, a lovely little spot he led her to. The trees provided some shade from the warm spring sun, and the horses seemed happy to have a drink and a nibble at the fresh grass.

Sam stretched out on his back with his hands pillowing his head. "This is what I've missed."

Isa sat next to him, leaning back on her hands. "Well, we did have a chance to do something like this when we went for our picnic in Goldalming."

"Godalming," he corrected her with a laugh. He became serious again much too fast, however. "That ended a little more abruptly than I'd hoped."

"Well, I do hope we will not be shot at here," she agreed.

"I'm certain we won't," he said.

"But we did end it nicely after the gunman rode away," she added, quietly remembering his sweet kisses that afternoon.

He sat up. His green eyes focused on her intensely as a small smile played on his lips. "Yes, we did," he said softly. He shifted closer to her and leaned in for the kiss she'd hoped for. Her mind settled into a happy, mushy state until a passing thought caused her to start.

Sam pulled back and looked down at her with a concerned expression. "What?"

"Nothing!" She pulled her lips up into a smile even as she pulled him back down to continue kissing her, only this time she put a great deal more enthusiasm into it as her disturbing thought settled into one of even greater joy.

She was in love with this man.

Chapter Twenty-Nine

-Day 32: Dinner and Promises of Help-

"So... tomorrow," Dev began as they all sat back after a wonderful dinner. The gentlemen had glasses of port in front of them or in their hands. Isa was still sipping at her wine.

"Tomorrow, we get back on the road," Isa answered Dev's unspoken question.

"You don't want to have one more day of this idyllic life?" Sam asked, giving Isa a broad smile. "We could go riding once again. Maybe take a picnic to the stream..." He left the suggestion hanging in the air. Isa felt her cheeks heat as she remembered their time that afternoon.

"It would be safer in terms of the men after you," Dev said, chiming in to offer his opinion.

Sam gave him a grateful smile.

"I suppose we might..." Isa said slowly.

"Excellent. We'll leave the day after," Sam said quickly before she could change her mind.

"And then we'll go to Canterbury or—" Isa began.

"No, no, Canterbury's only a few miles away. We'll go straight to Margate. It should only take us perhaps three hours to get there, maybe four—another reason why there's less of a hurry." Sam gave Isa a reassuring look.

"Probably closer to four, considering your coach only has two horses," Dev said.

"Yes, why don't you have four?" Wythe asked Sam.

"Didn't have them in my stable at Ranleigh. And it would have been much more expensive to travel all this way having to change four horses each time," Sam explained.

Wythe nodded his understanding.

"It's taken us a little longer, but then, considering we were being followed, it didn't really matter," Sam continued.

"No, we ended up taking as long as we possibly could anyway," Isa said, trying to keep the frustration from her voice. She knew it had been the right strategy, but that still didn't make it any easier considering she was in a rush to find her brother. On the other hand, she did so want to draw out the time she had left with Sam—who knew what would happen after she found Nik. She refused to even allow her mind to go there.

"Yes, so it's just as well," Sam said, looking quite pleased with himself.

"And once you get there?" Dev asked.

"We will look for my brother," Isa told him.

"Do you know where he may be?" Wythe asked.

"No. I will look first for his ship, but it may not be there. He may have had it moved just to trick the men after him into thinking he had left the country," she said.

"He has his own ship?" Wythe asked, sitting forward.

"Well, it belongs to our father, actually, but, er, yes. It is the ship that brought us here," she said, wondering if she'd made a mistake. She looked at Sam and Dev, but neither one of them seemed to think it was unusual that her father would own a ship. She relaxed just a touch.

"And beyond that? You don't know where else he might be hiding?" Dev asked.

"No, I am afraid I do not," she said, trying desperately to keep her spirits up.

"Well then, I suppose we'll just have to ask around," Dev said, giving her an encouraging smile.

Sam nodded. "We can ask at any of the inns near the pier. Perhaps they've seen him."

"And the other inns in town. It's not a very big place," Dev agreed.

"I'm sure there will be some word on where he might be. Certainly, someone has seen him," Sam said.

"You speak as if you and Lord Wythe will be joining us," Isa commented, looking from Dev to Wythe.

"I don't—" Wythe began.

"Of course we will!" Dev said, cutting him off. "We'd be happy to help you search for him." He looked over at Wythe. "You don't have anywhere else you need to be, do you Wythe?"

"I would be most grateful," Isa added.

"No, I, er, I don't have anything else I need to be doing," Wythe agreed with a touch of reluctance to his voice.

"Thank you so very much," Isa said, giving all the men a bright smile. "With your help, I am certain he will be found in no time."

~Day 34: On the Road Again~

A wave of nausea and excitement washed over Isa as she climbed into the coach when they finally left Dev's beautiful estate. After being in a traveling coach almost nonstop for so long, she was absolutely sick at the thought of having to sit in this one for the three to four hours it would take for them to get to Margate. On the other hand, she thought with rising excitement, it was only a few hours, and they would finally, finally be in Margate!

It had taken so much longer than she ever expected. However, she also hadn't anticipated being followed and having her life in danger. She hated the fact that she had inadvertently put others in danger as well. She would have to do something very special for all of them once Nik was located. She wasn't entirely certain what, but she would think of something.

Mrs. Brompton followed Isa into the carriage with a small groan. "Oh, I do beg your pardon!"

Isa just laughed. "It is all right. I feel the same way. But this is it, the last leg of our journey."

"Well, the last leg for you. I still need to get to my sister's in Dover," the woman pointed out.

"Oh yes, of course." The idea that had been circulating around in Isa's mind came to the tip of her tongue, but she pushed it aside for now. She wouldn't tease the woman with the promise of employment if it weren't possible. She would need to ask Nik first and perhaps write to her father. So for the time being, she merely smiled sympathetically at her temporary companion.

"We'll see you there," Dev said, popping his head into the coach.

"Very good, Dev. Enjoy your drive," Isa responded with a bright smile and a wave. She watched as Dev's fancy carriage drove past them. With their larger, slower vehicle they would probably arrive a good hour behind the sporting phaeton, but that was all right. They would be arriving in Margate. Isa could hardly wait!

-Day 34: Helping Out a Gentleman in Need-

They'd only been on the road for about an hour when Sam felt the coach slowing. He looked out the window, wondering why Davies was stopping the coach. They pulled up next to another traveling coach that was pulled off the road and sitting at an odd angle. It was clear one of the wheels on the coach had broken.

Isa had also been peering around Mrs. Brompton to see out the window but strangely sat back suddenly. He wondered what she had seen. Her eyes were now wide with fear and darting around the inside of the coach.

"I'm sure it's fine," he told her as reassuringly as he could. "It just looks like another nobleman's coach has broken a wheel. I'm certain it's not the men who've been following us."

She gave a short nod of her head and attempted to give him a smile, but it was clear she was anxious.

"I'll just go and see if I can help." He gave Mrs. Brompton a look he hoped conveyed a suggestion that she look after her charge. The woman seemed to understand because she gave him back a reassuring look of understanding.

He climbed down and went forward to see what they could do to help. He found Davies speaking with the coachman; the man who owned the coach was pacing back and forth in an agitated manner nearby. He was a fit-looking older man with slightly graying blond hair and narrowed eyes. He approached the owner. He vaguely recognized him as someone he'd seen at his club a few times but didn't actually know the gentleman.

"Good morning," Sam called out to him.

The man stopped his pacing and scowled at him. "I do not know I would say that," he snapped in a heavy German accent.

"Er, no, I suppose not. I'm the Marquis of Ranleigh. It looks as if my coachman and yours are working out some way for us to assist you."

The gentleman's expression cleared enough to be polite. He nodded at Sam. "Markgraf Kottenfurst. I do appreciate the help a great deal. I am in quite a rush, I'm afraid."

"I understand. Where are you headed?" Sam asked.

"Margate. And you?"

"I'm also on my way to Margate. Perhaps we can give you a lift. My man can take your wheel to be repaired, and then see it returned to your coachman with assistance to put things right again?" Sam offered.

The man's worried expression cleared up immediately. He came forward extending his hand toward Sam. "That would be excellent. I would appreciate that immensely."

Sam took his hand and gave him a reassuring smile. "Of course. Not a problem at all. Let me just speak with the coachmen."

He proposed his plan to the other two men who were discussing options as well. Lord Kottenfurst's coachman agreed that since his employer was in such a rush, Sam's idea would be best. He'd stay with the horses and the coach.

Everything was agreed upon, and the broken wheel was strapped on to the back of Sam's coach. As Sam climbed back in with Lord Kottenfurst behind him, he started to say, "I'm traveling with—" and then he stopped.

Isa wasn't in the coach.

He looked to Mrs. Brompton who shook her head quickly.

"Er, I'm traveling with my cousin's companion," he finished, quickly amending his words. "Lord Kottenfurst, this is Mrs. Brompton."

The woman gave the gentleman a nod since she couldn't stand to curtsy to him.

Sam settled himself next to the woman while his guest sat across in the forward-facing seat. "How do you do?" Lord Kottenfurst said politely. He then looked curiously at Mrs. Brompton. "You are traveling without your charge?"

"She is traveling with friends in another conveyance," Mrs. Brompton said quickly. "No need to worry," she added, looking at Sam.

He wondered where and how she was traveling, but he trusted both Isa and Mrs. Brompton and only allowed a small niggling worry to tease him. She would surely turn up... he hoped.

"I assume she is old enough to travel without you, then?" Lord Kottenfurst asked curiously.

"Oh, yes. She is eighteen," Mrs. Brompton said, giving the man a smile.

"Really? I have a niece that age studying here in England," Lord Kottenfurst said. "I assume your charge is a great deal more responsible than her." He gave her a smile.

"Well, naturally I wouldn't know your relation, my lord, but my charge is certainly quite responsible. I have no fears for her well-being," the woman answered.

He looked to Sam. "Are you bringing her to London for the Season? That would be quite a responsibility for a young man such as yourself."

"Er, uh, no. I'm just escorting her to Margate where she'll be meeting her brother," Sam told him, wondering at the man's curiosity regarding Isa. As soon as the words were out of his mouth, however, he feared he might have already said too much for the man looked even more interested.

"Really? To her brother, you say? Not her mother or another female relative?" the gentleman asked.

"Oh, I'm certain the two of them will go on to their family home," Sam said quickly. He was a terrible liar, never able to think of a story at the spur of the moment. He needed to get out of this situation, fast. "And what of you, my lord? You say you are in a hurry to get to Margate?"

"Yes. I have business there." He pulled out his watch. "I have a meeting I need to get to by early evening."

"No worries, then," Sam said, also pulling out his watch. "It's only half-past two. We should be arriving well before that."

"I do hope so." Much to Sam's relief, he turned to stare out the window, looking preoccupied with his own thoughts and worries. He turned back toward Sam briefly. "Your man did say he would take care of the wheel, yes?"

"Yes, I'll see to it he does. And he'll arrange for it to be returned to your coach and the vehicle repaired, so your driver can meet you in Margate."

"I will only be in Margate for a short time." He frowned and sighed heavily. "I may need to hire a coach to take me on to Dover," he added quietly to himself.

"It sounds like you've got a very busy schedule," Sam commented.

Lord Kottenfurst looked a little startled, as if he hadn't realized he'd been speaking aloud. "Er, yes. Well, a gentleman's work, you know." He returned to his contemplation of the passing scenery.

Sam didn't know what sort of work would take a man to two different port cities within a day, but he supposed it wasn't any of his business. Isa, however, was his business. He only wished he could be reassured they hadn't actually left her out in the middle of nowhere, attempting to make her way to Margate on her own. He wouldn't put it past her to suddenly decide to walk or somehow believe she could find a ride with someone else. He only wished he knew why she'd abandoned him. *Them*, he corrected himself. Why she'd abandoned *them*.

Mrs. Brompton patted his hand, resting on the seat between them, soothingly. "I'm sure she's fine," she said quietly.

"I do, er, worry a bit about these friends she's traveling with. She is my responsibility," he told her in an equally quiet voice.

"And it is quite commendable that you take that responsibility so very seriously, my lord. But have no fear."

He wished he could ask what she knew, but in their present situation with Lord Kottenfurst sitting directly across from them, he couldn't. He could only pray she was right.

Chapter Thirty

-Day 34: Arriving in Margate-

Isa jumped down from the bench the moment they arrived at the inn in Margate. Mr. Davies followed her. He'd not said a word to her the entire way since they'd picked up her uncle, the Markgraf Kottenfurst.

The moment she'd seen the crest on the side of the coach sitting off to the side of the road, she'd known she would have to do something fast or else her uncle would see her. Once again, her riding clothes had come to her rescue. As Sam had spoken with Uncle Alexander, she'd slipped out the door on the far side of the coach with her saddlebag. A quick change into her breeches, coat, and most importantly, her hat, and she'd been able to climb onto the bench without being noticed by anyone. The men had all been much too preoccupied with their plans, thank goodness. As she sat there, keeping her head down and face turned away, she gathered her uncle would be traveling to Margate with them, and once there, Mr. Davies would see to getting his wheel repaired.

Mr. Davies had only given the slightest pause when he'd climbed back onto the bench and found her there after seeing the pieces of the wheel secured to the back of the coach, and Sam and Uncle Alexander had climbed inside. She fully expected him to say something—whether it was to question her presence or scold her she didn't know. But he said absolutely nothing, merely taking up the reins once again and driving in silence to Margate.

As soon as he'd jumped down after her, he retrieved Sam's portmanteau from the boot and handed it to her saying gruffly and loudly, "Boy, take that up to his lordship's room. I'll see to that wheel after I attend to the horses."

Isa nodded, keeping her head down, and took Sam's luggage. Inside, she found Sam making arrangements for their stay and then followed him silently up to his room. She didn't like the expression on his face when he saw her there. He was clearly unhappy with her. At least she'd had time to come up with a plausible story as to why she was avoiding Uncle Alexander.

The moment the door closed behind them Sam turned on her. She could feel his anger from across the room. "All right, out with it. Why is it you felt the need to nearly give me apoplexy when I discovered you weren't in the coach?"

"I do apologize for that," she said quickly.

He just folded his arms across his broad chest and waited for her explanation.

"Markgraf Kottenfurst is a good friend of my father's," she told him. It was completely true. They were brothers but as close as friends.

"Is he from the same country as you?" Sam asked, releasing his arms and allowing them simply to hang at his sides. His anger, too, dissipated as quickly as it had come, much to Isa's relief.

"Yes. I knew if he saw me, he would recognize me. And if he did that, he would surely inform my father I was not at school and, quite possibly, that my brother was also not at university. We both would have had a great deal of explaining to do," she told him.

He nodded his understanding. "I just wish you'd said something the moment you recognized him—or, I suppose you saw the crest on the side of his coach?"

"Yes, I did."

"And that's why you sat back so suddenly and looked like you'd seen a ghost," he said, putting things together in his mind.

She smiled. "Did I?"

Thankfully, the corners of his mouth lifted as well. "Completely!" He then added, "Those riding clothes of yours have come in handy a number of times."

"It is lucky I had them with me," she agreed.

"If I had a sister, I almost believe I'd get a set for her."

Isa laughed but quickly found herself enfolded in Sam's warm, safe embrace.

"You scared me there. Please don't do that again. I was so afraid we'd left you on the side of the road to make your own way to Margate," he whispered into her hair.

"No need to worry for me, Sam. I have learned how to be rather self-sufficient these past few weeks."

"Yes, you have, haven't you?" he asked, pulling back a little to look down at her.

She nodded, smiling up at him. "It really is quite incredible. Before I embarked on this journey, I had never been alone, not once in my life. I have always had someone with me to look after me, see to my safety and comfort. Although I have had both you and Mrs. Brompton on this adventure, I have also had to figure out a lot of things on my own."

"And you've done an incredible job of it," he told her.

"Thank you. I think so too," she said, smiling up at him.

He gave a little laugh. "And that is probably the most important thing you've learned—to say thank you!"

She giggled and shook her head in wonder. "I cannot deny it."

"You are truly amazing."

"And so are you, worrying for my welfare," she pointed out.

"It is true. I think we've both come a long way on this journey."

He cupped her face in his hands and placed a sweet, gentle kiss on her lips. "I have definitely learned a lot."

"Oh, me as well!" she agreed, going up on her toes to kiss him once again.

-Day 34: Making Search Plans-

That evening after dinner, Dev sat forward and asked, "So, how are we going to go about searching for your brother? What is his name, by the way?"

"Nik," Isa told him. "Nikolas."

Dev nodded. "Nikolas Günter, got it."

Isa was immediately stricken. Nik wouldn't answer to Günter. It was a name she pulled from thin air when she didn't want to tell Sam her real last name. She'd got used to being called Miss Günter, but of course, Nik wouldn't answer to it. She didn't quite know what to do about that, though. She couldn't simply tell these men she'd been lying about her name when they were about to go out scouring the city looking for her brother for her. She could only hope Nik would understand and play along should they find him without her.

"But we don't know what he looks like," Wythe pointed out.

"That is simple." Isa reached around her neck and pulled out the locket she always wore. Inside was a miniature painting of her father on one side and Nik on the other. She unclasped it and held it out for the men to see. Dev and Wythe were sitting next to each other. Wythe held it in between them so they could both look at it.

"I take it the younger man is your brother?" Wythe asked.

"Yes. The other is my father," she told him.

Dev passed the locket over to Sam. He took a close look at it and then signaled for the maid who was just passing their table. "I am in need of a piece of paper and a pencil," he told her.

Isa looked at him curiously.

He just smiled as they waited for the woman to return which she did within a minute or two, along with a pen knife as well. Once he ensured the pencil was sharp enough to his liking, he proceeded to sketch a copy of the portrait. Isa watched in wonder as he easily captured her brother's features with just a few quick strokes of the pencil.

"That's incredible," she said.

Sam stopped and looked at her. "Did you not learn to sketch?"

She shook her head. "My governess tried to teach me, but I have absolutely no talent or patience. I did slightly better with watercolors, but my efforts were amateur at best."

"Sam, here, used to sketch the funniest pictures of our teachers when we were in school," Dev said with a chuckle.

Wythe smiled as he too remembered. "He would put them in compromising positions or make a nose overly large or eyes bulging."

Sam just laughed as he went back to his sketching of Nik. "I haven't done that since, although I must admit to pulling out my pencil every so often to sketch the people I see around me."

"And so you should. You are very good," Isa commented, smiling at him.

His expression warmed, but with a glance at his two friends across the table, he quickly went back to the drawing. He sat back, looking at it with satisfaction once he was done.

"It looks just like him," Isa said.

He nodded. "How about if you and I use this and go to docks tomorrow to ask around and see if anyone has seen him. If need be, you can also describe him to people."

"We can scour the inns around town," Dev offered.

"Yes, and take the locket so you can show people what he looks like," Sam said, handing it over. He turned to Isa. "That is all right, isn't it?"

"Yes, but please be careful with it. It is the only portrait I have of either of them."

"We'll make sure we keep it well," Dev agreed as he dropped it into the pocket of his waistcoat.

"And then we'll meet back here at midday or so?" Wythe asked.

"Yes." Sam finished the wine in his glass and then carefully folded his sketch.

"Tomorrow, hopefully, we'll either find or, at the very least, get some news about Nik," Isa said, wishing with all her heart they would indeed be successful in finding him.

-Day 35: Searching-

Sam and Isa set out early the following morning after breakfasting with Dev and Wythe. Isa was relieved to have met them in the common room of the inn where they were all staying. She had feared Sam's friends would have continued with their habit of rising late. Although Wythe didn't look happy about it, he was up and moving even though it was, as he said, an ungodly hour.

As they looked around the docks, Sam began to look wary. The wind was blowing hard enough to plaster Isa's dress to her legs, making walking a bit more difficult.

"What is wrong?" Isa asked him, tying her bonnet on more tightly.

He shook his head. "I was incredibly stupid, that's what." He sighed as they walked down the path, holding his hat on his head. "I should have had Wythe and Dev search here while we looked at the other inns in town. I'm not terribly certain this is the sort of area for a proper young lady."

Isa laughed. "But this is the most likely place we will find him or find word of him. And I can assure you, I do not care one whit for propriety."

"That I know," he answered quickly enough. "But you should."

Isa gave just a little shrug and headed for the first tavern they saw. It was a relief to step inside and out of the wind. She allowed Sam to take the lead, certain the barkeep would respond better to a gentleman than to her. Unfortunately, the man just shook his head when shown the sketch of Nik. "Never seen 'im afor, gov'na."

Sam nodded his thanks, and they headed back out to find the next tavern.

Isa was beginning to get discouraged by the fourth one. The Crown and Anchor looked exactly like all the other taverns, only ever so slightly cleaner. She was standing off to the side when a barmaid came next to Sam as he was speaking with the innkeeper.

"Oooh, 'e's a looker," she said, looking down at the sketch.

"Have you seen him?" Isa asked the woman.

"Naw, but ask Marie, she's got a memory fer faces you jus' wouldn't believe." The woman nodded toward the other barmaid who was standing next to a table of three men, laughing and chatting with them.

"Oy! Marie! Some toffs gots a question for ye!" the woman next to Isa called out across the room.

Marie looked up and then excused herself from her conversation. "Yeah?"

Sam showed her the sketch.

"Oh, yeah..." she said slowly, clearly thinking hard. "I's seen 'im. 'E was 'ere a few weeks ago, meybe a month?"

Chapter Thirty-One

"Really? You don't know where he went, do you?" Isa asked, her heartbeat kicking up a notch.

"Naw. I know 'e was interested in rentin' some 'orses, though. Asked where there was a stable nearby."

"And where did you send him?" Sam asked.

"Why, over ta Smithson's on High Street. Best one there is," she said with certainty.

"Thank you, thank you very much!" Sam said and passed her a coin.

She gave him a bright smile. "Anythin' else I can do fer ya?" She swayed her hips suggestively.

"Er, no, thank you. You've been quite helpful." He nodded to her and then took Isa's arm as they left.

"This is excellent. Some real information. I knew he had been here," Isa said excitedly as they walked over to High Street. It wasn't too far, and soon they found the stable with a large sign out front marking it as Smithson's.

Sam found a groom and asked for Mr. Smithson. They were shown into a dusty office. Sam once again showed his sketch. The man just shook his head, however. "Can't say that I remember him. He definitely rented a horse from me?"

"We're almost certain of it," Sam told him.

"It was a while ago, a few weeks or perhaps a month," Isa added.

"Aw, no, I get so many people in here renting horses, I wouldn't remember," the man said, shaking his head again.

Isa sighed and felt tears prick her eyes. It wasn't fair! They were so close, and she'd come so far.

Sam looked away for a moment, but then turned back to the man. Indicating the ledger on his desk, he asked, "Do you keep a log of everyone who rents horses from you?"

"Why yes, yes I do. You know this fella's name?" Mr. Smithson asked.

"Yes. It's Nikolas Günter," Sam told him.

"Perhaps look for the name Hofman," Isa suggested. "Friedrich Hofman."

Sam looked at her curiously.

"That's the name of his valet," she told him. He nodded, understanding immediately.

"Hofman? About a month ago," Mr. Smithson repeated. He ran his finger down one page and then flipped back to the one before it. "Ah! Here it is. Hofman, Friedrich. Yes indeed, they were here. Rented two carriage horses which they took to Dover."

"To Dover?" Isa asked excitedly. She looked up at Sam hopefully.

"It sounds like we're going to Dover," he said, giving her a smile.

"We needed to do so anyway since that's where Mrs. Brompton's sister is," Isa pointed out.

Sam just gave a little laugh. "That's right." He thanked the man, and they made their way back to the inn where they were staying to see if Dev and Wythe learned anything.

-Day 35: Plans Get Advanced-

Sam and Isa met Dev and Wythe as they'd planned back at the inn. His friends were already beginning to tuck into plates of cold meat and cheese when they joined them.

"And here I was fully expecting you to have a multicourse meal waiting for us," Sam said with a laugh as he helped Isa into a chair next to Wythe. He then took his own chair on the opposite side of the table next to Dev.

Wythe chuckled around a bite of bread. "You know me too well, Ranleigh. Sadly, Dev here convinced me to partake of a lighter meal. I assure you, were I to have ordered, it would have been roast beef with a side of potatoes and another of vegetables."

"Oh, what a shame, I would have been very happy with that," Isa said, giving Wythe a commiserating smile.

A maid came over and deposited two more plates identical to Dev and Wythe's in front of them.

"Well, at least this is fast, if not hot," Sam said, beginning to dig in. He was hungry, so he was happy for cold fare.

"So, how did your search go?" Isa asked the other men.

"There was one innkeeper who thought he remembered Günter having been there, but it's been too long. He would have been there between three weeks and a month ago, no?" Dev asked.

"Yes," Isa agreed.

Wythe shook his head. "It's been too long. There have been too many people coming and going for them to remember one unremarkable man."

"What about you?" Dev asked before taking a big bite.

"We actually had more luck. We met a maid with an excellent memory for faces. She remembered seeing Günter," Sam said. When Isa opened her mouth to continue the tale, he gave her a slight shake of his head. He didn't know why, but he wasn't so sure it would be a good idea to give away the rest of their findings. He wanted to wait for a bit of confirmation first. Luckily, Isa got his message and instead filled her mouth with food as if that would keep the words from tumbling out.

"Well, that's good news," Dev said. "At least we do know he was here."

"But he clearly isn't anymore," Wythe added.

"No, but we'll see if we can't follow his trail," Sam said, keeping his eyes down on his own plate. He wondered if he'd mentioned to Dev and Wythe they were going to have to deliver Mrs. Brompton to her sister in Dover. He couldn't remember if that had come up in earlier discussions. Isa, for her part, was doing an excellent job of staying quiet. He appreciated that a good deal. She wasn't one to jabber on in any case, so her silence was nothing out of the ordinary. Small things to be grateful for, but grateful he was.

-Day 36: Deceit-

The following morning, Sam sat down for breakfast with Mrs. Brompton, Davies, and Isa.

"I asked around yesterday when I took care of Lord Kottenfurst's wheel," Davies told them.

"How did you do so without an image to show people?" Isa asked.

"Just asked if there were many foreigners seen recently," he told her with a smile.

Isa nodded. "My brother does have a bit of an accent, more so than me." She was clearly quite proud of the fact she spoke better English than her brother. Sam nearly laughed at the smug look on her face as she said this.

"And has anyone seen or heard of him?" Sam asked, turning back to Davies.

"There have been a few foreigners come through," the coachman said, nodding. "Does your brother have blond hair and blue eyes like you?" he asked Isa.

She nodded. "His hair is lighter than mine, but we have the same eyes."

"Tall? Thin?" Davies asked.

"Yes, both. He is a sportsman who rides all the time," she agreed.

Davies nodded. "One fella said he'd seen such a gentleman a few weeks back. He was struck by the fact that the man was so suspicious, lookin' around, ducking in and out of his coach and the like. Said the gentleman looked like he was hidin' from someone."

"But of course he would!" Isa exclaimed, becoming quite animated.

"Did he say where the gentleman was headed?" Sam asked.

"No. He tried to chat up his coachman, but the fella either didn't understand English or was deliberately mum, not sayin' a thing to anyone."

Isa shook her head. "His coachman is English. He must have been given strict instructions not to speak with anyone."

"Well, he kept to 'em. He didn't say a word. All the fellow knew was that there was a blond gentleman with his man traveling in the coach and a silent coachman. Said it was a fancy new coach, too."

"Yes, it was bought for us when we arrived in England," Isa agreed.

Davies nodded. "But has no coat of arms or anything on the side. From the outside, it just looks like an ordinary black traveling coach. But apparently, the inside is quite plush."

Isa shrugged. "It is comfortable. It is very well-sprung."

"The man I spoke to said it was one of those new lighter models. He came in with four horses, although he only left with two," Davies added.

"So that means they can travel fast," Sam said, nodding.

"A lot faster than us," Davies said, sounding a little saddened by the fact.

Sam knew both his own coach and the one he'd borrowed from Newly were really made to be pulled by four horses, but he didn't want the expense. His decision to go slowly on their journey was definitely, in part, due to that. Although, he'd never mention it to Isa. She probably would have insisted he rent four horses and move along faster. Happily, she'd accepted his excuses for going more slowly, and it had worked out for them—for the most part.

"Well, Sam and I learned they rented two horses from a stable nearby and traveled—" she was interrupted by Dev coming over. He looked a little agitated and was frowning something fierce.

Sam stood up. "What is it?"

Dev motioned him to sit down and pulled up a chair to the end of the table. After he'd sat down, he leaned back and glanced toward the door. He then leaned forward again and looked around the table.

"Whatever it is, you can share it with everyone here. Both Mrs. Brompton and Davies are completely trustworthy and won't speak out of turn or share anything we ask them not to," Sam told his friend as he sat there looking hesitant.

Dev let out a breath and nodded. He spoke very quietly, so no one even at a nearby table would be able to hear him. "I just saw Wythe speaking to some shady-looking characters. Money changed hands, and the other men kept taking glances down this way."

"Bloody—" Sam started and then remembered the women at the table.

"I will get our things," Mrs. Brompton said, standing.

"I'll hitch up the coach," Davies stood as well.

Sam thought about his friend Wythe. Why would he sell them out? What had happened to their years of friendship? They'd shared everything since they had been thirteen years old. Granted, the first two years at school they hadn't been all that keen on each other. It was only after Sam saved Wythe from a pommeling by some older boys that they became close. And then Wythe had returned the favor the following year, cementing their friendship. But now... now he was stabbing Sam in the back. Why? He made a split-second decision.

"All of you go to Dover. I'll tell Wythe Isa is accompanying Mrs. Brompton to her sister and then will visit with her for a time. I'll meet you there in a day or so after I attempt to convince Wythe to return to London. Dev, you'll help me with that, won't you?"

"Of course! I'll even go with him, make sure he gets there," Dev said quickly. "And I agree, it'll look less suspicious if just Isa and Mrs. Brompton go and not you, Ranleigh."

Sam nodded and then looked around the table. He could see clearly Isa didn't like this idea. Her lips were pressed together into a thin line.

"Are you certain it is safe for you to stay?" she asked.

"They're not after me," he pointed out.

"No, but you know exactly where we are going," she pointed out.

"No, I don't. All I know is that you're going to Mrs. Brompton's sister's home. I don't know where that is precisely."

"Then how will you meet us there?" Davies asked.

Sam frowned at him. "Mrs. Brompton will tell me where her sister lives, but no one need know she has done so."

"Oh, right," the man said, turning slightly pink with embarrassment.

"And you don't think the men will do anything to get that information from you?" Isa asked.

He lightened his expression as a feeling of warmth flooded through him at her concern. "I think between me and Dev we can take them on."

"Not if they have a gun," Mrs. Brompton pointed out.

Chapter Thirty-Two

Dev looked startled at that.

"No, I'm certain they won't go quite so far as to threaten a marquess and an earl," Sam said, trying to calm all of them. "Don't worry. Please go, now." He looked at Davies and Mrs. Brompton, who both nodded and left. Isa stayed, taking his hand under the table so no one could see.

"I am frightened for you," she said quietly.

He squeezed her hand and smiled at her. "Don't be. I'll be fine, and I'll join you within a few days, I promise."

She sighed and then left the table.

"I just can't believe Wythe would—" Dev started.

"He'd damn well have a good explanation for this, and I will not hesitate to beat it out of him," Sam growled, finally allowing his anger to bubble into life. "To sell out the woman I love is beyond—" He stopped speaking, suddenly realizing what he'd just said. He exchanged a shocked look with Dev.

A smile quickly grew on Dev's face however, and within moments, he was laughing out loud. "Never... never in my life..." he said between guffaws.

A few heads turned his way to see what he'd found so funny. Of course, there was nothing to look at, and Sam's angry glare had them returning their attention to their own business.

"It's not funny," he ground out through clenched teeth. "Not funny at all."

"Oh, but it is! It's absolutely hilarious," Dev said, finally managing to calm himself. "I never thought I'd see the day when the famed Marquess of Ranleigh admitted to being completely smitten by a girl. Why, you were always the first one laughing when some fellow would be woozy in love, calling him an idiot for succumbing to such a ridiculous emotion."

"I have to admit I never really believed in it. Aside from those poetry-spouting puppies, I've never witnessed it," he admitted.

"But now?"

"Now I... my God! I just can't get her out of my mind. I need to be with her, to make her happy, to..." He paused and then added more seriously, "To protect her."

Dev, too, lost his smile as he nodded his understanding.

Sam stood. "Wythe will have hell to pay for doing this to Isa, I will make sure of that."

- Mrs. Brompton's Sister-

It was strange traveling in the coach without Sam. Mrs. Brompton sat across from Isa and stared out the window. Finally, Isa could hardly stand the silence anymore.

"Are you looking forward to seeing your sister?" she asked the woman.

Mrs. Brompton turned a smiling face toward her. "It will definitely be different."

"Oh dear. That does not sound very enthusiastic," Isa said with a little laugh.

Mrs. Brompton just shook her head. "We haven't actually seen each other for about ten years. We've corresponded but haven't actually got together."

"Why is that?"

"We don't really get along," she said with a slight shrug.

"Then why are you moving in with her?" Isa asked. She couldn't imagine why Mrs. Brompton would want to live with someone she didn't like.

The woman gave her a sad little smile. "Because she's all I've got. She's my only relative. Where else would I go?"

"Anywhere! Surely your previous employer gave you a generous pension after so many years of devoted work?"

"I was given a modest pension, enough to live on with Cordelia but only because she already owns her home."

"And what of Mr. Brompton's family?" Isa asked.

Mrs. Brompton chuckled. "There isn't a Mr. Brompton... well, except for my father."

"Oh! I thought using Mrs. meant you were married," Isa said, now becoming a little confused.

Mrs. Brompton shook her head. "Women in certain positions use it whether they've been married or not. It's a form of politeness, especially for older women like myself," she explained.

"Oh, so is your sister also Mrs. Brompton?" Isa asked.

"No. She married a man by the name of Jones. He died about five years ago," Mrs. Brompton explained.

Isa nodded. "Well, that makes things a little easier for me." She gave Mrs. Brompton a smile.

The woman laughed. "Yes, it will. And Cordelia is a very nice person, please don't think she isn't. It's just... well, she can be a little slovenly, that's all."

"In what way?" Isa asked, not entirely certain what the word meant.

"She leaves things about, doesn't wash up immediately after meals, that sort of thing. I end up feeling like a maid in her house, always cleaning and picking up after her."

"Oh, I see," Isa nodded. "Yes, that could be difficult."

"However, my pension will allow for me to hire a daily—someone to come in and clean every day."

"Oh, but that will be perfect, then!"

"Yes. It's only because I can afford such a person that it will make the situation bearable," Mrs. Brompton told her.

Isa once again thought of asking Mrs. Brompton if she might be willing to continue working for her, but she knew she truly couldn't do so without either Nik or her father's permission. She had no control over her purse. Hopefully, she would find Nik soon.

The sun was low in the sky when they finally rolled up to a small house at the end of a pretty little street. It had a small garden in front and a few steps leading up to the front door. Mr. Davies began unloading Mrs. Brompton's belongings while she and Isa knocked on the door.

A gray-haired woman who looked remarkably like a larger version of Mrs. Brompton answered the door. "Margaret!"

"Cordelia, how wonderful to see you again," Mrs. Brompton said with a bright smile. Even though she'd said her sister was difficult, it was clear the women were extremely happy to see each other. They embraced, giggling when they both reached to pat down their hair after moving apart again.

"Miss Isa Günter, may I present my sister, Mrs. Jones?" Mrs. Brompton said, turning to Isa. She turned back to her sister as she curtsied to Isa. "I've been looking after this young lady on our journey here... and at times, she looked after me," she added as an afterthought.

"Oh my! It sounds like you have had adventures. But please, come in. What am I doing, making you stand in the door," Mrs. Jones said, stepping back and inviting them into her parlor.

Mr. Davies came in with Mrs. Brompton's trunk just then.

"Oh! And you have all your things. Very good. Just bring that straight upstairs. The second door on the right," Mrs. Jones told Mr. Davies.

"Thank you so much, Mr. Davies," Mrs. Brompton said, giving him a warm smile.

He turned slightly pink and nodded before taking the trunk upstairs.

Mrs. Jones gave Mrs. Brompton a startled look and whispered, "You're going to have to tell me about that one, too!"

Mrs. Brompton giggled but didn't say anything. It was so funny to see the woman with her sister. It was as if she were a completely different person. No longer was she the quietly in-control lady's maid, or even the stern chaperone Isa was used to. She was much more relaxed, much more giggly, much more like a young woman rather than the reserved older lady Isa had always known.

"I do hope you don't mind. Miss Günter will be staying with us for a day or two until Lord Ranleigh—the very kind gentleman who brought me here—joins us," Mrs. Brompton told her sister as they settled on the faded pink sofa.

"Of course," Mrs. Jones said immediately. "But where is the gentleman?"

"He needed to stay in Margate for another day. Mr. Davies will be going back for him tomorrow," Isa explained.

"I see," Mrs. Jones said with a slight frown. She turned to her sister. "You will have to tell me all about this journey and how you came to be taken up by this Lord Ranleigh. I'd thought you were taking the mail and expected you weeks ago."

"I had been planning on doing so, of course, but then Lord Ranleigh and Miss Günter requested I join them as the miss was traveling alone," Mrs. Brompton explained.

"Oh! That wouldn't have been appropriate at all, unless..." Mrs. Jones turned a quizzical expression on to Isa.

"No, it wouldn't have been," Isa agreed quickly. "Which is why we asked Mrs. Brompton to join us."

"Indeed!"

Mr. Davies knocked on the door before coming through. "I've put your things up in your room, Mrs. B. I'm going to see to the coach, and then I'll be off first thing in the mornin' to return to Margate for his lordship."

"Of course. Then we'll see you the day after tomorrow?" Mrs. Brompton asked.

"Yes, ma'am," he said, doffing his cap.

"Excellent. I will look forward to it," she said, giving him a smile.

"As will I," he said, his face softening as well. He recalled himself quickly, however, and bowed to Isa. "Miss. Mrs." He gave Mrs. Jones a polite nod and then left.

"He seems to be a nice gentleman," Mrs. Jones said after he'd left.

"He is very nice," Isa said after waiting for Mrs. Brompton to say something. She seemed to be staring out the window, however, perhaps watching the coach pull away. She had a rather sad smile on her face, and Isa wondered how she was going to manage without Mr. Davies after they left.

She startled slightly at Isa's words and returned her attention to her sister. "Yes, he is a pleasant man." She paused and then said, "I'm afraid some of our delay was due to me falling ill, which was when our positions switched, and Miss Günter took to caring for me rather than the other way around," Mrs. Brompton told her sister.

"Oh dear!" the woman exclaimed before turning to Isa. "How *very* good of you, miss, to take care of my dear Margaret when she was unwell."

"It was the least I could do, considering how wonderful she has been to me," Isa said.

Mrs. Brompton gave her a slight nod and a smile. "We have managed to make a lovely trip of it, though. We went to Runnymede and picnicked under the Ankerwyke Yew, and we went for lovely walks in the Surrey Hills..."

"My, my, that sounds so nice! I'm quite jealous," Mrs. Jones said with a little laugh.

Isa kept quiet regarding all the other adventures they had when she realized Mrs. Brompton was deliberately leaving out the less pleasant parts of their journey.

"Oh, well, we had to do something to relieve the boredom of just sitting in a coach for days on end. Lord Ranleigh made sure we had moments of respite for which I was exceedingly grateful. Were not you, as well, Miss Günter?" Mrs. Brompton asked, turning to her.

"Absolutely," Isa agreed. "He was very considerate the entire time." Except, of course, when he wasn't, but that was really only in the beginning of the journey, and she had mostly forgot about that.

"Well, I look forward to hearing all about it over dinner," Mrs. Jones told them.

- Confronting Wythe-

Sam was so furious with his friend that he was ready to beat him to a bloody pulp. Unfortunately, Dev had a much cooler head and insisted Sam take some time to cool down and speak with Wythe later that evening. It was infuriating to have to wait, but he knew Dev was right. Nothing positive was ever gained when speaking in anger, and Wythe probably wouldn't tell him anything if he led with his fists.

Instead, he went for a brisk walk. When he returned, he was feeling slightly calmer—calm enough to think of booking the private dining room so he didn't make a scene in public. He found Dev and asked him to join him for dinner along with Wythe. He knew if fists were raised, Dev's cool head would prevail. Either that or he could act as Sam's second in a fair fight.

Sam took in a deep breath when Wythe entered the room. He'd already poured himself out a glass of brandy from the decanter he'd requested, and now upon seeing the man who he used to consider one of his closest friends, he finished it off in one gulp.

He watched as Wythe helped himself and Dev to brandy and then took one more calming breath before he began. "Wythe, would you care to tell us what you were doing earlier today?" There, that was innocuous enough. He received an approving nod from Dev.

Wythe lowered his glass. "Earlier today?" He smiled at Sam in all innocence. "What do you mean? When?"

"When I noticed you speaking with some disreputable-looking men and accepting money from them," Dev said as if he were passing comment on the weather.

Wythe blanched.

"You hadn't realized you were being observed," Sam noted.

"You don't understand..." Wythe started.

"Why? That's what I want to know," Sam said. "Why would you make a deal to sell Isa like that?"

"I didn't *sell* her," Wythe started.

"Sold information about her, then?" Dev asked.

"They wanted me to bring her to them," Wythe admitted. "But she left before I could..."

"And thank God for that!" The words exploded from Sam before he could catch them.

"But that doesn't tell us why," Dev pointed out.

Wythe had the grace to look ashamed.

"It was the money, wasn't it?" Dev asked. He always was very insightful.

Wythe just nodded.

"But—" Sam started.

Chapter Thirty-Three

"You both have so much," Wythe said, raising his voice. "I've got practically nothing. My estate is in trouble. My coffers are nearly empty, thanks to my efforts at propping up the estate, and my mother's damned redecorating every two years. My father spent more than he could afford to build a bloody dower house to her specifications, so she could live comfortably after I get married—if anyone would ever consent to marrying an impoverished nobleman. I've got nothing, and right now, I'm just looking down an endless well where I'm throwing everything I've got. Pretty soon it's myself I'm going to throw down there if things don't turn around."

Sam ran a hand down his face.

Dev sighed heavily and kept his eyes on Wythe's boots as the man turned and walked toward the window.

"I'm sorry, Wythe," Sam said finally after a good minute of silence. "I didn't realize things were that bad."

"Yes, well... they are," Wythe said quietly, keeping his back to them.

Sam went over and put his hand on his friend's shoulder. "I don't quite know what I can do to help, but you should know—should have known—that you can always come to me."

"And me," Dev added also walking over.

"I'll write to my steward and see if he knows of anyone who can take a look at the situation at your estate," Sam offered.

Wythe pinched the bridge of his nose and took in a deep breath. "Thank you. I've got a man but..."

"Perhaps a second pair of eyes will help," Dev said, backing up Sam's suggestion.

"And it won't cost you anything," Sam added.

Wythe just nodded.

Something occurred to Sam. "Those men couldn't have been offering you that much money..."

"A monkey," Wythe told him.

"Really? Five hundred pounds? For a girl?" Dev asked.

"Do you know who they are working for?" Sam asked. It had to be someone incredibly wealthy to offer that much.

Wythe sighed. "Some fellow named Kottenfurst? I don't know him, but apparently, he's a nobleman, or at least they called him Lord Kottenfurst."

"I know Lord Kottenfurst!" Sam said, shocked. "I met him on the road here. Bloody hell! I gave him a ride to Margate—a wheel had broken on his coach, and he said he had an appointment to get to here."

"Perhaps to meet these men," Dev suggested.

"It must have been," Sam agreed. "But why would he want Isa so badly? What's the connection?"

"Do you know who she really is?" Wythe asked Sam.

Sam opened his mouth immediately to say he did but then closed it again. "I know she gave me a false name when we met," he admitted.

"What?" Dev started.

"I couldn't really blame her. She was a young woman, alone and in trouble when I offered her a ride. She didn't know who I was or where I might take her," he told his friends. "I wasn't thrilled she lied to me, but I understood it."

Dev's eyebrows lifted. "And she hasn't confided in you since then?"

"She has been remarkably sparse in her personal details. I didn't even know she rode so well or was such an avid hunter until she told you at Blean. In fact, she divulged a great deal more to us there than she had the entire trip. All I knew before that was she was a student at a school for young ladies, and she needed to find her brother who was a student at Oxford," Sam said. "Other than that... well, you know as much about her as I do."

"That's not a lot of information, considering you've been traveling with her for weeks," Dev pointed out.

"I know," Sam admitted.

"Well then, I know a great deal more than you," Wythe said. "Just one moment. I promise, I shall return in just a minute. I need to show you what they showed me," Wythe said, putting his glass down on the table. He slipped out the door, and Sam could hear him climbing the stairs quickly.

A minute later, Wythe returned with a folded newspaper. He handed it over to Sam, saying, "This is who your Miss Günter really is."

Sam almost didn't want to take the newspaper. He suddenly felt as if someone had poured a cold bucket of water down his back. He stood ramrod straight and still, not even looking at the newspaper in his hand, trying not to shiver. This was the woman he loved... but did he? Still? He knew she'd lied to him. He knew he didn't really know who she was.

No, that's not true, he told himself. He knew she was a good, kind—

"It's there. Her picture is there," Wythe said, cutting into Sam's thoughts, indicating the newspaper.

Sam reluctantly lifted it and looked. Indeed, a sketch of Isa stared him in the face. Below the picture were the words, *Princess Louisa of Aachen-Düren*. Below that, an article concerning the princess's upcoming investiture as the heir to the throne of the small German principality.

Sam scanned it with growing dread. The moment he lowered the newspaper, Dev pulled it gently from his hand so he too could look at it.

"She's a princess?" Dev nearly shouted.

"Lower your voice!" Sam snapped.

"Yes, we don't want anyone nearby to know of her little secret," Wythe said with sarcasm. "*She* certainly doesn't want anyone to know. But that's the connection—Kottenfurst is the princess's uncle."

Sam turned and looked at Wythe. "He mentioned he had a niece when we were traveling to Margate. He was asking a lot of questions about the girl I claimed to be my cousin which, I have to admit, I thought very strange at the time."

"He couldn't have thought his niece was your 'cousin,' could he?" Dev asked.

"No, that would have been impossible. I'm sure he was just making polite conversation," Sam said.

"I can't believe Isa is a princess," Dev said with a shake of his head. He gave a little laugh and looked at Sam. "You're in love with a princess."

"That's currently up for debate," Sam ground out, his anger spiking again. "She lied to me. No. She didn't only lie to me, she didn't trust me. Not once during the past few weeks." And then, something else occurred to him, as if lying wasn't enough. "She put my life and that of Mrs. Brompton and Davies in danger—knowingly! She had to have known someone was trying to kill her because of who she is." He suppressed a growl of fury.

"Don't such people have bodyguards?" Wythe asked.

"She probably slipped away from hers when she embarked on this ridiculous journey," Sam said. He turned and looked out the window. It was dark. Curses slipped from his tongue. It was too late to ride to Dover. Too late to confront the conniving, lying... princess!

"It's too late," Dev said, immediately following Sam's thoughts.

"I know," he said, his voice was deep with anger.

"It's better you don't confront her as angry as you are, anyway. Sleep on this—"

"I've got no choice in the matter, do I? But I can assure you, my anger won't calm overnight, not after what she's done," Sam told his friends.

-Day 37: Confronting Isa-

Sam was, in fact, only slightly less angry when he woke up the following day. That didn't stop him, however, from renting a horse from the same ostler he and Isa had spoken to. He left for Dover before Dev or Wythe even woke up.

It was a long ride from Margate, giving Sam time to think and stew. It still infuriated him that she had put their lives in danger. And it hurt more than anything that she hadn't trusted him, after all he'd done, with her true identity. *Why hadn't she trusted him?*

He dismissed the question as unanswerable. His mind wandered back to a newspaper article. It said that Prince Nikolas had died a month ago, but Isa had told him she was coming here to meet her brother. Surely she knew... His heart plummeted to his stomach. Either she didn't know that her brother was dead or, more likely, was refusing to believe it. The thought made him feel a little sick.

And then, there was Kottenfurst. Sam knew there were two different sets of men after Isa—one who wanted to return her to school and one who wanted to kill her. The question was, which group of men had Kottenfurst hired. Of course, the men who'd offered Wythe money to turn her over to them hadn't said what they'd wanted to do with her, merely that Kottenfurst had been the one to hire them. Wasn't it more likely that her uncle was merely concerned for her safety and wanted to see her returned to where she should be?

He wanted to believe that was the case, but there was something nagging at the back of his mind. He rode on, allowing the horse to drop to a walk. What was it? Was there any reason why Kottenfurst would want to see Isa dead? She was a princess, but she was his niece... Sam pulled the horse to a stop and pulled the newspaper out of the saddlebags he'd brought along. There was something... he scanned the article beneath her picture again. It was about the investiture, which was to occur ten days hence. With Prince Nikolas's death the previous month, Princess Louisa would be crowned heir to the throne. Her uncle, Markgraf Kottenfurst was second in line and his son, Graf Adenheim, was third.

That was it!

If Isa died, Kottenfurst would become the heir to the throne. Sam let out a disturbed sigh. The horse under him sidled a little to the side, probably wondering why they weren't moving. Sam returned the newspaper to his bag and encouraged the animal to begin walking. Well, that answered that. He had to warn Isa. Her uncle couldn't be trusted and was in all likelihood the one who'd been trying to kill her. Unless she already knew that, which was the other reason why she'd disappeared the moment they'd stopped for him on the road.

Sam's fury—this time directed at Kottenfurst—reared again, and he kicked the horse into a gallop.

-Sam's Confrontation and Isa's Escape-

Isa was pacing back and forth in Mrs. Jones's front parlor. She wanted more than anything to go out looking for Nik, but Mrs. Brompton had insisted she wait until Sam arrived. Perhaps she could convince Mrs. Brompton to go out with her that afternoon. The problem was she wasn't exactly certain where to look. Would he have stayed at an inn? Would he have gone on to somewhere else or caught a ship... no! There were too many possibilities.

She would start by going to all the inns and asking if anyone had seen him. She had her locket back, so she had his portrait to show people. Hopefully, there'd be another person like that one maid who'd remembered him. She wondered if he were still in town, still in the area. She could only hope.

She nearly jumped at the sound of a knock on the door. For one wild moment, she wondered if it were Nik but that, she knew, was impossible. She heard Mrs. Jones come down the stairs to answer the knock through the partially open parlor door.

"Yes?" Isa heard the woman say.

Isa peered out the front window but could only see a horse tied up to a post outside. The person at the door was out of sight.

She heard the rumble of a man's voice, and then a minute later, Mrs. Jones entered the parlor followed by Sam. A spike of joy jolted through Isa. "Sam!" she said, giving him a bright smile and coming forward.

He didn't return her smile. That was strange. Even stranger still was the bow he executed. It was low and formal. "Your Highness," he said, his voice low and menacing.

Isa stopped and gasped.

"Yes, you very well might be scared. I've found out your secret," he told her. "And you lied to me. After all I've done for you, after all we've been through together, you never once even thought of trusting me with the truth, did you?" His voice thundered in the room.

"Oh, dear." Mrs. Jones's voice was little more than a whisper. "I think I'll get Margaret." She disappeared from the room.

"You put my life, and that of Mrs. Brompton and Davies, at risk. You knew someone was trying to kill you, and yet you never had the decency to tell us," he shouted.

"I did not—" Isa started.

"You lied to me!" he roared.

Isa straightened her back and squared her shoulders in the face of his fury. "I could not—"

"You *could* not? Or you *would* not? You didn't feel I was good enough? Important enough to trust with your truth? What was it, Your Highness?"

"Stop calling me that. You have been calling me by my name..."

"No, I've been calling you Isa, which is what you *told* me your name was," he corrected her.

"It is!"

"Your name is Louisa, not Isabelle. You are *still* lying to me!" he shouted.

"Isa is short for Louisa, you idiot!" she yelled back.

He scoffed as if he didn't believe her.

"And I did not know—" The sneer on his face stopped her from telling him she had no idea there would be people trying to kill her when she left to find her brother. She'd thought the men were from Herr Mueller, her bodyguard, trying to take her back to school—until they'd shot at her. She shook her head as a deep sadness and anger warred within her. "It does not matter. You will not believe anything I say, will you?"

"No, as a matter of fact, I won't. You have proven yourself to be completely untrustworthy."

Anger won out. "Fine. Then, there is no point." With that, she swept out of the room and was about to mount the stairs when she remembered the horse she'd seen out front. Sam must have rented it to get here from Margate. She was wearing a gown, but she didn't care. She just needed to ride out all the emotions swirling within her before they boiled over into tears of rage. Showing him how much he'd hurt her would never do. Princesses don't cry!

Chapter Thirty-Four

Isa ran out the door and mounted the horse. It was a regular saddle, so she had no choice but to straddle the horse. Her skirts bunched up around knees indecently, but truly, she didn't care. She kicked the horse into a gallop and headed out of town—at least she knew the way from having watched as they'd come in.

She *had* lied to him. She had withheld the truth, but not all of it, she thought with some resentment. He'd accused her of deliberately endangering the lives of Mrs. Brompton, Mr. Davies, and him, but she hadn't done so—not intentionally. How could she have known there was someone trying to kill her? She hadn't. She couldn't have known. If she had... she would never have allowed anyone to travel with her. She would have returned to school somehow and informed Herr Mueller. It was his job, after all, to see to her safety. She hadn't meant for Sam to take on that position.

And yet he had, and he'd done an incredible job of it. He'd protected her again and again. He'd stood up for her, he'd run with her, and then strategized how to avoid running into those men. He had been strong for her and had even taken the blame when she'd shot and killed one of the men. He had done so much for her, and how had she repaid him? By withholding the truth of who she was.

She kicked the horse harder, but really it was herself she wanted to kick. She had treated that man—that sweet, kind, generous man who she loved with all her heart—atrociously. She deserved all his anger, all his scorn. She had behaved like an entitled princess, just as he'd accused her early on in their journey. She'd thought—hoped—she had learned to do better, to *be* better, but clearly, she hadn't. She didn't deserve a good man like Lord Ranleigh.

She was wiping a tear from her cheek when the horse stumbled a little. He regained his footing immediately, but Isa felt it. She pulled him to a halt and got down. She felt his hind legs and then moved to his forelegs. Everything felt fine, she thought, as she lifted his leg to see if maybe he'd got a stone or something lodged in his hoof. His right hoof looked good, but then she lifted the left. The horse had lost a shoe, and yes, there was a stone embedded in his hoof. Poor thing!

She had nothing with which to pry it out. She looked around for a stick or something, but there were just fields of grain all around her. She turned to the saddlebags. She opened the first and found a newspaper. She wondered what Sam was doing—

She suddenly found herself staring at a picture of her own face. She gasped. So, that was how he'd found out. Beneath her picture was her name and then an article about her upcoming investiture. Investiture?

Isa stumbled, her knees suddenly going weak. She was to be made heir to her father's throne? But what about... of course. The world—even her father—thought Nik was dead. Only *she* didn't believe it to be true. She rested her head on the horse's neck, truly working hard not to give in to the sobs gathering in her throat. She didn't want to be made the heir to the throne. She didn't want that responsibility. She hadn't been trained as Nik had been.

The sound of an approaching carriage made her lift her head. It was coming from Margate, heading toward Dover. Perhaps she could get a ride with whoever it was. Surely, they would take pity on a young woman stranded in the road with a lame horse. She didn't know what she would do once she returned to Dover, but she would worry about that once she got there.

As the coach pulled up beside her, she was shocked to see that it was her Uncle Alexander. She'd hid from him when they'd run into him on the road to Margate a few days earlier because she didn't want him giving her away to Sam. Now she supposed she didn't need to worry about that anymore. The truth was already out.

"Louisa! What are you doing here?" Uncle Alexander said in German as he jumped from his coach.

"Uncle, I can't tell you what a relief it is to see you," she replied in the same language. "My horse has lost a shoe and has a rock stuck in his hoof," she explained.

"Well, goodness! Let's get him tied up to the back of my coach. We'll take him back to Margate, and then you need to be in London," he told her. He gave her a warm embrace, and for a moment, she thought she would truly begin to cry. It felt so good to be with someone she knew and trusted.

The sound of a galloping horse pulled her attention away, and she turned to see a man riding up to them at full speed.

"Coachman, get this thing turned around, quickly. We are going back to Margate," Uncle Alexander shouted to his coachman in English.

The man climbed back onto the bench, took the reins, and started the horses around. Luckily, the roadway was wide enough for such a maneuver.

The rider still approached at an incredible pace, but now he was close enough for Isa to see that... was it Sam? She couldn't believe it, but it was!

"Isa! Stop! Isa!"

"Quickly, Louisa," her uncle said. He bodily lifted her up into the coach since the steps hadn't been let down.

"What? Why—"

"Isa, no!" She could hear Sam's impassioned scream.

The door was slammed shut, and her uncle was banging furiously on the roof. Something was wrong.

Isa stuck her head out the window.

"Isa, stop! Jump out!" Sam called, now galloping alongside the coach. "I'll catch you!"

Her uncle grabbed her by her waist and pulled her back into the coach, putting a strong arm around her shoulders. "Oh, no. You're not going anywhere. I need to get you to London."

Isa couldn't move, and she had no idea why Sam was so insistent on her leaving her uncle. Perhaps he didn't know Markgraf Kottenfurst was related to her?

She watched Sam fall back behind the coach but had no way of knowing whether he would return to Dover or what. She turned to look at her uncle. She had grown up with this man. He was like a second father to her. So why was Sam so sure she needed to get away from him? She was certain he wouldn't insist if he didn't think she might come to some harm.

She turned toward her uncle. He'd loosened his grip on her but still kept a hand wrapped around her shoulder, ready to tighten his grip if need be. He was a strong man. He'd been in the army and had never lost his strength even as he grew older. No, there was no way she could overpower him, and she still wasn't entirely certain she needed to.

"Uncle, why are you so insistent I go to London? What is happening?" she finally asked.

He frowned. "You haven't been reading the newspapers, have you?"

"No."

He sighed and released his grip. "You know, of course, about your brother?"

"I know he was reported to have drowned, but I don't believe it. I believe he is still alive," she informed him.

He gave her a sad, pained expression.

"No! Don't look at me like that! I would *know*. I would feel it were he dead," she insisted.

"Well, your father believes it, and that's really all that matters. He's insisting you be crowned heir to his throne."

"But the throne can only go to a man. You are the next in line."

He nodded. "That was true until your father changed the law allowing a female to take the throne—you."

"Oh!"

"There is to be an investiture ceremony next week, and there is much to be done for you to prepare," he said, relaxing further.

"I see. And that is why you need to get me to London?" She didn't believe him. Parliament would never just change a law that simply. Why would they? He had to be lying to her.

He nodded. He then glanced out the window. He rapped on the ceiling and called out, "Why are we going so slowly?" in English.

"For the horse tied to the back, my lord," the coachman called back.

"Oh, the horse! I need to return him to the stable where he belongs! We need to go to Margate," Isa told him in their native language.

Her uncle frowned at her but nodded. "Very well. I'm certainly not going to make the journey all the way back to Town at this crawling pace." He rapped on the roof once again. "Head to Margate," he called to the coachman. "We need to return the horse."

"Very good, my lord," the man called back.

"Actually, if you don't mind, Uncle, I would like to stop and check on the poor thing," Isa said, giving him a worried look.

Markgraf Kottenfurst looked at her disbelievingly. "You really don't think I would fall for that one, my dear?"

"I would not lie to you! I am appalled you would think so little of me," she said, straightened herself and giving him her most affronted princess look. "The animal has a rock in his hoof. I told you so when you stopped for me if you recall."

"And how do I know you won't try to ride off?"

She allowed her jaw to drop. "I would never harm an animal! Surely you know me better than that?"

He thought for a moment and nodded. He knocked on the roof once more and called up for the coach to pull over and stop so she could check on the horse.

"Do you have a knife on you? I want to see if I can pry the stone out, so he isn't in distress," she told him.

He reached into a pocket and pulled out a small pen knife.

"Thank you."

She jumped out the moment the coach had stopped and was slightly amazed and grateful he didn't follow her. He wasn't as passionate about horses as Isa and her brother, and she knew this.

She could hear him call up to the coachman for him to assist her.

They had entered a wooded area, and she caught sight of Sam on his horse disappearing amongst the trees. She smiled. She hadn't been sure he wouldn't abandon her, and it felt good to know he was still nearby.

The coachman came around the vehicle. She could see the animal was in distress and stroked his nose, whispering words of strength and encouragement. Once the animal looked slightly calmer, she held the horse's leg up while the coachman pried the stone out. Immediately, the horse looked better and took a few experimental steps onto the road.

Isa took advantage of the moment and leapt on the animal's back and kicked him into a gallop back toward Dover, screaming out for Sam to join her. Within a moment, he was galloping alongside her.

She turned her head and gave him a smile. Somehow, he knew and turned to grin at her, too. As one, they rode as quickly as they could. The coach followed for a time, but they were too fast for it. Still, Isa made a quick decision and didn't head straight back to Mrs. Jones's home. She had already done enough to endanger the lives of those she cared about, and she wasn't going to do so anymore.

They slowed as they entered the city.

"Where is the stable where you need to return this horse?" she asked Sam.

He nodded. "Excellent idea not to lead them to Mrs. Brompton and her sister," he said approvingly. He led her to the stable where they returned both horses.

As they walked away, Isa asked, "Dare we go back there now? I haven't seen my uncle's coach anywhere."

"I think it may be safe," Sam agreed.

Chapter Thirty-Five

-Apologies-

They were greeted with sighs of relief from both Mrs. Brompton and Mr. Davies. Mrs. Jones just laughed and said, "I told them you'd be fine, but they wouldn't believe me."

"Thank you for your confidence, Mrs. Jones," Isa told the woman.

Sam smiled at her politely and asked, "I wonder if I might trouble you for some tea. I am rather parched after that ride."

"Oh! Of course! Where are my manners?" She giggled as she bustled out the parlor door.

The moment she had closed the door behind her, Mr. Davies said, "All right, out with it now. What really happened?"

Isa sat down on a chair, keeping her eye on Sam, but he was waiting for her to speak. It was her story; she would have to tell it.

Finally, she realized he wasn't going to make things easy for her, so she turned to Mr. Davies and Mrs. Brompton who had sat next to each other on the sofa. "Lord Ranleigh has discovered my true identity."

"Oh, ho!" Mr. Davies said, rubbing his hands together in anticipation.

“Is it what I had thought earlier?” Mrs. Brompton asked.

“Yes. I am sorry, Mrs. Brompton, for having had to lie to you. Well, I am sorry for having lied to you all for so long,” Isa said. Sam was impressed. Normally when a young lady apologized, she would lower her gaze and look contrite. Not Isa. No, she sat straighter with her chin in the air and owned her mistake.

“You know who she is?” Mr. Davies asked, looking at Mrs. Brompton.

“Well, I overheard something once. I asked Miss... I asked her about it, and she said it was something else,” the woman said as vaguely as possible.

“That tells me absolutely nothin’,” Mr. Davies said in disgust.

Isa just laughed. “Mr. Davies, Mrs. Brompton, I am Princess Louisa of Aachen-Düren. Isa is my nickname. It always has been. You may still call me Miss Günter if you wish, however. Günter is close to my actual surname, which is Guelf. Or I suppose you could call Miss—”

“We will call you Your Royal Highness, which is, I assume, the correct thing for us to call you,” Mrs. Brompton said, interrupting her.

Isa smiled at her. “Well, actually, unless I am crowned head of the country, I am not Your *Royal* Highness, just Your Highness.”

“Then that is what we will call you,” Mrs. Brompton said quickly.

“You’re really a princess?” Mr. Davies asked, as if it was just beginning to sink in.

“I really am. My father is Prince Heinrich, the leader of my country—a small country, but a country, nonetheless. My brother Prince Nikolas—”

Mrs. Brompton gasped. “He isn’t the one who, who...”

“Who what?” Mr. Davies asked.

“The newspapers reported about a month ago that he drowned while crossing the Channel on his way home,” Isa said. “He didn’t. I am absolutely certain of that, which is why I have been so determined to find him. I’m certain he is still alive. I just... just...” She paused for a moment as her eyes became glassy. She blinked them clear, however, and composed herself. “I do beg your pardon, but it’s been a rather long day.”

"The other thing I learned last night, along with the princess's identity, was that the man who hired the thugs who've come after us was her uncle, Lord Kottenfurst," Sam told them.

"My uncle?" Isa exclaimed. "Are you sure?"

"We know there were two sets of men hired to find you," Sam reminded her. "I don't know which set it was he hired—the ones who wanted to return you to school or the ones who wanted to kill you—but I do know he hired the men who tried to bribe Lord Wythe into turning you over to them."

Isa was clearly stunned. "So that's why you shouted for me not to go with him this afternoon."

"Yes," he said.

"You went with him? Where? How?" Mr. Davies asked.

"When?" Mrs. Brompton added.

"When I rode off after arguing with Lord Ranleigh," Isa explained. "My horse threw a shoe out along the road to Margate. My uncle drove by in his coach and picked me up, but just as I was climbing in, Sam galloped toward us shouting for me to go with him. My uncle pushed me inside and then held me there, so I could do nothing. He told me he was taking me to London."

"Oh, my word!" Mrs. Brompton exclaimed.

Her sister came in at that moment with a tea tray laden with tea and a plate of biscuits. "Oh, it's nothing, truly," Mrs. Jones laughed, clearly thinking Mrs. Brompton had exclaimed over the tray.

They all stayed quiet while Mrs. Jones poured the tea and offered round the biscuits.

"Well, have you two made up your little tiff, whatever it was?" Mrs. Jones asked, looking from Isa to Sam.

"Er, no. We need to have a conversation about that," Sam said.

"I take it you were able to, er, leave your uncle?" Mr. Davies asked Isa.

She smiled at him. "Yes. He is now, most likely, on his way to London by himself."

"Well, I am glad to hear that," Mrs. Brompton said, sounding very relieved, indeed.

"Yes. Perhaps tomorrow, my lord, we can continue my search for my brother?" she asked, turning to Sam. "We do know he came here to Dover. Perhaps we can find evidence he's either still in the area or has gone on somewhere else."

"I hope, back to university where he belongs," Sam said.

"That is my hope, too, if he isn't here," she agreed.

"But if he's trying to avoid your uncle as well, he might be... well, anywhere," Sam pointed out. He didn't want to scare her but rather to prepare her for the idea they might not be able to find him if he had gone into hiding.

"Yes, you're right. But I would like to try," she said hopefully.

"Well, you can't have come this far and then not try," Mrs. Jones laughed.

"Indeed," Isa agreed with her.

-Day 37: Making Up-

It took a little convincing, but finally Mrs. Brompton allowed Sam and Isa some time alone to talk.

"She takes her role very seriously," Sam said, giving Isa a smile.

She laughed. "Yes, she does. I would like to keep her on, but I'll need permission from my father to do so."

Sam nodded. "Isa, I—"

"Sam, I want—"

They both started at the same time and both immediately stopped.

"Ladies first," he said, indicating with his hand.

She cleared her throat. "I, er, I wanted to apologize and to thank you for your warning today."

"Thank you for that," he acknowledged.

"I understand why you were so upset and-and angry with me," she admitted. "It's just that once the lie had been told—"

"It's hard to come out with the truth," he said.

"Yes! To have to admit that I hadn't told you the truth to begin with..."

"Well," he laughed. "I knew that from the first. And I believe I did

give you a number of opportunities to share the truth with me. Sadly, you never did."

"You did know?" she asked, sounding surprised.

"I'm afraid you're not a very good liar, Isa."

She chuckled and sat back down on the sofa. "No, I never have been."

He joined her there and took her hands in his. "What hurts the most was that you never trusted me enough to tell me the truth."

"I… I could not. Or, well, I *felt* I could not."

"But it was a matter of safety for me and Mrs. Brompton," he pressed.

"Oh, come now. From the first time I was shot at during our picnic, you knew we were all in danger," she argued.

"Yes, but—"

"But what? Would you have abandoned me if you'd known *why* someone was trying to kill me?" she asked him, pulling her hands from his.

"No! Of course not." He took hold of her hands again. "But I might have dismissed Mrs. Brompton and Davies. I might have insisted we go on ourselves so as to not put the other two into harm's way."

She thought about this. Finally, she conceded, "It would not have been proper, but I can understand your concern for them, and I find it commendable."

A little war began to wage inside of Sam's mind. Did he tell her the truth of how he felt? Of his desire to be with her—forever? My God, that thought startled him! *Did* he want to be with her forever? Did he want to marry her? He wasn't entirely certain, not yet. He loved her. He knew that, but marriage…

"I probably shouldn't, but I do want to point out that, while I did not trust you with my true identity while we were traveling, I have always trusted you with my life," she said quietly. She looked directly into his eyes as she said this, so he could see the truth and the emotion behind her words.

He was filled with a warmth that defied reason. "I have always and will always protect you, Isa," he told her in all sincerity.

"I know. I know that deep in my heart." She paused, allowing her words to sink in. "It is why, when you came after me today and screamed for me not to go with my uncle, I knew that you must have had a good reason. If I could have got away then, I would have."

"But you did get away. You were very clever."

"Frankly, I was surprised my uncle fell for it. He almost didn't. It is only because he knows how much I love animals he allowed me to get out and check on the horse."

"Is that how you convinced him to stop?"

She nodded. "Once the coachman had pried the stone from his hoof, I felt better about riding him when missing one shoe. Before that, I knew the poor thing was in discomfort."

"You are good with animals," Sam admitted, rather relieved to be past the awkward part of their conversation.

"I only wish I was better with people."

"Oh, I don't know. You did an amazing job of befriending Dev. He'll do just about anything for you, you know."

She giggled. "He is a very sweet man."

"Don't get any funny ideas about him," Sam said as a spike of jealousy surged through him.

She looked at him, confused. "Funny ideas?"

"Er, he's, um, not interested in marriage," he told her.

"Oh! I never even thought of such a thing. Are... have you..." she started but was clearly at a loss or too embarrassed to continue.

"No! No, I just want to see you safe," Sam said immediately and then mentally kicked himself. Maybe he shouldn't have said that, and he certainly shouldn't have done it so quickly and definitively.

An expression of sorrow flashed on and off her face that he certainly would have missed if he hadn't been watching her so closely. She pulled the corners of her mouth up. "Good. Of course."

"So, tomorrow..." Sam started, needing to change the topic of conversation and fast.

"Yes. Tomorrow, we shall resume our search for Nik?" She latched on to the topic like a drowning person grabbed a rope thrown to them.

"Yes. We can go to all the inns in town and perhaps even a solicitor to see if there have been any houses temporarily let recently."

She widened her eyes. “What a brilliant idea! I did not even think of that.”

He smiled. “Tomorrow.”

Chapter Thirty-Six

-Day 38: The Search Continues-

Isa was enjoying the excellent breakfast Mrs. Jones had prepared for her when Sam joined her in the dining room.

"Good morning," he said, giving her a bright smile.

"Would you care for something to eat, my lord?" Mrs. Jones asked him.

"Oh no, thank you so much, ma'am. I ate at the inn where I'm staying," he said, taking a seat across from Isa.

"A cup of tea, then?" the woman persisted.

"Yes, that would be lovely," he agreed. She probably would have gone on offering him things unless he took something, Isa thought. The woman was almost generous to a fault.

"As soon as you're ready, I've made a list of all the inns in Dover where we can ask after your brother," he told her, accepting the cup from their hostess.

"Excellent. I will be finished—" Isa started.

"There's no hurry," Sam said, interrupting her.

She nodded and finished her breakfast. As soon as she was done, she collected her reticule and donned the shawl Mrs. Brompton insisted she take—one belonging to that lady—and they set off walking. Inn after inn after hotel and even a tavern or two, and there was not one person who recognized the small portrait Isa carried with her.

They had finally sat down at a tea shop to partake of a light luncheon when Sam reached out his hand and patted her own as it sat on the table.

"Don't worry, I also have the name of a solicitor known for letting houses and rooms to wealthy young men. Perhaps your brother rented some place instead of staying in a public inn."

Isa sighed and nodded. "I do hope you're right."

Bantham, Bantham, and Wright was only three blocks from where they'd eaten.

"We'd like some information on houses and rooms that can be rented in the area," he told the clerk who greeted them when they entered the offices.

"Do you have an appointment?" he asked with a lift of his chin.

"Er, no. I am the Marquess of Ranleigh and would simply like some information," Sam said, taking on a rather imperious tone and handing over his visiting card. Isa noticed he did not give her name and was grateful.

"Oh!" the man said, looking down at the card. "Of course, my lord. If you would just wait one moment, I'll see if Mr. Bantham has some time to spare." The man hurried down a long hallway. He returned a few minutes later followed by an elderly gentleman leaning heavily on a walking stick.

"Lord Ranleigh, how may I be of assistance to you?" the man asked.

"We are looking for some information," Sam told him. "We were wondering if you could tell us if a foreign gentleman rented a place to stay approximately a month ago."

The man looked taken aback for a moment. "You want to know if one month ago a gentleman of foreign origin rented..." he sputtered.

"I am looking for my brother," Isa said, stepping forward. She pulled out her locket and opened it to show the solicitor. "This is his picture. Might you have seen him or possibly his man?"

"Young lady, I am sorry you cannot locate your brother, but I have not seen him."

"Might you have records—" Sam started.

"My lord," the man interrupted him, "even if I did have such records—and I'm not saying I do—I would not be able to share that information with you. It is private and personal, even if the fellow is the miss's brother."

"Is there nothing you can tell us?" Isa persisted.

"Nothing. Good day," he gave them a bow and then turned around and shuffled back down the hall.

Isa just turned and looked at Sam. Her throat was closing up. She could feel it tightening. "There is nothing more we can do," she managed to whisper.

He looked at her sadly. "I'm so sorry, Isa. I don't think there is."

She blinked rapidly for a moment and then straightened her spine, scolding herself. Princesses don't cry! She gave the clerk, who was watching them closely, a nod and then walked out the door.

As they made their way back toward Mrs. Jones's home, she said, "I am so sorry, Sam. I seem to have led you on a fruitless search. I should have known we would not be able to find my brother. If he thought his life was in danger—as it most surely is, just like mine—he has probably gone into hiding somewhere. If he does not want to be found by those trying to kill him, it is unlikely we will be able to find him, either."

"I'm afraid you might be right," Sam admitted, which unfortunately only made Isa feel even more despondent.

"Then there is nothing..." She stopped talking and walking. There was a man standing just outside of a shop reading a newspaper. He was holding it up, reading the front page, which allowed Isa to see the back. Another picture of herself was staring back at her.

Sam kept walking for another few steps before he realized Isa had stopped. He came back and saw what she was looking at. "I beg your pardon, but did you purchase that newspaper from this shop?" he asked the man.

"Eh? Oh, er, yes. Yes, I did," the man said, holding the newspaper closer to his chest as if to say he wasn't about to let it go to anyone.

"Thank you. Wait here. I'll buy another," he told Isa.

She nodded and did as he asked. The man moved away from her to ensure she couldn't read his newspaper.

Sam was already turning the pages to read the story as he exited the shop. He stopped next to her so they could read it together.

Members of the beau monde were shocked and delighted when Her Highness Princess Louisa was seen at Lady Temberton's soiree last night. Despite being poisoned in the Queen's own home where she is currently staying, Her Highness seemed to be in, if not the peak of good health, not too far from it. She was overheard giving a very pretty speech on the importance of her upcoming investiture and that nothing was going to stand in the way of her taking up her new role. It was generally agreed and remarked upon that her strength and determination was exactly how the future leader of a country should behave.

Isa finished reading just a minute after Sam and found him staring at her with a grim expression on his face. He folded the newspaper, took her arm, and proceeded down the street at a smart pace. "If we leave immediately, we should be in London tomorrow."

-Day 38: Off Once Again-

There was absolutely no naysaying Mrs. Brompton's decision to join them on their journey to London.

"What do you mean I don't need to go?" she'd asked, clearly affronted. "A young lady may not travel alone with a single gentleman, no matter who she is! In fact, her position makes it even more imperative she be properly chaperoned. What in the world are you thinking, my lord?"

Sam had sighed and started, "But ma'am, you have already done so much—"

Isa had cut him off saying, "Mrs. Brompton, if there is one thing I have learned on this journey, it is that people must be paid what they are owed. I freely admit the idea had never once entered my mind before this—indeed, I had not even thought much of it at the start of our trip—but now I am fully aware that you need to be paid for your time."

"Oh, posh-tosh!" the woman had answered, waving a hand in the air.

"I must agree with the princess," Sam had added.

"Unfortunately, I am not in control of my purse. I have always relied on Frau Schmitz, my companion, and Herr Mueller, my bodyguard, to manage that for me. Together they see to all my needs and expenses. I need either my brother or my father to agree—"

Mrs. Brompton held up a hand to stop Isa. "Princess Isa, I have not asked for payment, have I?"

"No, of course you have not, but that does not mean—" Isa replied.

"Then stop worrying about it. I am coming of my own free will. I am, as you have pointed out, an unencumbered and free woman. If I wish to go to London, I may. If I wish to take care of a friend—if you would excuse me for being so bold and presumptuous—I may do that too," Mrs. Brompton told them.

A smile had brightened Isa's face. "We *are* friends," she'd said immediately.

"Then it is decided. I shall accompany you to London," the woman said as if the matter was closed. She turned and left the room saying, "Excuse me, I am going to pack."

There was clearly nothing Isa or Sam could do.

Less than an hour later, as they made their way out of Dover, Sam looked across the coach to Mrs. Brompton reading the newspaper article they'd just handed to her, he was grateful she was with them.

"But I don't understand," she said finally, looking up. "How could you have been seen at a party last night when you are here?"

"Clearly, there is someone there impersonating me—and she has even deceived the Queen!" Isa said, barely hiding her outrage.

"Oh! But that's awful!" Mrs. Brompton said, now understanding the situation.

"I wonder if that was why Markgraf Kottenfurst was so insistent you go to London with him," Sam said, thinking about it.

Isa just looked at him, wide-eyed. "But you said he was the one who hired the men after me!"

"Yes, he was—or the men told Wythe that he was. But they could have been lying, or they could have been the other men."

"Not the ones trying to kill me, you mean?" Isa asked.

"Exactly." Sam shifted in his seat. Could he have made a terrible mistake in accusing the markgraf of having bad intentions?

Isa thought about it for a few minutes. "I suppose... but he was oddly insistent," she said.

Sam sighed. "I don't even know how to find out. We can't exactly ask him."

Isa gave a little smile. "I could just see my note to him: 'Dear Uncle, please tell me, did you want me to come to London with you in order to stop the imposter or to kill me?'"

Mrs. Brompton giggled. "Somehow, I don't think he would appreciate such a question."

"No!" Isa agreed, also laughing.

Sam was just relieved Isa could see the humor in the situation.

They were silent for a little while as Mrs. Brompton opened the book she'd brought along, and Sam read the rest of the newspaper. Isa, as usual, simply stared out the window until suddenly she gasped and turned to Sam.

"We completely forgot about Dev and Wythe! They are back in Margate probably wondering what happened to us."

Sam just smiled at her. "They were heading back to Town after I left to come to Dover. Have no worries about them."

"Oh, good! Do you think we will see them there?" Isa asked.

"I suspect so," Sam agreed. He usually saw his friends a few times a week, although that was mostly at his club. But he suspected they might want to come and meet Isa while she was in London.

Chapter Thirty-Seven

-Day 39: Arriving in London-

Isa was very disappointed to learn they would have to spend the night, yet again, at an inn along the road.

"I'm sorry, Isa, but with this coach and only two horses, we simply can't go any faster," Sam had told her when they stopped for the night.

She hadn't responded, merely gone up to her room in silence and had ordered her dinner to be brought to her there, claiming she was too tired to come down.

Unfortunately, her mood didn't seem to have improved with the additional rest. She was curt or simply silent at breakfast and then continued to be so in the coach as they continued on their way.

"She is just anxious," Mrs. Brompton whispered to him as they left the inn.

Sam understood that. He was beginning to feel the same way. He had no idea what they would meet with in London, nor even what they were going to be able to do about this imposter taking Isa's place.

"Where will we be staying, my lord? I understand there are a number of hotels in the city," Mrs. Brompton asked as they began to enter the outskirts of Town.

"At my home, Mrs. Brompton. I have a house in Mayfair," he told her.

"I do beg your pardon, my lord, but that would be highly inappropriate," she said, her voice growing icy cold.

"We need to go directly to the palace," Isa said, suddenly turning away from the window. "That is where the imposter is staying, according to the newspaper."

Sam sighed heavily. "With your presence, Mrs. Brompton, I'm certain it will be fine if we all stay in my home. I have a small staff there now—I don't need a great deal when my mother isn't in residence—but a staff, nonetheless. And no, Isa, we cannot go directly to the Queen's House. Don't be ridiculous," he added, turning toward her.

"Ridiculous!" she nearly shouted. "I am most certainly not being ridiculous! I am being impersonated. There is some woman passing herself off as me!"

"I know and I understand that you are upset by it, but truly, you can't just march into the Queen's House and... and I don't know what you would do. Do you?" he asked, looking straight at her.

"I would... I would go straight to the Queen and tell her. That's what I would do," Isa shot back.

"Yes, and how does the Queen know you are not the impersonator?" he asked, trying his best to keep his calm.

"I... I..."

"What? Because you say so? I'm sure the imposter has said that she is Princess Louisa. She probably even speaks German fluently. If the drawings in the newspaper are anything to go by, she looks exactly like you as well," he pointed out.

"Do you have any cousins or other relatives who look just like you?" Mrs. Brompton asked.

"An excellent question. Perhaps this girl is a relation of yours," Sam said, grateful to Mrs. Brompton for turning the conversation.

Isa thought about it for a moment but shook her head. "No. My father had an older sister, but she died when she was relatively young and never had any children. My only other close relation is his younger brother, my Uncle Alexander, Markgraf Kottenfurst, and his son, Adenheim." She turned toward Mrs. Brompton. "I have absolutely no idea who this person could be, or how she has managed to fool everyone into thinking she is me."

"Well, it certainly will be interesting to learn more, but you must go about this in a clever way. If you simply walk into the Queen's House, as his lordship said, this girl could simply claim that *you* are the imposter. She is already known and trusted. You are not." Mrs. Brompton took Isa's hand and patted it consolingly when the girl looked horrified at her words.

"But then... what am I to do?"

"Let me ask around," Sam offered. "I can go to my club tonight and ask about the girl. With more information about what she's been up to, maybe I can even find a way to meet or..."

"You want to meet her?" Isa sounded outraged.

"Don't you think that would be a good idea? If I can perhaps—" he started.

"No! You cannot. *I* should meet her, not you," Isa insisted.

"Yes, but if I can meet her first, then I can figure out how you can do so," he pointed out.

She glared at him, thinking hard about this. "I will come up with an idea. I need to think of something." She turned and looked out the window again. They had entered Mayfair and would be at his home in just a few minutes.

-Day 39: Reconnaissance-

The footman bowed Isa, Mrs. Brompton, and Sam into the house Mr. Davies had pulled up to. It was on a very pretty square and was one of a row of houses. Sam's had a lovely bright red door which made Isa smile as she walked into the house. The foyer was elegant and understated, except for the sweeping staircase, which she soon found herself climbing to the first floor.

Sam led them straight into a lovely drawing room with pale-blue walls trimmed in gold. The furniture was of an elegant gold with matching blue upholstery. A harp and pianoforte took up one side of the room and a small round table the other, with the seating area in the center in front of the fireplace.

Isa wandered forward to inspect a painting of a boy in a blue velvet suit standing next to a pony, one hand on the bridle. She turned to ask Sam if it was a portrait of him but found him in consultation with an older lady who must have been the housekeeper.

"Thank you, Mrs. Fleming," he said as the woman curtsied to him and then left the room. He came forward and dropped into a chair with a sigh.

Isa laughed. "I don't know how you can sit when we've been doing nothing but sitting for the past two days and weeks before that."

He smiled but didn't say anything.

"You must be glad to be home, my lord," Mrs. Brompton said.

"Yes, that I am," he agreed. "And no, Isa, that's not me. It's my father. Apparently, he couldn't bear to be separated from his pony for long, so the artist included it in the painting."

She giggled. "That sounds like me when I was little. I had wanted to bring my pony right into my bedroom with me. Luckily, my governess managed to convince me she would be much more comfortable in the stable before my father found out I'd tried to bring her into the castle."

Sam chuckled. "So, you grew up living in a castle?"

"Oh, yes! It was a horrid, drafty old place, but it has been in our family for centuries," she said, moving to another painting. This one was of an elegant young lady dressed in the frills and fribbles of the previous century.

"My mother when she was first married," Sam told her.

Isa studied the woman. She was very beautiful with brilliant green eyes just like Sam's, and rich brown hair arranged artfully with a curl resting on one shoulder. "You have her eyes," she said.

"Yes. It's the only thing I inherited from her. Otherwise, I look just like my father."

She looked around for a portrait of the gentleman, but the rest of the paintings were just landscapes.

"His portrait is in the library. I'll show you later," he said as a maid came in with a tea tray. A footman followed, carrying another tray laden with meat, cheese, bread, and cake. Isa was very pleased to see it as she suddenly realized she was starving. It was well past midday, and they hadn't stopped for anything to eat on their way.

Over their meal, Isa asked, "When will we go out to learn more about this impostor?"

Sam raised his eyebrows at her. He'd just taken a large bit of bread and couldn't say anything for a good minute while he chewed. He finally washed his food down with a sip of tea and then shook his head. "*You* aren't going anywhere. I will go out and see what *I* can learn"

"What? But—"

"Isa, if you go out, you'll be recognized," he said.

"Well, I suppose that depends on how well-known this other princess is," Mrs. Brompton pointed out. They'd insisted she eat with them when she'd been about to go below stairs to find some nourishment of her own.

"She is *not* a princess," Isa said immediately.

"I do beg your pardon, Your Highness. I should have said *counterfeit* princess," Mrs. Brompton immediately corrected herself.

"I prefer impostor," Isa informed her, trying to keep the anger from her voice. She wasn't sure she succeeded. Whenever she thought of this person, fury welled up inside of her.

Mrs. Brompton nodded. "But as I said, if the other person is well-known among society, then you going out could quickly become embarrassing and difficult when people believe you to be her."

"She's right, Isa. You need to stay within the house until we get this figured out," Sam agreed.

The anger within her sloshed about like the sea before a storm, but she did understand their point. If she were greeted by someone she didn't know, but the impostor did, it could get very awkward indeed. "Very well," she agreed reluctantly. "For now."

"I am looking forward to an evening of relaxation and—"

"Sam! How could you?" Isa exploded. "I may have to stay in, but you have the freedom to go out and find out about this person. You *need* to go out. How else are we going to know—"

"She'll still be here tomorrow," he protested.

"And so will I! You must go and see what you can learn," she insisted.

"Must I? Tonight?" he asked reluctantly.

"Yes!"

He signed heavily and put a piece of cake on her plate.

"If you do not, I will! I will, I will—" She couldn't think of what she would do, or how she would find out anything, but she wouldn't hesitate to go to the Queen if it came to that. She was about to say as much when Sam held up a hand.

His lovely green eyes softened when he looked at her. "I'm sorry, Isa. I will go to my club and see what I can learn."

Isa relaxed a touch, then took a breath. "Your club? What could you learn there?"

"A lot! You think women are the only ones who gossip?" He gave a little laugh. "I can assure you, with a good glass of rum in his hand, I can get just about any gentleman to tell me everything he knows about this girl."

A smile tugged at Isa's lips. "Excellent!"

Chapter Thirty-Eight

-Powell's-

The comfortable masculine bastion of Powell's Club for Gentlemen had Sam heaving a sigh of relief as he entered its warm embrace. He took a stroll around the card room where he'd spent so many hours winning and losing, nodding to friends and acquaintances.

"Ho, Ranleigh!" Lord Kineton said as he passed by the faro table. "Here to line my pockets, I hope?" The man burst out laughing at his own joke. Sam just gave him a pat on his shoulder. "Sorry, Kineton, not tonight." Sam started to wander away, then paused, and turned back. "Say, you haven't seen Wickford around, have you?"

"Eh?" The man looked up from counting the coins in front of him. "Wickford? I believe he's in the Reading Room." He looked around the table, and there seemed to be a consensus that's where the owner could be found.

"Thank you. Good luck, gentlemen," Sam said, giving them a nod.

There were some chuckles. "Yes, with Kineton playing we'll need some!" one man said as Sam walked away smiling.

He went across the hall to the Reading Room and, as always, was astounded by the lack of noise coming from the gaming room so close by. He ordered a glass of rum and wandered the room, searching for both a place to sit—it was rather busy this time of the evening—and Lord Wickford.

He found Wickford first. The man, as always, was standing chatting with a few other gentlemen. Sam found a seat not too far away where he could keep an eye on the gentleman. As soon as he concluded his conversation, Sam beckoned him over.

"Wickford, how are you this evening?" Sam asked, inviting the man to take the seat next to him.

"Doing well, Ranleigh. I don't believe I've seen you around for some time," Wickford said, relaxing back in the brown, leather chair.

"No, I've, er, been in the country," Sam told him. "How's the family? Can I congratulate you again?"

Wickford's smile broadened showing his bright white teeth, which stood out in contrast to his darker complexion. "Yes. Lady Wickford delivered a beautiful, healthy boy the week before last."

"That's wonderful!" Sam exclaimed. "Congratulations. And how does his older sister feel about this new addition to the family?"

"Oh, she is in love with her little brother. We've named him Stephen, after my father."

"I am so happy for you. And how is Lady Wickford?"

"Yes, thank you. She is doing quite well, and my mother is thrilled to be a grandmother once again," he said.

"I'm not at all surprised." Sam took a sip of his drink. "Aside from this very happy news, what else have I missed while I've been out-of-town?"

Wickford widened his eyes before they crinkled with his smile. He leaned forward to speak confidentially. "Well, you must have heard about the newest diamond of the *ton*."

"No! Who is this? Not Lady Kettonwood's daughter? No, it can't be, this is her second Season, isn't it?" Sam asked, deliberately playing dumb.

"Miss Clemens? No, no! We have true royalty among us this Season," Wickford said. "The Princess Louisa of Aachen-Düren has been a guest of the Queen, and at Her Majesty's insistence, the girl has entered society," Wickford told him with the joy of sharing a juicy piece of gossip to a new listener.

"Princess... I don't think I've ever heard of Aachen-Düren. Where is that?" Sam asked since, in truth, he didn't know.

"It's a small principality in the region between Holland and France. Not too far from Brussels. But the Queen is apparently close with Prince Heinrich, the current ruler of the country. His son died not too long ago, sadly—drowned. Perhaps you read about it?"

"Oh! Yes, yes, I remember seeing something about that," Sam admitted.

"Right. His sister, Princess Louisa, is to be crowned heir to her father's throne next week."

"Where? Here in London?" Sam asked.

"Oddly enough, yes. Prince Heinrich, perhaps too scared to lose another child to the Channel, asked the Queen to see to it. While the princess is readying herself for the ceremony, she has attended a few parties and become quite the darling of society."

"Really?"

"She's quite pretty—although if you tell Lady Wickford I said so, I will deny everything!" he said with a laugh.

Sam burst out laughing. "No, no, your secret is safe with me!"

"What's even more interesting," Wickford continued, "is that the princess has not only captured the hearts of the *ton*, but that of the escort the Queen chose for her—Lord Melfield."

"Oh?" Sam leaned forward to make sure he heard everything Wickford was saying since he'd lowered his voice with this new bit of gossip.

"Yes. Not only has his lordship been seen escorting the beautiful princess all over Town, but he's watching her dance with such longing if not outright jealousy in his eyes—according to my sources," Wickford added.

"My, my. I guess the Queen knew what she was doing when she had him escort the girl."

"You can be sure of it."

"So, what do you think—if I attend a party or go to the park during the promenade, what are the chances that I'll get to meet this paragon of a princess?"

Wickford laughed. "I'd say you'd have a pretty good chance!"

-Day 40: Isa Gets a Glimpse of Lou-

The following morning, Isa cornered Sam in the breakfast room. She didn't even need to say a word before he held up a hand, halting her.

"I went to my club last night and spoke with Lord Wickford who is always up on the latest gossip," he told her.

"And?"

Sam shrugged. "And apparently this impostor has all of society in the palm of her hand. They love her."

Isa frowned.

"He told me she was beautiful—which I already knew because I know how beautiful you are," he said, smiling at her.

She continued to frown at him. He wasn't going to compliment his way out of telling her everything if that was even what he was trying to do.

He cleared his throat and continued, "She is liked a great deal, invited everywhere, and is seen all about Town. They say she is both regal and not so high in the in-step that people feel intimidated by her. Something you might—"

"Sam! If I want a lesson on how to conduct myself, I will ask for it," Isa snapped.

"Right." He paused and took a sip of his coffee. "Well, that's it really. Oh, and apparently, the gentleman the Queen chose as her escort in society, Lord Melfield, is madly in love with her. But that's not relevant to you, I don't think."

Isa sat down at the table, completely ignoring the food on the sideboard. What was she going to do? What *could* she do? She still didn't understand how this woman had managed to take her place so thoroughly. Did Frau Schmitz and Herr Mueller not even realize that this person wasn't her? Just how much did this woman look like her?

That's it! She needed to see this person for herself. She turned to look at Sam who was thoroughly involved in eating his breakfast—a hearty one by the looks of it with steak, eggs, toast, and even a good helping of vegetables.

"I want to go out today," she announced.

His gaze shot up to hers. "That would be a really bad idea."

"I can wear my riding clothes and keep my hat pulled down over my face," she told him quickly. "Do you have a horse I could borrow?"

"Isa, you can't just go riding around Mayfair looking for this girl," he protested.

"Well then, what do you suggest? I want to see her. I need to see just how closely she resembles me."

He thought about it for a moment. "I don't think it's a good idea, but I know you. You'll do this whether I want you to or not, won't you?"

She nodded. "I will."

He sighed heavily and took another sip of his coffee. "Very well. I will go out in my curricle this afternoon for a drive in the park at the height of the promenade," he told her.

She shook her head, not understanding what the significance was. "And how will that allow me to see the impostor?"

"Perhaps I can get Dev or Wythe to accompany me, so I don't look like a complete fool," he added, clearly thinking out loud. He turned back to her. "You will dress in livery and play the role of my tiger."

A smile grew on her face. "Excellent! I like that idea very much." She stood and started out the door.

"Are you not going to eat?" he called after her.

"No. I need to have Mrs. Brompton find me some livery. Oh, and when you ask Dev and Wythe, don't mention that I will be there, too. Let's see if they notice."

Sam chuckled as he went back to his breakfast.

In the end, it was Dev who finally agreed on accompanying Sam. Wythe was probably still feeling guilty for having nearly given Isa away to the men after her. Sam told her he would give his friend some time to get past it.

Isa wasn't terribly surprised when Dev didn't even take a second glance at her standing up on the back of the vehicle. Mrs. Brompton had been amazing, as always, finding her a set of livery that nearly fit her perfectly. The woman had shortened the breeches a bit and made the waist a bit smaller. The top hat she wore did a good job of hiding both her hair and her face, but still she tried to keep her head down as she clung on to the back of Sam's curricle.

"So, what made you decide to go to the park this afternoon?" Dev asked as he climbed into the carriage when Sam picked him up from his home. "Want to see this impostor yourself?"

"I do," Sam agreed. "And so does Isa," he added with a smile.

"Isa? But—"

Sam motioned with his thumb.

Dev twisted around to look behind them. He looked straight past her and strained to see, perhaps, if she was riding behind them on a horse. "Where…?"

Isa waved and then waved again to catch Dev's attention.

"Oh, my God!" The words suddenly burst from Dev's mouth when he finally caught sight of her. "What the…"

She put a finger to her lips, signaling for him to be quiet and then gave him a wink.

He turned back around. "I can't believe—"

"It was the best solution I could come up with when she insisted on going out to see the girl," Sam said, cutting him off.

"But won't someone notice?"

"You didn't even see her," Sam pointed out.

Dev huffed, then clearly thought about it for a moment. "No, you're right, I didn't. I suppose no one even looks at a tiger on the back of a carriage."

"It's a perfect disguise."

Chapter Thirty-Nine

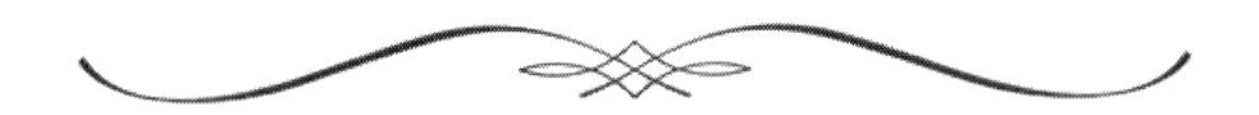

As Sam drove the curricle through the gates of the park, Isa suddenly had the hardest time not staring at all the beautiful people out, strolling along the pathways and riding or driving along the road. There were young ladies in pretty white and pale-colored gowns, some holding lacy parasols above them to ward off the harmful sun. Older women usually accompanied them in bolder colors. There were a number of young ladies with gentlemen, either unaccompanied in open carriages or walking along the path to either side. The gentlemen's clothes were nearly as magnificent as that of the ladies in bright blues, greens, even some red, and one man in lavender!

Isa had thought Sam's pair of matched bays impressive, but they were practically ordinary compared with all the magnificent horseflesh that suddenly surrounded them. It almost seemed as if every gentleman had to outdo the others with the quality and beauty of their horses. She was absolutely in heaven.

"Isa!" Sam's sharp whisper reached her and tore her attention away. She looked toward him. She caught him turning back around and replacing his hat on his head, presumably from having just lifted it to greet a lady. "Keep your head down," he said softly. "Your face can be seen clearly."

"Oh!" She immediately lowered her face and pulled her hat lower. It was harder to see this way, but she knew the danger of being recognized.

They made their way down the road at a snail's pace, frequently stopping and starting as either the line of carriages in front of them halted, or Sam paused to greet some acquaintance or other. About twenty minutes into the journey, Isa caught sight of a horse she would recognize anywhere—it was her own Blume! A low growl of fury came from Isa's throat before she could stop it.

"What was that?" Dev asked, briefly turning around to look at her.

"That's my horse!" she whispered, nodding her head at the animal still a few carriages and riders away.

He turned back around and let out a gasp. "My God, it's her!" Luckily, he'd kept his voice low as well.

Sam's mouth had dropped open. He closed it, but it only opened once again. He seemed to be at a complete loss for words. "But it's... it's remarkable," he said finally. "She could be your twin sister."

"She is a horrid, thieving impersonator!" Isa whispered, giving vent to the anger bubbling up inside of her. She watched in fury as the "princess" stopped to chat with a couple on horseback in front of them. She was clearly happy and very comfortable in her role. And why wouldn't she be? She was thought to be a princess. She was bright, animated, and—Isa hated to admit it—pretty. She looked elegant in her military-style riding habit and comfortable atop Isa's horse. What else could anyone want?

A stomach-churning anger mixed with a deep-seated hollow feeling inside of her. She wanted nothing more than to leap off her perch and claw this woman's eyes out, to rip that smile right off her face, to scream at everyone who bowed, laughed, or smiled at that charlatan.

"If you make one move, Isa..." Sam started.

"Yes!" Dev immediately agreed, smiling and nodding to a lady passing them by ahead of the impostor. "If you give yourself away, you will risk ever being able to resume your position."

Isa growled again and clung tighter on to her handhold, as if that would keep her from lunging at the woman taking her place. As the "princess" passed, Sam and Dev both raised their hats and gave her as much of a bow as they could from their seated positions. The woman smiled and nodded, acknowledging them.

And then Isa caught sight of Herr Mueller riding right behind the impostor—and he was staring straight at her! For a moment, she froze and locked eyes with him. She suddenly came to her senses and ducked her head down, praying he wouldn't make a scene. He rode so close she was afraid he would reach out and grab her.

"Come to the palace servants' entrance. I will tell them to look out for you," he said quickly in German as he rode past.

Isa didn't even have the chance to respond before he was behind her. She turned and looked back. He had his back to her, probably knowing that it would cause others to look if he turned around.

She quickly turned back to face forward. What was she going to do now? And why had he told her to go to the servants' entrance?

- Isa's Despondency-

Isa hadn't said a word after the woman posing as the princess passed them in the park. Her face had grown pale, and her eyes had taken on an emptiness that was a little unnerving. When she had jumped down and begun to unhitch the horses from the curricle after they reached the stable, Sam mused he wasn't entirely certain what to do.

"The grooms will take care of that," he told her.

"It's fine," she said and continued with the work.

He knew she loved the animals, so maybe it made her feel better to care for them. He joined her, helping her remove the bridles and brush down the horses in silence. He waved off the grooms who stood around watching in confusion. Once the horses were back in their stalls, fed and watered, he gently led her back to the house.

"Are you all right?" he asked as they walked through the garden, which was the shortest route from the stable.

She gave a short nod but didn't say anything.

Once inside, she merely went up to her room in silence. Sam could do nothing but go to his own to change and clean up. That evening, she took dinner in her room, leaving Sam to eat by himself.

After two days, when she hadn't left her room, he knew he needed to do something… if only he knew what. He was pacing in his study, thinking it through, when there was a quiet knock on the door. He rushed to the door, hoping it was her but was only slightly disappointed when he found Mrs. Brompton standing on the other side.

He motioned for her to come into the room.

"My lord," the woman started. He noticed she was wringing her hands. "I just don't know what to do. She won't talk. She won't say anything. I've tried speaking with her, asking her what happened, whether she had seen the impostor. She wouldn't say anything. She just stared off into space as if I wasn't even there." The woman looked as if she were about to burst into tears.

He patted her shoulder. "She didn't say a word to me after we got back, either."

She looked up at him, worry writ large on her face. "I take it you saw the 'princess'?"

"We did. It was remarkable. She was absolutely identical to Isa. The only difference I could tell was that, well, I suppose she held herself differently. That may have been because she was riding sidesaddle." He gave a little laugh. "I've only ever seen Isa ride astride." He sobered again quickly. "But she was just as beautiful, just as poised and regal as you would expect a princess to be—as Isa is."

"Oh, the poor dear—Her Highness, I mean, not the impostor. She must be devastated to have been so completely and perfectly replaced."

Sam could only nod. "I must admit I've been thinking along those lines as well—how very thoroughly this other woman has taken up Isa's identity."

"You need to say something to her, my lord. You need to cheer her up in some way," Mrs. Brompton pleaded. "I just can't bear to see her this way!"

"I don't…" He started to say he didn't know what he would say to her, but an idea tickled in the back of his mind. Instead, he nodded. "I'll go up immediately."

"Thank you," she said in relief. He didn't know whether he would be able to do any good, but he would certainly give it his best.

-Proposal-

Sam was certain he had gone mad. Surely what he was thinking of doing was absolutely the definition of such a condition, was it not? And yet... his feet continued onward, and words began forming in his mind of what he was going to say.

Well, there was absolutely no doubt, he *was* mad—in love. Sadly, it would probably end in nothing, and he would end up nursing a broken heart for the rest of his days.

He knocked on Isa's bedroom door. "Isa? Could I have a word?"

There was a muffled sound which he took to be a bid to enter. He found her sitting on a chair, her knees drawn up by an unlit fire, staring vaguely in that direction.

He went over to her and extended out a hand. She looked up at him, her eyes brimming with unshed tears. After a moment, she took his hand, placing her feet on the floor.

He pulled her up and into his arms. For a few minutes, he did nothing but hold her. Instead of calming her as he'd hoped, she seemed to become even more upset and even began to cry. His heart clenched. Could there be anything worse in this world than to hear the woman you love in such distress and know there was absolutely nothing you could do about it? He wasn't sure there was.

"If only I could, I would go straight to the Queen's House and drag that impostor out. I wouldn't care what anyone said, what anyone did. I would drag her out by her hair and throw her into the gutter where she belongs," he told her, rubbing her back in long soothing strokes.

Isa gave a hiccoughing sound that almost sounded like a laugh. He bent to the side a little to see if he could catch a glimpse of her face nestled against his chest. Yes, indeed, there was a tiny, tremulous little smile on her face. His heart soared.

He straightened again and held her tighter.

"I wou-would like t-to see that," she said. "I-it's such a sh-shame you cannot."

He sighed. "I know."

"I-I was thinking, th-though," she said. She paused to sniffle and pull back a little from his embrace.

He pulled out his handkerchief and handed it to her.

She took it with a nod and then used it to wipe her nose and eyes.

"What were you thinking?" he asked while she did so.

"That maybe I should take advantage of this situation." She looked up at him. Her beautiful blue eyes were tinged with red.

He tilted his head in curiosity. "What do you mean? In what way?"

"Well, I've never really wanted to be a princess. When I was little, I always wished I could have been an ordinary person. That way I could ride and hunt and not have to worry about..." She waved a hand vaguely in the air. "Being political or setting a good example for others," she finished.

He nodded. "I suppose there are a number of pressures that come with being royal that most people don't consider."

"Yes, a great many pressures. If I just let this other person continue to impersonate me, then I can live my own life and let her be the princess since she clearly wants to very badly."

He frowned. "That's an interesting thought. You'd never be able to see your family again, though."

"I could. I would just have to do so in a hidden way."

"Hmm." Her idea, oddly enough, played right into his own secret wishes. "I have to admit I like your idea."

Her eyes widened in surprise. "You do?"

"Yes. In fact, I like it very much." He smiled at her and took her hand. "If you weren't the princess, then I would be able to ask you to marry me. We could go and live at Ranleigh. You could hunt and ride to your heart's content." He paused at her shocked silence. "I say this only because I am, in fact, a selfish man. I want you all to myself, and if you *were* the princess, I wouldn't be able to have you. I wouldn't be able to propose to you when that is truly what I want to do more than almost anything." He cupped her face in his hand, rubbing his thumb down her soft cheek. "I love you, Isa. I want to spend the rest of my life with you. But I know with you being a princess I wouldn't be able to do that. So..." He shrugged. "I like your idea very, very much."

Chapter Forty

Isa took a step forward and lifted herself onto her toes so she could kiss him. Her lips gently pressed against his at first, but he could hardly bear such a sweet, light kiss. It tore at his heart. He pulled her closer and deepened the kiss, running his tongue over her lips until she parted them to allow him access to the sweet heat of her mouth. He put all his love, all his heart into the kiss. He wanted her to know without any reservations that he meant every word he'd said. And the fact that she had initiated the kiss made him wonder if she didn't love him, too.

He loved the feel of her. He loved her sweetness. He loved that she was running her fingers through his hair, sending shivers of delight down his back and straight into parts below. At that thought, he forced himself to put an end to this before he embarrassed himself. With great reluctance, he stepped away.

"I would love nothing more than to accept your proposal," she told him, putting a hand to his cheek and looking up into his eyes. "Because I love you. But you would be so very unhappy if we stayed at Ranleigh."

He lowered his eyebrows.

"I saw you, Sam. I saw you when you were gambling with those men in Frimley. You lit up. And I saw how you dimmed when you turned Dev and Wythe down when they wanted to play cards with you. You like gambling. You like playing cards." She quickly held her hand in front of him to stop him from speaking when he opened his mouth to refute her words. "That doesn't mean you should gamble like your father did. He took it too far from what I understand. But I don't see any reason why you shouldn't enjoy yourself if you keep it to reasonable limits. That would be the responsible thing to do. Have fun, but don't go beyond what you can afford."

"And what of you?" he asked because, if he were honest with himself, she was absolutely right. It actually wasn't so much that he liked to gamble. He liked to be social, and he liked playing cards.

She shrugged. "I am a princess. I don't know—even if I let this girl continue to impersonate me—that I could ever be anything else."

"But you are a sweet, considerate princess," he told her. "You can be both a princess and respectful of others. You've shown that. But could you also be happy living in London?"

She smiled. "I could, so long as we have the opportunity to go out into the countryside every so often."

"We absolutely could and will do that. I do have an estate to run." He paused. "But there is still the matter of that impostor."

Now it was her turn to frown. "Yes, there is, but I have an idea about that."

-Day 43: Speculation-

The following morning at breakfast, Isa had returned to her normal habit of enjoying a good breakfast. There was something about love that made her hungry. She glanced over at Sam who had just sat down at the head of the table, his plate brimming with his hearty breakfast. Oh yes, she could definitely get used to this, she thought. Having breakfast with Sam every morning, perhaps dinner every night. He'd stolen a quick kiss after he'd sent the footman off for a pot of coffee, and she'd had to keep from giggling when the man returned much too soon.

Sam must have felt her gaze upon him because he looked up and smiled at her as he picked up his knife and fork. "Will you excuse me if I read the newspaper while I eat? If you would prefer I didn't..."

"No, no. That's perfectly fine. We are at our ease," she said, picking up her teacup.

He nodded and opened the newspaper that had been placed next to his plate. "My God!" He said, dropping his cutlery before he'd even had a chance to use it.

"What is it?" Isa asked, setting down her cup.

He read out loud from the article,

"The Princess Louisa of Aachen-Düren, guest of the Queen, was kidnapped yesterday on her way to Lady Colburne's picnic at Kensington Gardens. The young lady got into a coach at Buckingham Palace thinking it belonged to the queen but, instead of being delivered to the party, was whisked away. The Earl of M.—"

"Melfield, I assume," he surmised.

"—caught sight of the rapidly retreating coach and rode after it, rescuing the princess from a horrible fate. She is now resting comfortably in preparation for her investiture ceremony scheduled for..."

"And it goes on about the investiture," Sam concluded.

"My goodness! Someone went so far as to kidnap her?" Isa asked. She couldn't imagine!

"They wanted you dead. Perhaps the same people thought you were now at the Queen's House?" he asked.

"But she's been there for... well, we don't know for how long. A week, probably two, at least?"

"At least. But whoever is after you may not have known that," he pointed out.

"Yes. But that means that *her* life is in danger," Isa pointed out. "I may despise the woman for impersonating me, but I don't wish her dead."

"No, of course not! But now you will have to be even more careful than we thought. If anyone discovers you are here, they could try to kidnap you next. I'm certain they're not aware there are two of you."

"Goodness, yes."

Sam turned to the footman standing by the door. "Would you please inform Simmons I would like a word with him?"

The man nodded and went off to fetch the butler.

"I will have Simmons tell the staff they are not to speak a word about your presence here to *anyone*—it could mean your life were anyone to find out."

-Day 45: Herr Mueller and the End-

For two days, Isa did nothing but fret about her position. She didn't know if it was wise to carry out her plan. She went back and forth and back and forth until finally she couldn't stand it any longer. She hated being cooped up, and she hated being indecisive. Even Sam's calming presence was no longer enough.

She finally made her decision, not at all certain it was the right one, but she had to do *something*. Dressing in her riding clothes, she tucked her hair up under her cap and pulled it low over her eyes. She only needed to ask for directions to the Queen's House twice since she somehow made a wrong turn somewhere.

The palace was impressive. Finding the servants' entrance, however, was easier than she expected. There were a great number of tradesmen going in and out making deliveries. She slipped in completely unnoticed. She wondered if it was always this busy. There were people running this way and that, food and flowers being delivered, maids and footman scurrying every which way. Finally, a maid stopped and asked if she was a temporary footman waiting for someone to tell her where to find some livery. "Although, I'm sure no footman was ever as short as ye," the girl said, looking Isa over from head to toe.

Isa did her best to keep her head down so the girl wouldn't get a good look at her face. "Er, no, not a footman. I'm here to see Herr Mueller. He said he'd leave word I was coming."

The girl frowned. "I don't know nothin' about that. Better ask Mrs. Thornton. She's in there." The girl pointed to a door not too far away.

Isa nodded, then went and knocked on the door.

"Come!" a woman's voice called out with force.

Isa opened the door and found a very serious-looking woman standing behind a desk piled high with papers. She looked busy and completely ignored Isa as she walked in. "Mrs. Thornton? I am looking for Herr Mueller. He said he would leave word—"

The woman looked up, her eyes piercing into Isa. "Please remove your hat, young man. Have you no manners?" she snapped.

Isa laughed. If she removed her hat, her disguise would be gone. She seriously doubted he had told this woman who would be asking for him. "I'm afraid I cannot do that. If you could please just call for Herr Mueller."

"You can't?"

"No, I cannot. Now, Herr Mueller..."

"You are the rudest boy!" the woman said, rising to her feet. And then she stopped as if she'd remembered something. "Do you speak German?" she asked, narrowing her eyes at Isa.

"*Ja. Es ist meine Muttersprache*," Isa told her.

She nodded. "Just one moment. I'll send someone to inform him you are here. Is there a name...?"

"Isa," she told the woman.

"You're not a boy, then."

"No." Isa did still keep her hat low and her head down, looking up at the woman from under the brim of her hat. She didn't want to give away her identity quite yet.

The woman scowled and then walked from the room, closing the door carefully behind her. Isa could have sworn she heard her say, "Of all days..." as she left.

About ten minutes later, Herr Mueller entered the room. He was a bit out of breath as if he'd been running, but he paused to bow low to Isa the moment the door closed behind him. "Your Highness, I could hug you and yell at you—both at the same time!" he scolded her in German, coming forward.

Isa just laughed. "It is good to see you, too, Herr Mueller."

"Where have you been? I've had men scouring the country for you."

"I've been searching for my brother. Where did you think I was?"

"But we looked in Dover and couldn't find you there," he said with a shake of his head.

"I took a little while to get there. There were men trying to kill me."

"What?" At that, he came forward and grabbed her arms, looking her over carefully as if she might show some evidence of the attempts on her life.

"I wasn't hit!" she laughed. "In fact," she said, sobering immediately, "I killed one of the men after me. Lord Ranleigh, who was escorting me, was kind enough to take the blame with the local magistrate. It set us back a few days, but there was nothing for it."

"Lord Ranleigh? I don't know him." Herr Mueller was clearly confused.

"I met him in Oxford after my—it doesn't matter. It's a long story. Just know that he has been taking excellent care of me and even hired a chaperone to see to my needs and ensure that everything was proper."

"Well..." He sighed with some relief. "I am glad to hear that. But still, you had us so very worried."

"I am sorry for that." And then she remembered the imposter, and her anger rose. "But it seems as if you didn't miss me so much. You found a replacement for me?"

"Er, yes. It was the greatest good luck, actually. The young woman came into the Abingdon School looking for a teaching job, and both I and Frau Schmitz mistook her for you. The only difference is the color of her eyes—they are brown."

"She is a schoolteacher?"

"She did not want to take your place and fought hard against it, but we convinced her of the necessity when the summons came from the Queen."

"And then she was more than happy to impersonate me, I assume."

"Well... no, not really. But she has been very good. She has worked hard at—" He stopped suddenly.

"At being me?" Isa prompted him.

"At preparing for the investiture. It is to begin any minute now!"

"What? She is going to be crowned the heir to my father's throne?" Isa nearly screeched.

"Come this way." He ushered her out the door, through a warren of corridors, and finally up a set of stairs. They proceeded down a wide, grand hallway. There was a trumpet blast that had Isa and Herr Mueller sprinting down the hall. He stopped before a set of double doors painted white and gold.

Isa didn't even stop but burst through the doors just as there was a second call of the trumpets. At the far end of the room, a young woman in a fantastic white gown lavishly embroidered in gold with a long train stood prepared to walk through another set of double doors. A nobleman in red robes was stepping away from her as the doors before her opened.

"Her Highness Princess Louisa Catherine Anneliese—" the crier began.

"*Warten*! Wait!" Isa screamed out as she ran into the room. "Halt!"

The woman at the other end stopped and turned toward her, a look of absolute shock and... was that relief on her face? Isa was so stunned to be face-to-face with her double that she stopped halfway across the room. As she did so, a man's voice could be heard screaming from the hallway and then into the room. It was a voice Isa knew as well as her own. She spun around as he called out.

"Halt! Halt! Stop!" He nearly barreled into her. "Isa!"

The End

Thank you for reading *Princess on the Run*!

A prince in hiding, a British spy on her first real mission... In the dark alleyways of London and in the brilliance of the ballroom these two will match wits, share information, and work together to find a killer. Don't miss the exciting conclusion of the Royals & Rebels series, *A Prince Among Spies*!

Read a sneak peek

A PRINCE AMONG SPIES

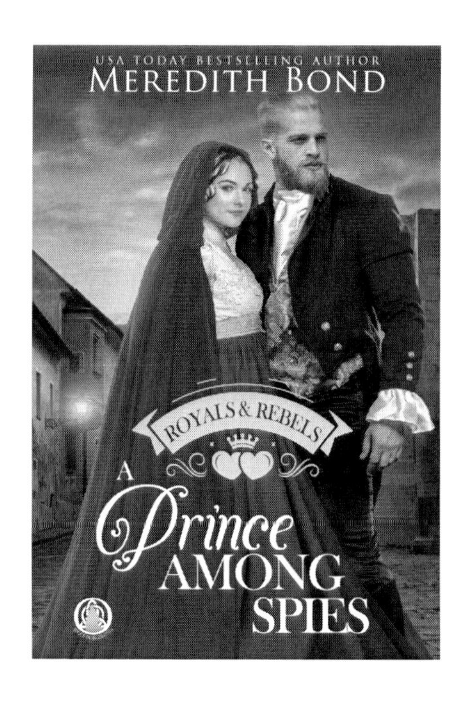

Chapter One

Prince Nikolas of Aachen-Düren tossed his last card down onto the table, crossed his arms over his broad chest, and watched as his friend Lord Newly pulled the pile of coins toward himself with a grin.

"I do not know how much more of this I can take, Newly," Nik said with a rueful shake of his head. In fact, he knew precisely how much more he was going to lose to his friend because he was doing it on purpose. Nik had a very generous allowance from his royal father, while Newly's father was struggling just to keep their estate afloat. Nik knew this and was doing what he could to make things easier for his friend. He had done the same for Sumerton and Marron, the other two gentlemen at the table. Tonight it was Newly's turn.

He was about to lean forward to reach for the deck of cards when a delicate hand began running its way over his shoulder and down his chest reaching inside of coat and waistcoat to the fine linen of his shirt. A woman's lips began nipping at his earlobe as she blew her hot gin-scented breath down his neck.

Newly and his other friends just smiled.

"On the other hand, I think I may need to call it a night," Nik said, correcting himself. He reached his hands behind him to the woman, found a round firm bum and gave it a gentle pinch. The woman stood quickly with a playful screech.

He turned to see Marie, the woman who he had been known to hire on occasion to sate his needs. She was a professional, as were many of the women who frequented this tavern in the center of Oxford, and enjoyed the company of a good many of the university students and dons. Nik didn't mind so long as she was clean. He didn't even say goodnight to his friends, but merely allowed the woman to lead him up the stairs to one of the rooms.

As the first vestiges of dawn were beginning to lighten the sky, Nik felt something cold against his bare chest as he slowly began to awaken. He sighed, felt whatever it was removed from his chest, only to press to his temple a moment later. He opened his eyes and found Marie staring down at him, a serious expression on her face. He shifted his head to see what it was that had been touching him and discovered the barrel of a little pistol pointed at his head.

He looked back up at Marie curiously.

"I'm sorry, Nik, but I've got no choice," she said.

"Of course you have a choice," he told her calmly.

She shook her head.

"If it is money, you know I will pay you more than whatever you are getting."

She shook her head again. "If it were just that..." A tear started to roll down her pretty, pale cheek. "They've got me mum," she told him quietly. "Said I'd get 'er back when they saw yer dead body in this bed."

Nik sighed. "I am so sorry, Marie... so very..." With a sudden move, he grabbed the gun from her hand, jumped to his feet and tossed it out the window.

"No!" she cried.

"As I say," he said, pulling on his clothes as quickly as he could, "I am so sorry." He shoved his neckcloth and stockings into his coat pockets, his bare feet into his boots, and threw on his waistcoat and coat on his way out the door.

He paused for a moment to toss some coins onto the table and then sprinted down the hall and headed for the stairs. Unfortunately, he was met at the bottom by two very large men who seemed to have been waiting for him.

There was no escape back up the stairs. He would just have to deal as best he could. He hoped surprise would slow their reactions. He threw himself at them from half-way down the stair. They all ended up in a tumble of arms and legs, but Nik was quick to his feet and running out the door before the men could sort themselves out.

He was sprinting down the street toward his rooms when his coach pulled up next to him. The door was thrown open, nearly hitting him.

"Jump in, your highness," his man, Friedrich, called out.

Nik did so, pulling the door closed behind him as Friedrich knocked on the ceiling and called out "Spring'em!" to the coachman. Friedrich didn't know a lot of English, but that was one word he'd learned early.

Nik nearly ended up on the floor as the coach shot forward. He righted himself as the clatter of the galloping horse's hooves filled the empty, early morning streets.

"How did you—" Nik started, speaking in his native German.

"I told you, your highness, that I would keep my ear to the ground. I wish I'd heard sooner what was planned, sadly my informant only told me about an hour ago. He tried to extract more money from me, but we came to an agreement," Friedrich responded in the same language.

"I hope no one was hurt?" Nik asked.

Friedrich gave a little, noncommittal shrug as he examined his reddened knuckles. "The blood only touched my shoes. I was able to clean it away."

Nik gave his servant a long, hard stare. The man blinked back at him and then sighed. "I only broke his nose. It will mend."

Sitting back against the comfortable seat, Nik crossed his arms over his chest.

"And it was necessary. Otherwise, I wouldn't have known to come and get you when I did. I have your valise, by the way, and I informed the doorman you would be away for a little while. He will keep an eye on your rooms while we are gone."

"I'm not worried about my belongings, and appreciate your efforts on my behalf. What did you learn?"

"Not as much as I would have liked, I'm afraid. Only that a great deal of money was offered for your life."

Nik frowned. "But do you know who—"

Friedrich shook his head and sighed. "No matter what I threatened, I could discover no name. I apologize."

"Well, we'll continue through with our plan, then."

"Yes, your highness. I've sent word to the ship. It will be ready to leave the moment we arrive in Margate. We'll find some place nearby to stay until we can discover who is behind the attempt on your life."

Nik nodded, but was unable to contain the huge yawn that overtook him. "Very good. I'll just close my eyes for a time, then."

"Of course, sir." Friedrich passed across the pillow he'd brought. Nik chuckled as he settled himself as comfortably as he could in the traveling coach. The man thought of everything.

Also by Meredith Bond

The Royals & Rebels

#1 In Lieu of a Princess

#2 Princess on the Run

#3 A Prince Among Spies

Prequel: Christmas Intrigue

The Merry Men Quartet

An Exotic Heir

A Rake's Reward

A Merry Marquis

A Dandy in Disguise

My Lord Ghost

My Gentleman Thief

A Spanish Dilemma

Under the Mango Tree

When Hearts Rebel

The Storm Series: Regency-set Paranormal Romance

Storm on the Horizon

Bridging the Storm

Magic in the Storm

Through the Storm

The Ladies' Wagering Whist Society

A Hand for the Duke

Jack of Diamonds

The Games She Played

Christmas in the Cards

A Trick of Mirrors

A Bid for Romance

An Affair of Hearts

Love in Spades

A Token of Love

The King of Clubs

Deck the Halls

The Children of Avalon Trilogy: Arthurian Fantasy Romance

Air: Merlin's Chalice

Water: The Return of Excalibur

Fire: Nimuë's Destiny

Falling Series, Time-Travel Paranormal Romance

Falling

Falling for a Pirate

About Meredith Bond

USA Today bestselling author Meredith Bond's books straddle that beautiful line between historical romance and fantasy. An award-winning author, she writes sweet, fun, traditional Regency romances, medieval Arthurian romances, and Regency romances with a touch of magic. Known for her characters "who slip readily into one's heart," Meredith loves to take her readers on a journey they won't soon forget.

Connect with Meredith:

https://meredithbond.com

facebook.com/meredithbondauthor
twitter.com/merrybond
instagram.com/meredith_bond
bookbub.com/authors/meredith-bond
amazon.com/Meredith-Bond/e/B001KI1SNE

Made in United States
North Haven, CT
31 January 2023

31862237R00169